Riverland

. D. Chase

This is a work of fiction. Names, characters, businesses, places, events and incidents are either the products of the author's imagination or used in a fictitious manner. Any resemblance to actual persons, living or dead, or actual events is purely coincidental.

Riverland Press

Pittsburgh

Copyright 2017 – Words and Pictures - D. Chase Edmonson
Back cover – Adam Edmonson
All Rights Reserved - Printed in the United States

ISBN 978-0-692-77580-6

RiverlandPress.com

For my grandparents, who filled their homes with books; my parents, avid readers and boaters; for sister Ann, and brothers Jim and Mark; for my wife Beth and sons Adam and Ian; with special acknowledgements to Jim Edmonson, Brian Moss, and Todd Ray for all their help, and a tip of the cap to all Waterboys up and down the river.

A weekend in July - mid 1980's

St. Clair River

On the United States - Canadian Border

St. Clair River

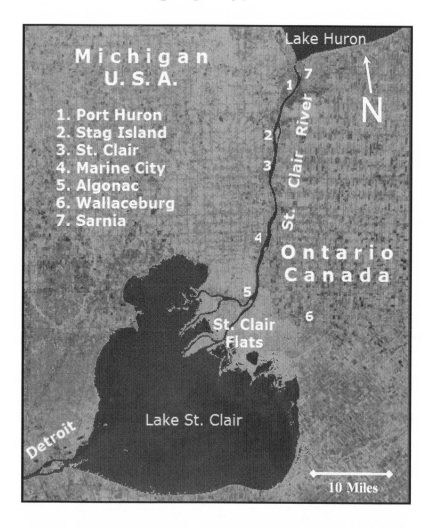

Michigan
U. S. A.

1. Port Huron
2. Stag Island
3. St. Clair
4. Marine City
5. Algonac
6. Wallaceburg
7. Sarnia

Lake Huron

St. Clair River

Ontario
Canada

St. Clair
Flats

Detroit

Lake St. Clair

10 Miles

St. Clair Flats

- The Great Lakes Delta -

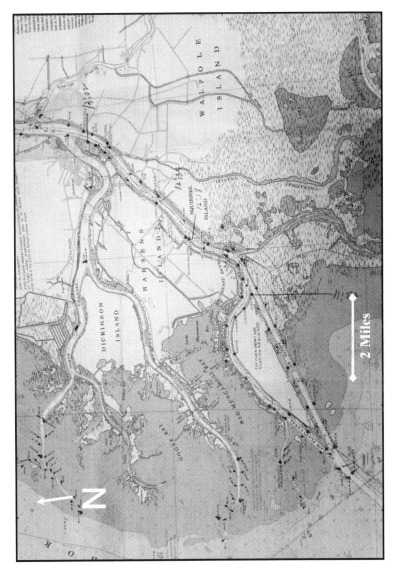

Friends

I had a friend who had friends by a river
They too had friends who had friends of their own
All seated round takin' port after dinner,
Port that was brought by the friends that were known

No one ever seems to care
Just as long as they were there
Friends beside you
Friends to guide you
Friends beside you, everywhere

- *Terry Reid*

CONTENTS

CHAPTER 1

The Accidental Bender

"The great thing about this river is it presents us with endless possibilities," Jeff Waters mumbled from his seat in the back of the boat. The comment hung in the night air, along with the fog which engulfed them as they drifted with the current. Lights from ashore burned through the mist, out of focus, large and surrealistic. The only sound an occasional light slap of water against the old cruiser's wood hull.

No reply came from Tom "Whitey" White who sat on the engine cover, mechanically moving his fishing pole up and down, up and down, bouncing a sinker off the bottom, somewhere in the darkness below.

From his seat at the steering console Kevin Casey turned and peered down stream, searching for lights on the channel markers through occasional breaks in the fog. He hadn't been on the river in years and was struggling to distinguish channel lights from shore lights. Was that a buoy or a fishing boat, he wondered? Was that a shore light or a freighter sliding slowly up stream, an eight-hundred-foot ore carrier headed for Lake Huron, unable to turn or stop if they drifted into its path?

Neither Jeff nor Tom scanned the river, there was no need. They'd spent their lives on the river and possessed radar minds and sonar souls. They knew exactly where they were.

Kevin Casey gave up his watch and turned towards Tom, the only one still fishing. He admired such patience and persistence, a true fisherman. It had been a long day, turned to night, but he was still at it. Jeff had long ago cleaned off his crawler harness and stowed his gear below. For him, fishing was an excuse to get down to his boat and onto the water. While Tom chugged for walleye, Jeff trolled for dreams. Kevin was along for the ride.

"You see," Jeff continued as he stared overboard at the dark, still water, "this river can take us anywhere. It's all the same water. It all runs together, anything is possible. We could drift from here to the sea, down the river, through the lakes, out the seaway to the ocean. Passed islands and towns and hidden bays, by opportunities and untold adventures and chances at life. It would be great, stop when we want, where we want."

"Man," Tom exhaled, "you must be buzzed! We're not goin' any further than the power plant."

"No shit!" Jeff sighed as he removed his ball cap and ran his hand through his curly, matted hair. "That's what I like about you Whitey, the cavernous depths of your mind. Where's your imagination?"

"Where's the beer?" Tom answered with a laugh. "Where are the freakin' fish?"

"Man oh man, Whitey," Jeff moaned as he reached for the cooler next to him, sloshed through its icy contents and continued undeterred. "You see, living along this river offers us a route out of here. But it's more than that, it's the water of life. It's timeless. It's everywhere at once, at the mouth, at the Flats, the lake, and here below this boat right now! This river is a water road to adventure, a liquid form of life. And, some say," he added with a sudden sense of revelation, "that a river is a liquid form of God!"

"He always gets like this when he's been out here too long," Tom said turning to Kevin. "Ocean my ass, we never make it past the Flats. He must be buzzed."

"I'm not," Jeff sighed as he placed a beer on the engine cover next to Tom. Then turning his attention towards Kevin continued, "I know we've never passed the Flats. But, it's knowing we could, it's knowing the possibility exists. It's always there, the water could take us, if we wanted, at least we can dream it," he said yanking his cap back on. "Sometimes, the dreaming is better than the doing.

Sometimes, the dreaming is all you get. But hey, that's better than nothin'."

"Oh man," from Tom as he began reeling in his line. "He gets out on this water and babbles on, like this river is some goddamn cosmic connection to who knows where. I'll tell ya, it's more canal then cosmic," and he added turning toward Kevin, "Your Captain Jeff here is nuts. Yep, Jeff, the Waterman, is nuts and I think he scares the freakin' fish off."

Kevin Casey wasn't going to argue with that, not after an entire day and half the night on the water with these two river rats, known around Riverland as the Waterboys. He'd learned anything was possible and that the unexpected had become the routine. What had begun as a quick cruise on the river of his youth, with two childhood friends he hadn't seen in years, had become a trip on waters not traversed by him in years. Most knowledge gained growing up along the waterway had been rendered useless by years ashore, and like a true landlubber, he'd strolled from the desk to the dock, without charting out a course, or checking up on the crew.

He'd discovered too late who he'd gone to sea with. A dreamer, who thought he was drifting through a fog on the Indian Ocean, and a fish head, who never got too far from a body of water, or a bottle of beer. Not two part-timers out on a two-hour blast across the water because the sun had popped out. They weren't beach boys, wearing baggy swimsuits, stylish sunglasses and smelling of Coopertone, at least not anymore. They were river rats, they were Waterboys.

He'd been shanghaied, should have seen it coming. He should have realized by the glow in their eyes that Whitey and the Waterman had plans for transporting a chance meeting on the deck of the Rocky Dock Restaurant into a reunion of some measurable magnitude. After all, years ago, the three had been inseparable. As youngsters, they were teammates in the games boys played growing up in the sporting class. Hours of pond hockey, touch football – down and out around the oak tree – hitting home runs onto the church roof, slanted like bleachers, or fouling one off – through a window. Endless games of hoops, traveling around town from one

11

driveway court to the next. They attended the same schools, left home together as travel pranksters and returned veterans of the psychedelic wars, before eventually drifting apart. They had much to talk about. Mostly they exchanged water stories, remembering tales of river adventures and high jinks, each followed by communal praise around the back deck of Jeff's cruiser, the *Lucky Lena*, for having the good fortune of growing up on the big blue water when they did.

Times like, when on an early summer morning, on a dare, they would defy the No Wake Zone and slalom ski down the Pine, the small river that cut through town and fed into the St. Clair. Starting on the straight away along the golf course, where the early duffers stared in wonderment at the high arc of sparkling water sprayed skyward as the ski cut into the river. Around the bend, past the boathouses and sleepy boat harbor where a dock attendant stood with hands on hips and a smile plastered on his face. He wasn't reporting anything. Around the next bend, digging hard to the right to throw a huge spray into the park, watering the flowers, they laughed, and under the bridge, into the St. Clair, the big river, before the napping draw bridge attendant rose from his chair. It was against the law. It was dangerous. It was there. It's what teenage Waterboys did. It was over before anyone knew what happened. Then Tommy T did it, barefoot.

The times on the big river when they skied up to freighters to bang on the steel side hulls with their fists then skied past docks that lined the shore, in search of girls sunbathing, to throw sheets of cold river water onto the unsuspecting tanners, sending them into shrieking spasms and fist shaking.

The times they played hockey on the river every chance they got throughout the long winters, when the ice froze thick and smooth between docks and pilings served as goal posts. If they were lucky they actually had a puck, or at least until it disappeared into a snow bank piled along the shore. Worse, was when it skimmed across a section of really good ice only to splash into open water along the dock line. Then they improvised, a chunk of ice, or a frozen pine

12

cone worked well. Goalie sticks were unheard of. A broom or snow shovel was the standard. Skates were pretty common but not required and the best skater always played the water side, skating up and down the wing closest to the river, where the ability to pull off a "hockey stop" or sharp turn was required to keep from falling onto stacked ice shards, or worse, over the edge into the deep and possibly deadly blue water.

The shenanigans of the Three Stooges, Soupy Sales, and Popeye era continued as the Waterboys grew older, including when the drinking age was 21 in Michigan, it was 18 in Canada, and Ontario was a mile away, just across the river, and everyone had a boat or knew someone who did. When they spent more hours a day on water then ashore, and when they got too burned out they were revived by a jump in the crisp cold water and rejuvenated by a hit on a joint, or was that the other way 'round, either way, they raced forward, experiencing more in an afternoon then many would in a week, a month, a year, or ever.

Now, he was stuck at sea with these two, now veteran marine cowboys, more duck than men, who often enjoyed a damp, dismal day as much as a hot summer one. A grey and soggy setting, when most boaters who plied this stretch of the Great Lakes would be tied up safe and sound at the local marina, leaving the rivers, lakes and Flats to the real Waterboys: the fisherman, freighter crews, and as Kevin Casey would soon discover, smugglers.

A breeze moved down river turning the boat slowly as it drifted on the calm water. A layer of fog lifted, clearing the night sky. Lights dotting the Canadian shore appeared to the east over a mile away. Above the *Lucky Lena* the fog suddenly parted, revealing a night sky filled with stars. The breeze cleared away a layer of mist that hung atop the water, and the Michigan shoreline became

13

visible. They drifted closer to the western shore, the American side, where boat houses lined the bank, dark silhouettes sitting on the water connected to shore by long, narrow docks. Elegant homes sat high on a hill above sweeping lawns running down to the water. The florescent blue glow of a television emanated from one of the homes. Sounds from ashore carried easily over the water; the laughter of teenagers hanging out in a boathouse, a car accelerating up River Road, a barking dog. It became still, very still. The breeze subsided. Calm settled over the river. The water so still it seemed one could step out of the boat and walk to shore on the black, marble surface.

The silence broken when Whitey calmly announced, "We got a down bound."

The *Lucky Lena* had swung 90 degrees to starboard, her bow pointed towards Canada. Kevin was sitting sideways in the pilot seat at the steering console facing north, the direction from which a down bound ship would appear, and though he'd searched the waterline on occasion, he'd missed this sighting.

"I don't see it," he said straining to find the telltale red and green running lights.

"Look for the masthead lights," Whitey reminded him. "The white lights high on the shoreline, above the shore lights. Focus on a group of lights and see if the taller ones are moving. When you find the shorter of the two drop down a few degrees and find the red and green running lights."

Easy for him, Kevin thought, as he pushed his hat back on his head and pressed his glasses tight against his face, squinting hard. This would be the fourth or fifth freighter passing of the night, and he hadn't found the lights before spotting the ship yet. The last one that passed, the *Middletown*, slid up bound, lit up like a party boat, her 730 feet strung with lights from bow to stern. Looking south from two miles away, Kevin thought they were lights from the town boardwalk, till the Waterboys mentioned they were moving.

Kevin struggled to focus across the darkness of the river to the shore lights upstream at a bend in the river two miles away. The

14

lights from the American shore on the west entwined with the Canadian lights to the east at the bend. The ships lights should appear near that spot, slipping between the American shore in the foreground and the Canadian shore in the background.

"There, I think that's it," Kevin half shouted.

"Good, hold it," from Whitey.

He hadn't taken his eyes off the lights, but now couldn't tell if they were moving, or only appeared to be because the *Lena* was moving on the current. That's it, he thought, but it was fading.

Suddenly the lights were gone, as quickly as they'd appeared, as a wall of fog rolled across the river from the northeast to engulf the *Lucky Lena* once again. Kevin hopped out of the pilot seat, making room at the controls, in anticipation of Whitey or Jeff firing up the engine to move the boat out of harm's way, but neither moved. Jeff remained seated on the back bench while Tom continued working with his fishing rig as he leaned against the engine box.

The fog became thicker, cutting visibility to a few yards in every direction. The Waterboys must be screwing with him, Kevin thought, waiting to see him panic, again? Was it another trick from the tricksters? Why now? On other freighter passages throughout the night they had simply started the motor, chugged a short distance, then shut down the engine to continue the drift. Each time a giant ship slid silently and safely past.

Kevin circled the engine box before leaning over the side hull. He peered towards the bow of the *Lena*, straining to find a break in the fog. There was none. Then he realized if the boat was still slowly turning, that might not even be the right direction anymore, and that he was once again, totally disoriented. The long night was wearing on him and the boy's apparent lack of attention stressed him. He was thinking of returning to the steering console to check the compass when Whitey calmly stated,

"We're O.K. man. Remember, we're only about 50 yards or so off the boathouses. There's plenty of room."

Kevin looked to Jeff for a confirmation but the Waterman sat motionless, staring into the back of the engine box, apparently on a drift above and beyond the current one, still pondering his water as life theory.

"Are you sure?" He inquired, knowing Whitey was right, but still not comfortable about drifting in an impenetrable fog, while somewhere nearby, a monstrous ship headed towards them with a good chance it would crush the *Lena*.

The seconds turned to minutes as the crew of the *Lena* sat in silent anticipation of the coming ship. Only Kevin seemed concerned that visibility was no more than ten yards in any direction. A chill shot through him. Was it the damp night air from standing on the open back deck, or the impending freighter? Either way, he'd been yanked to attention once again by yet another unforeseen event on this increasingly long voyage.

How long was it? He couldn't tell anymore. Then without warning, the sound of rushing water came from somewhere off their starboard bow, and moments later the fog rolled away enough to reveal a giant ship closing fast. It sat high in the water, empty of cargo, her raked bow pushing a wall of water that roared like a waterfall. The *Lena* had swung back to port as the vessel began to pass off their starboard side.

"A salty," from Jeff, now following the ship. "Wow, now those are some Waterboys for ya, Indian, Chinese, maybe African, certainly strangers to these waters."

Anyone who'd spent any time along the river knew the difference between a "salty," an ocean-going ship and a lake freighter of the fresh water inland seas. Even Kevin, who'd been gone for years remembered his freighter spotting. Lakers were long and narrow with the pilot house all the way forward and the powerhouse with stack aft and nothing in between but open deck. Its cargo of iron ore, coal, cement or grain loaded in holds below the string of hatch covers running the length of the sleek vessels.

Ocean freighters, like the one slipping by, were generally shorter, with the superstructure of cabins, wheelhouse, bridge and stack located in the center of the ship. On some, booms and derricks covered the decks fore and aft. Other ocean ships had superstructures all the way aft, or a combination of midship and aft.

"Just look at her," Jeff remarked with admiration, "sliding out of the fog like that, she has intrigue and adventure written all over her, don't you think?"

Neither Whitey nor Kevin responded. For Whitey, another of the countless ship passages of his life along the river. From what Kevin could see the ship looked a bit decrepit and in need of a paint job. But for Jeff, that's what added the romance.

"What a tramper. I hope we can read her home port," Jeff stated as he joined Kevin at the side rail. "What a tub she is," he added. "Look how beat up her bow is, dented and rusting. I bet she's put into many a port, Marseilles, Bombay, Dubai, Hong Kong, and now here she is, on the St. Clair."

"I bet there are characters aboard that crew," he continued. "You know, the way she appeared out of the fog, all dark and mysterious, I bet Bogart and Greenstreet could be aboard, in some cabin below the pilot house. There," he pointed at the ship, "those two dimly lit portholes, behind the steps coming down from the life boat station. There in that murky cabin, drinking scotch, smoking Turkish cigarettes, hatching a plot against the Captain who's hijacked them for a sizable cash payment upon arrival in some stinking backwater."

The ship passed close by, very close by in Kevin's opinion, and close enough that two figures moved out of the blackness of the wheelhouse onto the wing of the bridge to observe them. They leaned against the end of the bridge and peered down at the *Lucky Lena*.

"And there's the captain," Tom chuckled. "Let's hope we're not about to join Humphrey and Sidney."

The *Lena* was close enough to the ship that the angle allowed them to see only the heads of the crewman that leaned over the bridge to peer down on them. Kevin waved, but there was no response, then suddenly wished he hadn't.

"Friendly sort," Tom added.

17

"They're probably a little confused," Jeff said, again removing his cap to run his hand through his hair. "They can't figure out what we're doing out at this hour, especially adrift in the channel, in the fog, with lights out."

Kevin was wondering the same thing.

"Maybe they think we're the cops," from Tom.

"Cops?" Kevin inquired.

"Yeah, Coast Guard or immigration, or weekend sheriff boys," Tom added. "The Waterman's right. Just look at that tub. She could easily be hiding something, or somebody. Maybe even Humphrey and Sidney, eh Jeff?"

Jeff didn't hear the comment, or ignored it. He was onto something else. As the ship slid past, the sound of the bow wake gave way to the splash-splash-splashing from the approaching stern as the huge, half exposed prop chopped rhythmically into the river. The sound suddenly made the close passing seem more ominous.

"There, look at the light coming from the engine room," Jeff stated. "We'll be able to look straight inside her."

Moving along the top of the water a reflection of bright light emanated from a large opening in the ships side, where the hull began to bend towards the stern. As it approached, the sounds of the ships engine mixed with the splashing of the prop, the hiss of its steam turbines, sporadic clangs of metal on metal, and as the opening reached the *Lena*, the occasional outburst of unintelligible voices.

The opening was low on the waterline, and for a moment they peered straight into the ships power house. It glowed brightly against the darkness of the hull and blackness of the night. They stared into a steamy, loud, busy scene of shirtless men, shiny with sweat, working on different levels of a catwalk that surrounded the vessel's huge engine.

As it passed they were hit by a blast of heat that escaped the engine room and rolled over the *Lena*, followed immediately by abrupt shouts, and a wave from two figures leaning on the edge of the opening. Then as quickly as it had appeared the reflection of

18

light on the water disappeared off the *Lena's* stern, it's smoothness disrupted as it passed into the turbulence of the ship's wake, the engine room sounds engulfed by the thrashing of the huge prop now directly on their amidships, not more than 100 feet away.

"She's registered in Monrovia but flying a Greek flag," Jeff shouted as he stared up at the stern. "From the looks of the engine room probably an Indian crew, maybe Indonesian."

"Look at her rudder," Tom added, "she's swinging hard," and after a quick glance shoreward for a reference point, "we must be at buoy 52, it should come up on the other side of this tub as she swings 'round."

The *Lucky Lena* slipped under the stern of the ship now moving quickly away downstream. Unlike the unfriendly officers on the bridge, crewman hanging out on the ships aft deck shouted greetings, and made excited gestures as the cruiser unexpectedly appeared under their stern. The crew of the *Lena* couldn't make out what they yelled. When they were close enough the voices were washed out by the noise of the ship's prop, then they moved out of range.

Suddenly the mysterious ship and her crew were gone, enveloped in another fog bank as she rounded the buoy. A world entirely unknown to the Waterboys, and a life unrecognizable from the one just 100 yards ashore had slid silently by, self-contained, and carrying her secrets with her. Capitan Jeff, the Waterman was right, Kevin Casey thought. The river was full of mysteries and contained endless possibilities. He'd forgotten about the magic of the river, of the water. He had been away too long.

Whitey swung his fishing rig over the side of the boat, the sinker landing with a thud on the wooden deck. He took the can of beer from the engine cover and snapped it open. Lifting the crawler off the deck, "I've still got a worm, but it looks shot."

"Got any fresh ones left?" Jeff inquired.

Tom set down the rig and began digging through a plastic butter container full of moss and night crawlers.

"Oh yeah, I got a few swimmers."

"One more run?" Captain Jeff asked, already knowing Tom's answer would be yes.

"Why not," from Tom as he took a pull on his beer, "But, let's try some place else, there's nothin' happenin' here."

"Where to?" Jeff inquired as he returned to his seat on the back bench of the cruiser and Tom moved towards the console. Kevin noticed throughout the long voyage that even though it was Jeff's boat, Whitey did much of the piloting.

"How about Fawn Island, south tip, maybe there are boats down there?" Tom said. "Nobody's fishing up here tonight."

"Let's go," the Waterman replied, and turning to Kevin inquired, "Beer or coffee matey?"

"I think I'll grab a coffee," Kevin said before ducking through the cabin door and going below. He switched on a light and flopped down in the booth. A soft, yellow glow filled the cabin. He poured the hot brew from a thermos, and wrapped his hands around the cup to warm them. It was summer. It had been a bright, blistering morning when the *Lucky Lena* left the dock, but that seemed like ages ago. He'd spent the long hot day soaking up the sun, the beers, and the memories, but as soon as the sun set he was overcome with a piercing chill, and hadn't completely warmed since.

The news that the Waterboys were going to make one more river run to begin another drift didn't surprise him, but he'd hoped this voyage was about over. It had been a roller coaster ride. An exciting, stimulating rush of emotions, but coming out of the last loop, he was thrilled it was about to end, only to find there was one more lap to go. Now there would be one more run and one more drift down river.

On deck Jeff and Whitey made ready to get under way. The hum of the engine blower came on, followed by the louder sound of the pump sucking water from the bilge below. Suddenly the calm and quiet that accompanied them while drifting was gone in an explosion of sound as Whitey rolled the engine over. The big Chris-Craft groaned once, and then roared into action, sending a brief shutter along the boat's keel. After a few revs on the throttle, Tom idled back and slid the engine into gear. The cruiser slid forward, as the motor found its sweet spot, and settled into a smooth-running rhythm, the solid lifters clicking along beautifully, sounding like an old Singer sewing machine.

Kevin took another drink, switched off the cabin light, and moved to the couch opposite the booth to stretch out. He leaned back on several life jackets pushed against the cabin bulkhead. He steadied the cup as the *Lena* began to roll, and rise in the bow. Side to side, up and down she went. From out the sliding, cabin window he could see they were crossing a fairly sizable wake. The *Lena* had swung south and was running down river, catching up with the ocean freighter. The ship's lights appeared as they cleared her starboard side wake. They were running at a good clip and at a greater distance from the freighter, but she still maintained a shroud of mystery as she moved in and out of the patchy fog before being left behind. He took another sip from the cup and closed his eyes, emitting a weary sigh, realizing once again, he'd lost track of time on this Gilliganesque voyage.

Earlier in the long night, before the wind switched to the NNE bringing fog down from Lake Huron, the clock on the church steeple in town was nearing 1:00 as they drifted past. At that point they'd been out over 12 hours, motored more than 50 miles down the St. Clair River and back, anchored off Gull Island to clean the bottom of the boat, and gawk at the bikini's, cruised the marshes in the Flats, stopped to refuel the boat and reload the coolers. When night settled in, he discovered the crew had no intention of returning to port as they broke out the fishing gear.

All day, and long into the night, he'd been a willing participant in the raucous reunion. He was thrilled when Whitey and the Waterman plucked him off the deck at the Rocky Dock. Seated at a table overlooking the Pine River, he'd been reading a program from the Riverland Antique Boat Show, organizing a day of picture taking and interview ideas for a magazine feature he'd landed.

As he studied a row of brightly colored boat houses on the Pine, an excellent back drop for shooting the classic runabouts, he noticed an old wooden cruiser rounding the bend. He watched with admiration as she approached, then slid perfectly into a spot between two other boats on the break wall. A crewman stepped off the old cruiser, hopped up the stairs onto the deck, and was headed towards the restaurant entrance when, after inquiring glances, recognition came simultaneously.

It was at that point Kevin's day, his night, and his life changed dramatically, all his plans waylaid, and his comfortable little schedule altered, by that great deliverer of change and destroyer of all complacency, the accidental bender.

He hadn't seen Tom White in years, but though heavier and sporting a small beard, his saunter was unmistakable. After much expressed surprise, handshaking and back slapping, Tom hurried into the restaurant to pick up beer and ice while Kevin went down to the cruiser idling at the dock to greet Jeff Waters. Shortly after, he was aboard the *Lucky Lena,* headed under the Pine River Bridge, and into the mystic.

He thought about how easily he'd agreed to every suggestion and each additional escapade on the river voyage. About the boisterous belly laughs they'd shared throughout the long, midsummer, day of fun in the sun. He smiled as he recalled how they laughed at each other's new, decade's older appearance. How Jeff had retained most of his curly, not grey yet blond hair, still worn on the long side, or at least uncut, always matted down under a ball cap sporting a variety of team or beer logos. How he was certainly rounder, which made him appear shorter than Kevin remembered, and like many of his generation his protruding belly preceded his arrival.

22

A few hours into the voyage Whitey silently exited the cabin, snuck up behind Kevin to snatch the ball cap from his head, revealing a balding dome surrounded by the familiar, longish, straight brown hair they remembered. The Waterboys howled at Kevin's new look, barking they understood now why he wore a hat. Kevin was clean shaven, wore a style of wire-rim glasses it seemed he always had. Although heavier than in the past, his six foot two frame minimized any added weight had on his appearance. He thought his preference for wine and scotch may have helped him avoid the beer protrusions of others.

Kevin marveled at Tom "Whitey" White. He had changed the least, a small, precisely trimmed beard the only difference. He looked great, like he could still play football. Sure, a little heavier like most, but not by much, probably more muscle, solid and sturdy. After all he still worked hard, up and down the paint ladders he toted around all day. Unlike Kevin and Jeff, Whitey never wore a hat of any kind, ever. Why would he, his hair was perfect, always was. Still full, deep, dark brown with only a hint of grey beginning to show around the temples, parted on the left and Brylcreemed in place. Kevin announced numerous times on the voyage, "Your hair man, it never freakin' moves, not even in the wind." To which Jeff added, "It never did, and never does."

Their wardrobes were simple, and rarely changed. Captain Jeff wore an unbuttoned, nautical themed Hawaiian Shirt over a T-shirt, cut-off jeans and Samba's. Kevin, who thought he'd be working, wore a new blue golf shirt, clean Nike's and beige cargo shorts, pockets full of pens, notes and film canisters. Whitey preferred his white painter pants if coming from work, cut-off for summer, or Bermudas, plain T-shirts, and paint spattered Chuck Taylors.

Kevin shifted around on the cabin bench seat of the *Lena*, trying to get comfortable. He was exhausted, not to mention desperately behind on his assignment, and ready to call it a night, or morning, but was too tired to argue with the Waterboys. If they weren't going to call it quits, he was. He placed the cup on the table, turned

23

out the light, leaned back on the jackets and closed his eyes. He needed to regroup.

The sound and vibration of the Chris-Craft engine filled the cabin, the drone aiding his drift into an altered state of flashbacks ranging from recent hours to distant years. Adventures past and present swirled about in a gumbo of experiences, his mind unable to lash them down to their proper time and place.

He tried to block out anything to do with his assignment; the runabout shots missed on a perfect picture taking day, the appointments he'd blown off while darting and drifting on the water all day. But he couldn't. He battled to focus on a timeline, but couldn't as he drifted slowly off. He had taken shots while cruising down the river. Were the last ones taken at Harsens Island, he wondered, at the Old Club?

Images of the club on the tip of the Island drained into his mind as he floated toward sleep. Earlier in the day they'd slipped into the dockage area of the club in search of beer and ice. The Old Club was a private resort, but the Waterboys motored in, acted as if they belonged, and went about their business. A few retiring gentlemen along the docks were impressed enough with the *Lucky Lena* that they paid little attention to her crew.

They found themselves alone inside the club and while Jeff and Whitey went in search of the barkeep, Kevin roamed about the lobby. The walls were covered with pictures, a collection of portraits and party photos of the rich and famous who, in the early 1900's made the 35-mile trip from Detroit, across Lake St. Clair on excursion boats and private craft. After the turn of the century Detroit was flush with work and money and was on the cusp of becoming the Motor City, THE City, the technological and industrial center of the world. The city had just dropped the most user-friendly piece of technology into the laps of the masses the world had ever seen, the automobile. The four-wheel freedom machine. Hard working Detroiters needed a place to play and Harsens Island, with spots like the Old Club, Tashmoo Park, and the Idle Hour provided a resort that rivaled Newport and Atlantic City.

Other photos and renderings reflected the days when the island was known for its abundant hunting and fishing. Pictures of great groups of Hemingway like men, arms loaded with ducks or geese and stringers full of fish.

One wall of pictures and paintings depicted the multi-colored homes that lined the Old Club's boardwalk which ran south from the main club house into the lake, forming the southern tip of the island. Many of the cottages remained, built on pilings over the water, bedecked with wood railing porches. A few built with trap doors to allow residents to fish from the comfort of their living rooms.

Kevin walked into the empty bar, looked past the empty pool tables, out the picture windows to the docks and river beyond. The weight of déjà vu grew heavy as his numerous trips to the Old Club during his youth began to stream into his mind. He had been there before. To that exact spot, to the same pool table he now leaned on. He and Chip Morris played many a game of pool on that table, the last time when he was 13, maybe 14.

As he drifted off in the cabin of the *Lucky Lena* he dreamt of those times when he hung out all day in Chip's boat house on the St. Clair River. After the lawns had been cut and the papers delivered, too old to play with toy cars, and too young to drive the real ones, he and his pals were drawn to the water where they whiled away the long and lazy summer days by the water's edge. They swam, dove from dock pilings, fished, drove golf balls at freighters, played tag, and splashed about in small row boats. Days when it seemed summer would never end.

Inside the boathouse, hung in straps above the water, was a 1939 Chris-Craft runabout that belonged to Chip's father, Leo. The sleek mahogany machine, named *Bullet*, was 19' long, had twin cockpits, and as Chip's dad liked to say, "Went like a bat out of hell." The boys lounged in her red leather seats to escape the heat of the midday sun, but were never allowed to take it out, or drive it, except on those grand occasions when Chip's dad went down river to the Old Club.

The boys would hurry to load the runabout with duffle bags of clothes, a picnic basket, a jug of his dad's pre-mixed gin and tonics, then hop in the rear seat and wait in excited anticipation for Leo to slowly lower the *Bullet* into the water. Leo was always accompanied by a young lady on these excursions, Kevin knew Chip's mom didn't live with them, but was never sure who these girls were, or where they came from. He never asked and Chip never talked about them.

Adorned in a white captain's hat Leo backed the boat out of the slip, put one hand on the big, Packard style steering wheel of the Chris-Craft, the other around the young lady, and off they'd go. For Kevin, riding in a runabout was like riding in a convertible, except you were traveling on water. He sat in the auto-style back seat with his elbow resting on the side hull, just as he did when riding in his parent's car. He was taking a ride, top down, but instead of the confining grids of concrete roadways on land, they were roaring across the sparkling blue-green openness of the water.

Down the big river they ran, past Marine City, past Robert's Landing, past the State Park. They didn't talk much, it was hard to hear above the roar of the engine located just behind them, but there was no need to. The speed, the wind in the face, the spray of water making rainbows along the water's surface was enough.

On arrival at the Old Club Leo would pull into the closest slip, bounce around off the spiles till they could tie off, and then head for the club, with his young companion in tow, not to be seen again for hours.

While Leo and the girl sat in the bar the boys hung out on the docks all day. They passed the summer hours watching the endless parade of water traffic; the skiers, the freighters, the fisherman, the cruisers, and the rafters who floated slowly by on large inner tubes with no particular place to go and in no hurry to get there, the voice of Ernie Harwell calling the Tigers game on the dock attendant's radio a soundtrack to it all. When the afternoon sun drove them to the coolness of the club they ordered burgers and Cokes and shot pool, game after game.

As the long summer day turned towards evening Leo and his lady would emerge from the club's restaurant, loaded to the gills, and fall into the back of the Chris-Craft. That's when Chip and Kevin came to life. Now, after waiting all day, they were allowed to drive the runabout home. This is what they'd waited for all day, all week, all summer, all year. This made everything worthwhile. This made the summer. While Leo was groping his girl, or simply passed out, the boys didn't know or care, for they were completely focused on the *Bullet*. They went over the check list, repeating each step before function; open the hatch to air out the engine compartment; bilge pump; running lights; stern light; neutral; before turning the key, and finally pressing the starter button. As the engine rolled over and roared to life, and the runabout rumbled in the slip, it seemed too much power for too little a boat. With a glance and a nod Kevin undid the lines and Chip eased the throbbing engine into reverse.

Out of the slip at the Old Club, into the remaining light of a red ball summer sunset, they slid the sleek machine into the cuts and channels of the river, towards the long adventurous ride home. They ran the engine up slowly, as not to alarm Leo, until they were powering up the South Channel, planed off and running good. The power of the runabout surged through their bodies. A perfectly symmetrical wake streamed from the stern. They felt a surge of pride when a passing boater waved admiringly. By the time they reached Algonac nighttime descended over the river and they slowed to a safer, more comfortable speed. That's when the real challenge began.

The boy's were on a mission, alone, in the darkness. A mission as adventurous, as dangerous, and as compelling as any Huck Finn or Tom Sawyer ever experienced, they'd recall later, as they rehashed every detail while hanging out in the boathouse the next day. They needed to get hapless Leo and the girl home, safely. But even more important, they needed to return the wonderful watercraft to safe harbor.

They took turns driving, but the navigator was always just as important. All eyes were needed to help distinguish channel lights from shore lights. Was that a buoy or a fishing boat? Was that a shore light or a freighter sliding slowly downstream? An eight-hundred-foot ore carrier headed for the lake, unable to turn or stop if they steered across her path. And though neither ever mentioned it, they both prayed the fog wouldn't roll in off Lake Huron.

CHAPTER 2

Night Crawlers on the Canadian Bayou

The roar of *The Bullet's* engine faded together with the drone of the Waterman's cruiser. Suddenly, the *Lucky Lena's* cabin was filled with laughter. Chip and Kevin sat facing Leo and the girl at the cabin table. Leo's ruddy face was flushed with drink and jocularity. His commodore cap, too small for his bulbous head hung to the port side on his stringy white hair. His eyes wet from laughter, his arm around the babe.

Kevin was laughing also, at what, or why he wasn't sure, for he couldn't understand a thing Leo was saying. The words fell out of his mouth in the letters of the alphabet, turning to liquid as they hit the table top, before running off into their laps.

He noticed the babe though, for the first time really. So beautiful, and so young compared to Leo, and so bombed. With each burst of laughter she threw back her head, revealing her long, sensuous neck. Kevin stared at the spot where her neck met the top of her chest and formed a perfect little V. She must have noticed his attention, for under the table she kept running her bare foot up and down his ankle. Then up to his calf, then his knee. The cabin was spinning. He couldn't even remember her name!

Voices swirled in as the laughter faded away. Kevin tried to speak but couldn't. All of a sudden he realized nobody was driving the boat. Everyone was in the cabin. But *The Bullet* was a runabout, not a cruiser. It didn't have a cabin, or a table! He tried to rise, for someone needed to be at the wheel. He couldn't move. His ears buzzed and his head swam. As the strange mix of voices grew ever louder, and more unintelligible, the babes toe slid up his

29

leg, past the knee, higher, all the while the hum of the engines building to a crescendo before fading quickly to silence.

"Hey, Kevin, wake up man."

Startled, he opened his eyes, squinting against the cabin light.

"Knocked off pretty good, eh?" He heard a voice say.

"Yeah, I guess so," he grunted as Jeff Waters flopped down in the forward seat at the cabin table.

As Kevin drifted towards consciousness he realized his fellow dream travelers were gone, left to motor their way down the river of vapors without him, their memory returned to the storage of his mind.

"How long was I asleep?" he inquired.

"Oh, I don't know, an hour or so I suppose," Jeff replied.

Kevin swung his feet down to the floor. He felt like shit, worse than before he drifted off. His neck and back were stiff, his head pounded, and the anxiety from dumping out on the first day of his assignment grew with every waking second. He needed to get off the boat.

"Where are we?" He inquired as he turned to pull back the curtain and peer out the cabin window.

"Still on the river, but quite a ways downstream," Jeff replied as he removed the lid from the thermos.

"How far," Kevin asked, noticing it was still dark, then turned toward the Waterman seated at the table, "You know Jeff I'm ready to get back. I gotta get back to the Inn and get ready for….."

"I know," Jeff interrupted, "It won't be too much longer."

"Too much longer?" Kevin repeated as he shifted across the aisle to the booth seat opposite Jeff.

"Yeah, not too much longer," Jeff answered as he tipped the thermos to pour. "Damn, we're out of coffee, I better brew some more."

Before he could get up Kevin reached across the table to grasp his arm, "How much longer? I mean, I don't think you understand. I really need to get off this boat!"

The Waterman looked up from the thermos and paused before responding. "We need to make a quick, little delivery, before we go home."

"What?"

"We have to run an errand before we can head back upstream."

"An errand, a delivery, what kind of delivery and to where," Kevin blurted out? "What the hell are you talking about now," Kevin asked, still holding on to Jeff's forearm across the table.

"Smoke and booze," Jeff replied calmly, "to Canada?"

Kevin released his grip on Jeff's arm and fell back into the booth seat. He couldn't believe what he heard. He must still be dreaming he thought. He asked Jeff to repeat what he had just said.

"We're going to make a quick, little delivery, before we head home," Jeff said. "We're dropping off smoke and booze in Canada."

"Pot....... You're taking pot into Canada?"

"No, no man, cigarettes and whisky, no big deal," the Waterman replied as he searched the cabin for the percolator.

"No big deal," Kevin exclaimed, his voice rising above the noise of the *Lena's* engine. "No big deal? Jeff, it sounds like smuggling to me and if I'm right, it's still illegal, right? I haven't been away that long."

"I meant it's no big deal in that it's easy. We'll be in and out with no sweat."

"You've done this before?" Kevin asked.

"Well, yes."

Once…twice?"

"We've been doing this on and off for a while now," Jeff said.

"We?"

"Whitey and I," the Waterman replied as he rose from the table, "and another guy we've been working with the past five of six years."

"Working with?" Kevin said incredulously, his heart starting to pound. "You make this sound like just another job."

31

"Really, Kevin, it's no big deal. I mean once you get by the illegal part. We only do it occasionally. It's like a side job, you know, like moonlighting. And," he added as he sat back down in the booth with the found percolator and a package of coffee, "it's so damn easy."

"Well, I'm having just a little problem getting past this illegal part," Kevin replied rubbing his temples, trying to fathom what he was hearing.

"You know Kev, we're just workin' stiffs, tryin' to make ends meet. Nobody's gettin' rich off this. It's not about illegal or not. You know about that, right? Like the old days, it hasn't changed, the government trying to save the world, telling us how to live. We're makin' a little extra cash, and having some fun doing it. The way it is now things cost twice as much on that side of the river as on this," Jeff stated pointing with a flip of the wrist. "There's a demand and we're supplying."

"What if you get caught? What then? Don't you ever think about that?"

"No. Not really."

"No? You never weigh the risk involved," Kevin inquired. "Never think about jail? You mean Whitey never thinks about his kids, his family, putting them at risk?"

The Waterman emptied the packet of coffee into the percolator and plugged it in before replying. "We are not moron's Kevin. We have it worked out. Only the morons get caught. We pick our spots, are in and out, and know who we're working with. In certain instances, we don't go. Really though," he added looking Kevin in the eye for the first time. "It's no big deal. We're professionals."

"What about tonight?" Kevin asked. "You mean this entire night was just about waiting around for some smuggling gig to come up? Waiting for some secret signal or something? You guys didn't seem too prepared for anything tonight. Certainly not very freakin' professional," his anger rising.

"Little schedule change, that's all. No big deal."

"Hey! Jeff, I'm getting a little tired of hearing about this no big deal shit!" Kevin declared as he rose from the table. "And further more maybe this is a very fuckin' big deal for me! You stop to think about that?"

"Of course," Jeff replied calmly. "We discussed it at some length. We decided we can't put you at risk."

"Well, that's nice to know," Kevin sighed as he flopped back in the booth seat, then added with relief, "So you're dropping me off somewhere first?"

"No."

"No?" Kevin exclaimed. "What do you mean no?"

"No time really."

"No time for what?" Kevin asked.

"Well, no time to figure out what to do with you hanging around on shore, at a strange boathouse, or on some dock, or in someone's backyard, at three or four in the morning, 25 miles from your hotel, looking like, well, you'd been up for a few days."

Kevin stared at Jeff but didn't respond or couldn't. This protracted river run of excitement that turned stranger as the night wore on had now drifted into the scary, and was drifting dangerously close to the absurd.

"Think about it," Jeff continued. "We can't have you stay at the boathouse."

"What boathouse?" Kevin inquired.

"Our pick-up spot, we can't have you hangin' around there in case someone shows up. You'd be stuck with a lot of questions to answer that you couldn't. If you walk out to the road, well, now you're open to suspicion, just hanging out there at this hour, no car, lookin' like a damn ragamuffin. Hell, you know how that goes."

The Waterman paused but Kevin remained silent, staring towards Jeff, but more through him, then at him. The percolator began bubbling on the table.

"We felt it was better, not to mention easier, if you went with us," Jeff continued. "There would be a lot less that could go wrong

33

on the boat, fewer unknown variables on board than if you were ashore, alone. It's always better on the water."

"No alibi on shore," Kevin said, half joking.

"Exactly," the Waterman replied. "Too much we couldn't explain. Plus," he added with a smile, "well, I thought you might be into it, maybe a little anyway. I thought, you know, you might be up for going along."

"Really?" Kevin replied, caught off guard by the Waterman's remark.

"Sure. I just thought that after being together again like this, you know, I was thinking there was a time in the past when you'd be all for such a gig. I thought you might be up for some high sea adventure."

"I don't know man," Kevin groaned. "I can't even think straight anymore. I'm so burned out. So damn tired, give me a minute or so here could you?"

"Can't," Jeff answered as he reached over and opened a drawer below the galley counter top. "We'll be at the boat house any time now."

Kevin Casey reached for the muscles in the back of his neck and shoulders with his right hand and massaged the stiffness as he twisted his head around. "It appears I might have no choice at all," he sighed with a sense of resignation. "Like everything else on this voyage."

"Well, that's about it," the Waterman replied as he set a chart he'd removed from the drawer on the table. "Trust me Kevin, everything will be fine. And hey, look at it this way. It'll give you something more exciting to write about than that freakin' boat show!"

"What did Whitey have to say about this?" Kevin inquired.

"Oh, he was against it. So was Clayton."

"Who?"

"Clayton, our partner."

Kevin stopped stretching and rubbing his neck. "When did you talk to him?"

"While you were knocked out."

"What?"

"He found us while we were fishing off Fawn Island. You were still down here asleep."

"Found us, how?"

"With his boat," Jeff replied as he poured a cup of coffee from the steaming pot.

"So they were both against taking me along. How did you sway them?"

"Oh, I convinced them you'd be fine. Plus," he added with a smile as he rose from his seat and headed up the steps, "don't forget it's my boat and I'm its Captain. Many things have changed on the inland seas, but one thing that hasn't is, the Captain still has the last say."

"What if something happens," Kevin asked?

"Just jump overboard and swim for it," the Captain said as he disappeared up the cabin steps leaving Kevin alone in the cabin, the strong aroma of fresh brewed coffee filling the air.

Whitey slid the old Chris-Craft cruiser out of the fog just north of the designated boathouse. From his spot along the side rail Kevin watched as the wheelsman slipped the engine into neutral and rode the current past the boathouse, then at the precise moment, spun the spoked wheel, leaned heavily on the brass gear shift, powered up the motor, and swung 180 degrees dead on the boathouse door.

They crept forward against the current toward the two story, box shaped building set on pilings, 25 yards offshore. Kevin could make out houses and cottages onshore above and below their location, but the dock which ran from the darkened boathouse emptied into a thicket of bushes and trees. Two large doors occupied the south side of the boathouse and as they approached one began to slowly rise. Whitey pulled under and into a slip inside. The door closed behind.

Whitey left the motor running as he hopped out of the *Lena* with a line and secured the boat. A stranger appeared near a door on the dock side of the boathouse. As he reached a support beam by the bow of the *Lena* he dialed up a rheostat that brought a soft glow of light to the interior. He was a large man dressed in shorts, a dark sweatshirt, sneakers, and wearing a ball cap. Kevin assumed it was Clayton, the Waterboys' partner.

As Kevin stepped to the other side of the boat to help fend off, the three smugglers became a blur of activity. Jeff had gone below to open the front deck hatch and could be heard rummaging about in the cabin. Whitey pulled a canvas tarp from a pile of boxes along the boathouse wall nearest the *Lena's* starboard side as Clayton stepped onto the bow deck.

In fire brigade, water bucket style, they began loading the *Lucky Lena*. Whitey pulled a case of booze from the pile, swung it over the bow of the cruiser to Clayton who lowered it through the hatch to Jeff. They moved in a smooth rhythm, like they had done it before, and with no idle conversation. The Waterboys were all business.

Kevin inquired if he could help, and Whitey instructed him to remain where he was, hold the boat off, and be quiet. From the boxes that were labeled Kevin could see that most contained vodka, whisky, rum, and scotch. In short order the larger, heavier cases were aboard and the three began loading cases of cigarettes. As Kevin watched, he realized that the boxes changed from simple cases of liquor and cartons of cigarettes to illegal contraband as they were loaded aboard the *Lena.*

With a sigh of resignation he turned and sat down on the damp back seat of the cruiser. The sound of her engine exhaust spitting water bubbled in his ear. He still held onto the pilings but knew it was more an assignment to keep him out of the way than anything else. Was it exhaustion that caused his acquiescence, he wondered?

Was he so burned out he couldn't bring an end to his participation in the Waterboys' maddening voyage? He had no answer.

He scanned the interior of the boathouse. On the wall above where Whitey was working hung signal flags, shipping company banners, and a few ship nameplates. A stack of fishing poles stood by a door leading onto the small porch that sat over the river. The boathouse was constructed of wood with large beams framing the walls and running across the ceiling. A steel hoist sat directly above the slip the *Lena* sat in, and as he followed the workings was surprised to find a boat hung in straps, high in the ceiling, over the slip to his left. In the dim light it was difficult to make out in detail, but it appeared to be a wooden inboard, much smaller than the *Lena*, probably a runabout.

Along the shoreward wall of the boathouse were a picnic table, a fridge, and numerous tools hung above a work bench. Next to the fridge was a door that led to the dock going ashore. Staring at it he thought it wasn't too late to get out of this adventure, before it turned into a misadventure. He would simply tell the Waterboys no thanks, climb out of the *Lucky Lena*, and walk out that door, down the dock to shore. He didn't need to make it back to the hotel, or to anywhere. He would lay down under a damn tree and go to sleep. For that's all he really wanted to do.

Kevin got the feeling Clayton wouldn't mind such a move. He hadn't said a word to him, but based on the occasional glares he shot in his direction, then towards Jeff, he didn't appear too happy to have a stranger in his smuggling den.

"All right, let's go," Whitey suddenly announced from the deck above.

And they were off, as quickly as they had pulled in and began loading, they were finished. The lights went out, the door rose behind, Whitey hopped aboard with the lines, pulled the gear shift into reverse, and they were back in the darkness of the river.

The *Lucky Lena* backed safely clear of the spiles protecting the entrance to the boathouse, then swung slowly to starboard as the prop dug into the still water when Whitey put her in gear. As they headed into the dark expanse of the big river Clayton appeared in a fishing boat under the closed boathouse door. He sped south down river, same direction as the cruiser, only closer to shore.

The *Lucky Lena* lay in a small pool of still water just off the Big Bassett Channel, tucked among the high reeds and cattails that towered over the cruiser. She sat in Canadian waters, two miles below the Harsens Island Light, in the heart of the St. Clair Flats, a 200-square mile delta formed where the St. Clair River emptied into Lake St. Clair. At Algonac they'd taken the cut, leaving the shipping channel behind. Shore lights dwindled as they headed further into the Canadian Bayou. The on again, off again fog banks which drifted with them much of the night vanished when they reached the delta. The light from a nearly full moon washed across the low-lying Flats. They'd slowed the *Lena* and continued down the channel, and after their eyes adjusted, ran with her lights off. The powerful current of the big river dissipated with each turn into ever smaller distributaries, till they reached the spot where the water lay still.

"What time did Clay say?" Jeff asked for the second time.

"3:30," Whitey answered.

"He's late," Jeff stated, looking at his watch.

"I know," from Whitey, "I know."

The two stood on the back deck scanning the channel off the port side. The ten-foot cattails stood against the starboard side and most of the bow deck and transom were hidden. All lights were out as they waited.

Kevin stood behind the passenger seat holding an anchor line over the side, which wasn't necessary as they sat in four feet of water and the wall of reeds held them in place, but it kept him occupied and helped him relax. The tall reeds rustled in the light breeze, their tall tops swaying gently.

They waited, and waited, their anxiety growing, until the stillness of the marsh was broken by the distant sound of an approaching boat. In moments the Waterboys determined it was an outboard, and it was on the Big Basset. The boat approached from the north, then began to slow, more and more, until it was running at an idle.

"That's not him!" Whitey announced.

"What?" Jeff exclaimed in a hush.

"That's not Clay's motor! That thing's running way to smooth at idle, it can't be Clay."

"Lines over," they ordered in unison.

In a flash the Waterboys had fishing poles over the port side with sinkers pulling crawler harnesses to the shallow, sand bottom. A small wake preceded the arrival of the boat, rippled through the reeds, and lapped against the cruisers wooden hull.

"Don't say anything," from Jeff Waters.

"No shit," Whitey snapped back.

A small fishing boat slid out of the darkness, past the last reed beds, into space right next to the *Lucky Lena,* not twenty yards away. There was one person aboard, sitting at the idling outboard motor peering forward, searching the channel, then looking away left, then turning right, directly towards them. A moment later the fisherman returned to tracking the channel, floated beyond more reeds, and disappeared.

The boys waited in silence, exchanging anxious looks.

"Do ya think he saw us?" Jeff finally asked Whitey in a hushed, nervous tone.

"I don't know. I couldn't tell."

"Hell, he looked right at us, didn't he?" Jeff said as the outboard idled further on, then powered up and raced away.

"Who do you think it was?" Kevin whispered.

"I don't know," Whitey answered. "Probably some guy fishing and now he's lost, or taken a short cut home."

"He seemed to look right at us," Jeff repeated.

"Yeah, but I don't know, maybe he didn't see us. The moon is behind us so any light was in his eye, and we're tucked in here pretty good," Whitey said as he surveyed the scene. "If he was concentrating on finding a channel he may never have noticed us."

"What? We're a freakin' cruiser!" Kevin stated.

The Waterboys stood silently against the port side rail.

"And if he did, then what?" Kevin inquired. "It seems the jig may be up."

"What the hell are you talking about?" Whitey replied, obviously agitated.

"Well, if he did see us, what's next?" Kevin asked nervously. The more he thought about what just happened the more fearful he became.

"Hey Kevin, just keep it down for a few minutes here, O.K.?" from Jeff.

"Yeah, just shut the fuck up!" Whitey snapped.

"Hey, I just want to know what your big plan is now," Kevin cracked back, his voice rising. "Bein' seen wasn't part of the plan, was it?"

"Maybe he didn't see us," Jeff answered. "He didn't react like he saw anything."

"What if he freakin' saw us Waters, huh? What's next? I thought you said this was going to be no big deal."

"Damn it, calm down Kevin," Jeff said, then turned to Whitey, "What do you think?"

"Well, we had the poles in, if he saw us, he probably thought we were fishing," Whitey replied after a short pause.

"And if he was lost, and saw us, why didn't he hail us for help?" Kevin asked.

"I bet he was just rushing home, we're O.K.," Whitey answered with a lack of conviction.

"Oh boy, that's realfuckinassuring," Kevin mumbled as he turned to climb into the seat, convinced that his high sea adventure was on the brink of disaster.

Whitey was about to reply when the distant sound of a boat again grabbed their attention. It came from the south, the opposite direction from which the first arrived.

"He's coming back!" Jeff announced.

The Waterboys stood at the side rail of the *Lucky Lena* listening intensely as the approaching sound drew closer.

"It's not the same guy," Whitey said. "It's another outboard, but it's not the same one."

"Is it Clay?" Jeff inquired, hoping, as the boat began to slow.

"Yes, I think so, listen to that thing," Whitey stated. "It sounds like a blender full of bolts."

Once again an unseen boat was working its way through the marsh, toward them as they lay in wait. Kevin turned and asked the crew, "Hey, is this normal, all this traffic? I mean, it seems like too many damn boats to be safe."

"Just shut up will you," Whitey groaned, and then turning to Jeff, "Keep that pole working, till we are sure it's Clay."

The three waited silently till the boat finally slid into view, approaching from the south. It was another fishing boat, with one passenger, its silhouette nearly indistinguishable from the other. The crew of the *Lena* waited, staring at the boat.

Suddenly, it turned toward them and a bright light burst forth, first scanning the side hull of the cruiser, then flashing across the faces of the crew.

"Well, this is it," Jeff whispered.

Kevin felt a tingling that ran from the base of his spine to his armpits. He couldn't breathe. He was either having a heart attack or an adrenalin rush like never before. What the hell was happening? What was going on? Why had he allowed the Waterboys to get him into this?

The outboard motor went silent and the light went off, leaving them blinded, blinking into the darkness.

Waiting.

Waiting for jail, Kevin wondered as he turned in his seat to observe the Waterboys? They stood at the rail holding the fishing poles over the side. They gave no indication of panic, or any other emotion, as they starred silently at the small fishing boat now drifting toward them.

"Clay, is that you?" Whitey finally whispered into the marsh.

"Hell yeah it's me," a voice answered. "Who the hell did ya think it would be?"

"Didn't know there for a second," Whitey replied as he and Jeff leaned over the side hull to catch the bow of Clay's boat and guide it alongside the *Lena*.

"Another fishin' boat just passed through here," Jeff said. "It stopped right out there," he stated pointing into the channel, "and the guy was looking about. We didn't know if he saw us or not. Then he split, headed south."

"Yeah, and then you come headin' right back up the channel he went down," Whitey added.

"We thought it may have been him again," Jeff said as Clay's fishing boat swung alongside the cruiser. "Did you see him?"

"Hell yes, I saw him!"

"Did he see you?" Jeff inquired.

"I don't think so," Clay answered. "I saw his running lights, so I ducked into the reeds. I was running dark so he wouldn't have seen any lights and he never shut his motor down, so he would never have heard me."

"Did he pass you?" from Jeff

"Yeah, within about ten or 15 yards."

"But did he see you?"

"Na, I don't think so," Clay said. "He looked lost. He had a few poles hangin' over the side, he'd been fishin', must'av been lost, eh?"

Great, Kevin thought as he slid out of his seat and joined Whitey and Jeff at the side rail. Clay twisted his large body in the small boat to focus on Kevin.

"Well matey, what do you think? Did he see us or not?"

"Me?" Kevin answered. "I don't know. I mean, you're asking me? You guys are the pros, right?"

"Sure, we're the pros," Clay answered, scratching at his unshaven face, "but sometimes you have to go by feel, by instinct, by reading the play. This is one of those times."

"Yeah?"

"Yeah, so what's your gut say?" Clay asked as he shifted about in the fishing boat. "Should we proceed or not, did he see us or not? You're a reporter I heard, right? Your instincts should be good. Do we go or stay, sailor?"

Kevin looked toward Jeff and Whitey but neither said a word as they reeled in their lines.

"Well, I don't know," he replied.

"No time to think. Go with the feel, eh?"

"It doesn't matter what I think, or feel, does it?" Kevin asked turning towards Clay. "We're goin' in no matter, aren't we?"

"Hell yeah, we sure are," Clay laughed, rocking the fishing boat against the cruiser. "I just wanted to see how you felt, eh boys?" Clayton said turning to Jeff and Tom who made no reply as they moved about the deck of the *Lena*.

Jeff grabbed a pike pole and began pushing the bow of the cruiser towards the cut. Whitey hopped into the seat at the steering console and fired up the engine. Clay wrapped a line around the spring line cleat and snugged the fishing boat against the *Lena's* side hull and they were off, slowly into the darkness of the marsh. They crossed the channel in the cut and moved into a small opening in the reeds. Clayton gave directions to Whitey at the helm. The *Lena* proceeded at idle speed. Kevin and the Captain stared forward from the side rail.

The cruiser motored down a channel that turned ever smaller, till the marsh grass and reeds rubbed along the side hulls and forced Clay to clear a path for the fishing boat with his arm. In the moment the marsh became most impenetrable, they burst into an open pool of water.

"Now," Clay hollered above the motor noise, and Whitey powered up the old cruiser sending Kevin flying down the side rail, onto the rear bench seat.

"Oh yeah, I forgot, hold on," Jeff said as he held his position with a shift of his weight.

"Thanks," Kevin groaned as he pulled himself to his feet, struggling to balance the tilt of the deck to the increasing speed of the *Lena*.

"Now," Clay yelled again.

With that Whitey pulled back the throttle lever and shut down the engine and Kevin flew forward, crashing into the side of Captain Jeff.

"Shit," Kevin exclaimed, "What the hell's he doing?"

"Sorry," Jeff Waters repeated, "but we're here. Hang on."

With that the old wooden cruiser ran aground, knocking Kevin against the back of the steering console seat and again the Waterboys jumped into action. Whitey left his place at the wheel and ducked below into the cabin. Jeff followed. Clayton hopped out of his fishing boat into knee deep water and waded ashore. Kevin, tired of being bounced around, climbed into the pilot seat. Through the windshield he saw the front hatch fly open and Whitey climb through. On shore Clayton huddled with two indistinguishable characters that appeared through a thicket.

The *Lucky Lena's* bow rested on a narrow sand beach below a clump of small trees and bushes. Her stern, with rudder and prop, floated safely in three feet of water. Again, as in the boathouse, the smugglers were a whirl of activity. Jeff lifted the goods through the hatch to Tom White, who lowered them over the bow to Clay who handed them to the two guys who disappeared into the thicket, before returning to repeat the act, over and over.

Kevin's heart pounded in his chest. This was it, he thought. It was actually happening, right before his eyes. They were smuggling contraband across a border. He was smuggling contraband across a border, an international border. If they were going to get busted, now's when it would happen. When the cops would have them red handed. He waited for it. Agents from the Border Patrol, Coast Guard, OPP, State Police, RCMP, Sheriffs, ATF, to burst through the bushes and appear from the marsh, guns drawn, to bust them. Guns! Hell, he didn't know these guys on shore, he didn't know Clay. He certainly didn't expect this from Jeff and Whitey when he stepped on board for a "little boat ride." What if these guys on shore tried to shoot their way out? If he wasn't in over his head before on this long overdue cruise, he certainly was now. Everything building to this point was mere playful pranks, now, this was very serious shit.

His exhausted imagination reeled. He pictured the bust and later its aftermath. They all stood, he, Captain Jeff, Whitey, Clay, and the two strangers from shore, with their hands cuffed behind them on the back deck of the suddenly *Unlucky Lena*. They turned and saw a solitary figure in a small fishing boat, poles hanging over the side, emerge from the cattails, and motor slowly over to the stern of the *Lena*. As he moved closer they saw he was wearing sunglasses, at night, under the brim of a canvas bucket hat.

"Boy's, didn't you see me back there off the Big Bassett?" the figure asked. "I can't believe you didn't. I can't believe you still went ahead with it."

The thud of Whitey dropping the hatch cover closed snapped Kevin out of his pumping paranoia. Suddenly, the boys were finished. Clay waded back to his boat, Jeff and Whitey emerged from the cabin door and the two accomplices on shore pushed the *Lena* off the beach, bow to starboard, in anticipation of a quick departure.

In a moment they were idling back through the marsh. Clayton, the only one to speak, gave directions from the fishing boat as he retraced their route. Although it was a damp, cool night in the bayou, Kevin was soaked with sweat.

They emerged from the wetland and found the main channel. Clay untied the line from his fishing boat, fired up the outboard and headed back north, up the cut. The *Lena* swung south and ran down the Big Basset towards the lake. The first hint of light appeared on the eastern horizon as they left the narrow cut of the channel and entered the open expanse of Lake St. Clair. Whitey had the old

45

Chris-Craft cruiser running at top speed as Kevin joined Jeff at the port side rail.

"Beautiful isn't it?" Jeff shouted above the wind and the roar of the engine. It was the first time anyone had spoken since the exchange point back in the marsh.

"Sure is," Kevin agreed as he surveyed the scene then added, "How come we're heading this way, down into the lake?"

"We always try to leave by a different route than we enter, if we can."

Whitey began a wide turn to starboard in preparation of rounding a buoy that put them in the St. Clair Cutoff, the freighter channel which cut through the Flats connecting Lake St. Clair to the South Channel and the St. Clair River. As they swung round Kevin was amazed to see a tall, lit building on the distant horizon, across the lake to the southwest.

"What's that?" He inquired.

"Oh, that's the Renaissance Center in Detroit," Jeff replied.

"Downtown, that's downtown Detroit, it's that close?"

"Yeah, from here, straight across the lake it's about 35 miles."

Kevin was so disorientated, again. The entire night of drifting on the water and creeping around in the uninhabited Flats, the stillness, emptiness, the sense of vastness of the delta, was like being lost in an endless swamp, and yet when they emerged from the Canadian Bayou, there was metropolitan America, blinking on the horizon. He turned and plopped down on the back-bench seat, his senses overloaded.

Whitey never pulled back on the throttle till just off Algonac, back in the big river, where Clay pulled alongside and climbed aboard. Jeff tied his boat off the stern cleat of the *Lena* and they continued their run up river. Jeff and Clay invited Kevin into the cabin where they opened four cold beers from the fridge, handed one to Tom at the wheel, and toasted the success of the night's events. Then upon the insistence of the captain, gave Kevin a cut of the night's earnings. The three joined Whitey on deck as they sped north. Not a lot was said, it was hard to converse above the engine noise, a few belly laughs were had, but mostly they rode in silence, consumed by fatigue and what had just transpired.

Kevin stepped back from the protection of the windshield to let the wind hit him in the face. He leaned his head back to watch the dawn sky change colors by the second. Clouds to the west highlighted in shades of violet. As Whitey slowed to maneuver the *Lena* off the big river and under the Pine River Bridge the sun hit the horizon above the Canadian shoreline behind him. Kevin felt becalmed. He was exhausted. He was exhilarated. He was a rumrunner.

CHAPTER 3

The Waterfront

The mahogany Chris-Craft runabouts slid around a bend in the Pine River, gliding through mirror like water side-by-side, a blend of machine, style and soul seldom seen. They appeared so quietly Kevin Casey didn't see them till they were upon him. He quickly reached for his camera and began shooting the craft, their red-brown hulls and decks glistening below a dozen coats of varnish. The craft moved silently by, the high polished chrome cutwaters slicing through the still water. As the boats passed the rumbling of the powerful engines suddenly filed the air, a rhythmic combination of low-idle and water spitting from exhausts forming a deep, guttural sound Kevin felt in his chest.

"Beauties eh," A voice next to him shouted above the noise.

"They sure are," Kevin replied as he fired off one more shot as the runabouts moved away. He glanced at the man.

"A fifty-four Sportsman and, I'm not quite sure on the barrel-back, late thirty's, maybe forties."

"Is that right," Kevin replied as he fumbled with his camera.

"I'm pretty sure."

The stranger, dressed in boater apparel: baggy, khaki shorts, no socks, brown top-siders, white golf shirt and large brimmed ball cap was ready for more conversation. Kevin, however, wasn't. Not yet. He was fried. He was still possessed with the events of the night before. He returned to the shelter of the viewfinder as bits-and-pieces of the previous 24 hours replayed in his mind. He was coming off two hours of sleep, and hadn't eaten since, well, he couldn't even remember. And though it was only mid-morning, the bright sun was baking his brain. He felt like he might throw-up at any moment.

"I'm pretty sure," the man repeated, "But hey, don't quote me, I'm a cruiser guy, mine's over there," he said pointing across the harbor.

"Yeah, is that right?" Kevin stammered, staring into the screen of his camera.

"Yes, would you like to have a look at her?"

"Well, I have to, ah," Kevin mumbled, suddenly realizing this guy wasn't going away, and somehow he had to pull himself together. He began to sweat. He started to feel light-headed. "I have to get some info here," he continued. "I really need to," and with that Kevin pulled a notepad from his bag then watched as a pen fell from the pad, onto the dock, and rolled in slow motion toward the edge, before dropping over the side into the water. "Shit," Kevin spit, his hands shaking. He spread his feet a little to steady himself. He was surprised how long he could follow the silver sparkle of the pen as it floated down, and away, like a fishing lure, before it disappeared. It was his favorite, a gift. He stared into the water for some time. "Shit."

"Say, you all right?" the man inquired, moving closer to Kevin. "If you don't mind me saying, it looks like you could use a chair. Why don't you come aboard my boat and have a cool drink, coffee, or lemonade, get out of the sun."

Kevin turned to really look at the man for the first time. Much of his face was hidden below the cap, and behind sunglasses, but his smile was sincere and welcoming. He was offering an oasis, and Kevin accepted.

"I'm a little, uh, tired. I mean, sure let's have a look at your boat," he answered.

"Great!" the man exclaimed as he turned and led Kevin down the crowded dock.

Kevin had spent the morning at the boat harbor, concentrating mostly on the runabouts, walking the docks, and shooting the antique machines from all angles. He wondered how he missed the marvelous Chris-Craft cruiser tied off the end of dock three.

"I'm Jack LaCroix, and welcome aboard the *Captain Jack*, grab a chair and take a load off."

Kevin stepped aboard and found a seat at the table on the back deck and flopped down, under its umbrella, with a sigh. The coolness of the shade swept over him.

"So, you we're up a little too late, eh? Must have been quite a party?"

"Well, I...." Kevin stammered, a little embarrassed that his present state was apparently so obvious.

"Hey, that's all right. Were you over on the long wells, down at the picnic area? The Otsi Keta Yacht Club gang had a blow out there. I was there, but I don't remember seeing you. Say, are you the fella doing a story on the boat show? They said someone was coming. So, what will you have to drink? What you say your name was?" Jack's questions flew fast and furious.

"I'm Kevin, Kevin Casey, and water would be great. Do you have any water?"

"Sure," Jack replied as he retrieved a bottle from a small fridge built into the bulkhead and handed it to Kevin. "Say, those runabouts are quite the machines, eh?"

"Beautiful," Kevin replied before taking a long pull on the bottle.

"You know," Jack went on without waiting, "the reason they built those boats was to run booze over from Canada during prohibition. Well, actually, they first build them to race, but it didn't take folks long to figure out what all that speed was good for, eh?" he said with a laugh.

Kevin could only nod in agreement. Before he knew it, he received a brief history of runabouts on the local waterways as his host scurried about making sure the deck and steering station were ship-shape. The famous names of wood boat history rolled off his tongue. Chris Smith, Gar Wood, John Hacker. But, as one would expect from a Chris-Craft owner, Jack revered Smith the most. He told how Smith started building small fishing and duck boats, down the river in Algonac, in the late 1800's, to allow sportsman to enter the fertile St. Clair River Flats to hunt and fish. How it was only a natural progression for the gas engines that were being built for the burgeoning automobile industry to be placed in boats. How Christopher Columbus Smith and four of his sons built a craft in 1914 that went 50 miles per hour. Then came the racing, which led to the Gold Cups, the "Miss Detroit's" and "Miss America's," bigger and faster, always faster. How Smith collaborated with Wood, put twin aircraft engines in a 27' foot boat and blew the Brits out of the water to gain international fame.

"Nine hundred horses in a 27-footer, in 1919!" Jack exclaimed in awe, as he paused only long enough to drink from his jumbo coffee thermos. Kevin thought he should be taping this guy or taking notes, but couldn't. Jack was flying while Kevin was crashing. He closed his eyes, hiding behind his sunglasses, as the cool shade tugged at him. Jack talked about one of Smith's sons, Hamilton, who came up with the name "Chris-Craft" in the early twenty's, when the business switched from strictly racing to the rapidly growing, and more lucrative private pleasure craft market. Another son Jay, he thought it was, started dropping auto style engines into boats, and helped perfect Chris-Craft's own motors. Then, the Smith's adopted Henry Ford's idea of assembly line production and began producing the wood pleasure craft in greater numbers.

Soon after, the Smiths became kings of the new runabout rage. The boats became the new toys of the rich and famous, and not long after, the infamous. Harvey Firestone and Charley Chaplin owned Chris-Crafts, and in short order, so did Al Capone. It wasn't long before Chris-Craft unwittingly become the unofficial suppliers of thirsty Americans.

"Now, Chris Smith and his son's boat company of Algonac, Michigan never condoned such activity, but man, business was good," Jack beamed. "There were demands to be met. The people were thirsty, even if the government wasn't. Smith's sleek and powerful craft not only raced ovals up and down the rivers and lakes, they raced across them, back and forth to Canada, carrying prohibition booze."

"My old man told me stories." Jack continued, as he quit cleaning and flopped in a chair across from Kevin. "How, when he was young, he pumped gas at a filling station on River Road, and now and then these big, expensive roadsters would pull in, full of guys in coats and wearing fedoras, you know, brimmed hats, pulled down, in the summer. In hot weather! They would gas up, pay with large bills, and pull out. It was then my old man would see the Illinois plates. Everybody knew they were smugglers. The only chatter around the station was if any of those mugs were Al Capone. My old man always insisted Al was in one of those cars."

For the first time since they stepped aboard, Jack stopped talking. Kevin waited, thinking it was only a pause in the oral history of Chris-Craft and rumrunning, but the story seemed over. He wanted to tell Jack that he knew all about that smuggling stuff. Something like, hey, speaking of smuggling, I just did a little of that myself, last night. Tell him that the days of Capone and rumrunning still existed. That Americans were now returning the favor, sending booze and smokes back across the border to Canadians who were paying twice the price for the same stuff, some of it made by them, exported to the states, now coming back at half the price. Last night, he made a run to the Flats himself, but in a cruiser, an old Chris cruiser, similar to his, only smaller. He took another drink. It was all too surreal, too weird.

"But hey, if you're the reporter, you are, right?" Jack inquired

"That's me, I guess," Kevin replied.

"Well, you probably already know all that."

"A little, but nothing like you, how do you know so much? You sure know a lot about runabouts for a cruiser guy," Kevin smiled.

"Ha," Jacked laughed. "It's a hobby I guess. Yes, my hobby. Everybody should have one, eh? Need to keep the mind active. I do a lot of reading. I'm retired now, so I fill time reading. Hey, I've been on the lakes for years, I've seen a lot of runabouts."

"Keep those synapse snapping, right dad?"

53

Kevin quickly turned to see a young woman emerge from the shadows of the cabin entrance and climb the steps into the bright sun washing over the back deck.

"Hey, good morning girl," Jack said, rising to greet her with a hug. Then turning to Kevin, "this is a fellow I met, here to cover the show, say, I'm sorry, what was your name again?"

"Kevin."

"That's right," Jack laughed. "This is my daughter Renee."

Kevin sat in the shade of the table umbrella. Renee stood before him bathed in sunlight. Short brown hair, white T-shirt, cut off jean shorts, tan and bare-foot, a vision. She shielded her eyes from the bright sun with one hand and reached out to Kevin with the other.

"Hey, nice to meet you, I'm Renee."

Kevin took her hand and stood, bumping his head on the umbrella, which pushed his ball cap down onto his sunglasses, which slid down his nose. Jack and Renee had a good-hearted chuckle. Kevin felt like a complete asshole.

"He's had a rough night, and a long morning," Jack said as Kevin stumbled out from under the umbrella to adjust his lid and glasses.

"Is that so?" Renee smiled.

"I suppose so," Kevin half-laughed, humiliated, the bumbling fool with a hangover. If they only knew, he thought. And for a fleeting moment he was going to tell his tale. That would show them he was more then what he appeared to be. He was more than some geeky reporter. He was a rumrunner damn it. Not some idiot bumping around the back deck of their cruiser. That would impress her.

Jack began scurrying about again. Renee was still smiling at Kevin who said nothing. The pause broken only when Jack announced he was late and had to run.

"Hey you two, I'm supposed to be at the judge's tent for a meeting. Damn, I got rattling on a little I guess. Well, you two get to know each other and I'll see you later." And with that he stepped off the *Captain Jack* and started down the dock, only to turn and shout back, "Say honey, tell him about the trip to the island tonight. Invite him along." Then he disappeared into the crowd.

Renee, like her father, had a gift for gab. After stepping below for a cup of coffee, she returned topside to join Kevin, once again seated at the table. She had no problem telling her story, and Jack's. They were cruising around the lakes on a sort of, 'get to know you again' trip. He was a retired sailor who had spent years working on freighters around the Great Lakes. He was gone much of the year, leaving her and her mom, alone, together at home. Her mom had passed, dead from Alzheimer's a couple of years now. All those years Jack was gone, and when he finally returned, she was gone, long gone, onto a different plane completely. Jack was on Lake Superior when Renee was born, and he pretty much missed most of her coming of age moments, which helped with her becoming an independent kid, and a very grown up teenager. Only her mom's illness brought her and Jack together, for the first time really. During the struggles of watching over her mom's demise, they promised each other this trip. It was early on in the reflection and reconciliation cruise, not much had been talked about, but at least they were together.

Kevin wondered what encouraged these people to open up in his presence. Give him histories about themselves. Tell stories. He hadn't asked any questions, not on this morning. He usually did, with the, who, what, when, where, why foundation of reporting he carried at all times. But not this time, he just sat there and listened, everyone has a story to tell, if you listen, and in this instance, watched Renee, who was easy on the eyes.

She told of having a hard time getting her father to sit still, and talk, really talk, about his life, especially his life with her mother, and their life, or lack of one. He was always moving about, or heading off if her questions got to personal. Sea stories, boat questions, weather reports, shipwrecks, history lessons, book plots were all O.K. He could be moved by a good book, but never wanted to open the pages of his own story.

When she spoke, she rarely looked at Kevin, but stared at her coffee cup or scanned the parade of people strolling up and down the dock. On the occasion she glanced his way, there was a sparkle in her eyes, no remorse or regret. Wonderful, brown eyes, he observed. He was, he thought, smitten.

He was certainly the most relaxed he'd been since arriving in town. He was exhausted, true, but resting in the shade, in the company of Renee, becalmed him. He had taken enough photos of the runabouts that morning to ease the anxiety over his assignment. The intense excitement of last night's adventure was behind him. Now that it was over, he reflected on the glory, safe in the knowledge he had survived a frightening experience, never again to be repeated. Now, he found himself in the presence of Renee. She leaned back in her chair to stretch, a full wake-up, morning stretch. Her tan, angular body stretched before him. She stood and moved to the boat's side rail. He joined her

"What a beautiful morning," she said without turning.

"It sure is."

They stood in the morning sunshine, on the port side of the *Captain Jack* overlooking the Pine River. It was a sunny, summer Saturday and the river was busy with activity. Boats of all types began to back up on the river, waiting for the bridge to open. Small fishing boats and larger ones with inboard/outboards and down riggers, an open bow ski boat, a pontoon party boat, Sea Rays, and a couple of antique runabouts from the show. The larger boats jockeyed in position in the breeze; forward-neutral-reverse, forward-reverse, to stay in place, waiting their turn, while the smaller boats snaked through the pack, under the closed M-29 bridge, into the big river.

Across the river small, colorful, brightly painted boathouses lined the west side of the Pine. Most with doors open, the morning sun brightening busy, boathouse activity, small boats ramped into the water and picnic tables being set, fishing gear being prepped, children jumping from docks into the cool water, laughing and splashing, the seagulls calling, gliding onto the water, or sunning atop pilings.

Kevin looked at Renee. Her eyes closed, head tilted slightly back as she soaked up the sun. He looked at her face, her eyelashes. He traced the line of her nose, to the shine on her lips. He changed the angle with his mind's lens, zooming back to half her profile, and half the boat life landscape in the background. It was a perfect portrait. He wanted to take her picture. No, he wanted to kiss her. He would take her picture, he thought, then kiss her. He refocused again, beyond her face. It was a perfect shot, an impressionistic landscape with a beautiful woman in the foreground. Monet would be happy.

After a moment, his attention was drawn to the water, where drifting out of the nautical landscape in the background, and into focus came a boat, towards them, closer.

Was that the *Lucky Lena* he wondered as he refocused his minds camera?

"Kev? Hey, thought that was you?" a voice hollered as the cruiser approached.

It was the *Lena*. It was Jeff Waters, the Waterman.

Kevin's heart sank as the *Lena* slid alongside.

Tom White enjoyed the solitude and silence atop a forty-foot extension ladder; it was the Zen of house painting, high above the madding crowd. In amongst the treetops, with the birds and squirrels, tucked up, under the eaves, painting the wood trim, carefully cutting along the brick. No people, no phone, no desk, no noise, nothing. Alone, it was his Sistine Chapel.

And this job came with a view. Red Holtz' great stone home sat on the hill overlooking the river. Tom was positioned on the southeast corner of the house, the riverside, the sunny-side. From his perch, three stories up, he could easily see Canada across the river to the east, and the fields well beyond. Below, the lawn terraced down to the river, its water dancing with sparkles in the morning sunlight. To the south, through breaks in the trees, he could follow a distant bend in the river.

"Hey Whitey, come on down, take a break," came the gravelly voice of Red from below. "I see a cloud over there."

It was one of Red's favorites. Search the clear blue sky for any cloud, anywhere, near or far, small or large, on any horizon. When he found one, he would approach Tom, warn of the impending rain and storm and order a halt to the painting.

"You'd better knock off. I think something is building up."

"I don't know Red. I should finish up around this overhang."

"Oh, don't worry about that," Red replied, "You've got all damn summer."

Like always, Tom complied. He unlatched the bucket and climbed down the ladder. Red greeted him with a smile and a tumbler of vodka and grapefruit juice.

Hours of prime painting weather were left, but Red was the boss on this one, it was his house, and he was paying by the hour. Tom was being paid the same to paint, or to drink with Red. To accompany him on one of his last summer sojourns. Sometimes Tom wondered if Red wanted the house painted at all. On day's he needed to make serious progress Tom would wait till late afternoon before showing up, when Red was usually knocked out napping. Or drive by his house to see if his car was gone before showing up. He knew it would be late fall before this gig was done.

Tom cleaned out his brush, placed a lid on the paint can and plopped down in the Adirondack chair next to Red. They sat on the small terrace at the back of the house, in the shade of a huge oak tree, overlooking the river. Both men took a drink then sat quietly as a breeze rustled the leaves and cooled the scene.

"So, Carol and the boys are well?" Red inquired after a while.

"Doing fine, thanks for asking," Tom replied. It was the standard opening salvo from Red in these come-down-from-there-let's talk conversations. Before long, Red would be rambling on in a stream of conscious tale of some sort, but he always started with the inquiry about Tom's family, always heartfelt.

"Boy's growing fast, eh?" Red asked.

"Very, very fast and you know Red," Tom added, "I'm feeling now I missed something. They went from being little boys, to, I don't know..."

"Little men," Red added.

"Yeah, I guess, I mean it just happened overnight," Tom said. "And I was paying attention. I was there all the time. I knew it was going to happen and I still missed it."

Red's daily inquires about his boys had gotten Tom thinking. He had listened closely when people told him to hug and hold 'em, and cherish them early and often because soon enough, things would change, and somehow wouldn't be the same. He knew they were right. So he was there, watching, staring. Still, he missed it, the change. It had happened to Tom Jr. and was happening to little Leon. He'd missed one and couldn't grasp the other.

"You did better than most. Much better than most," Red stated, and after taking a long pull from his tumbler added, "When are you bringing 'em by? You said you'd bring 'em along. They can swim off the dock."

"Soon Red, soon," Tom replied.

Red and Rose Holtz never had any kids. Tom never knew why. Red never said. Tom never asked, but often wondered. The huge house on the hill had plenty of room. Was he too busy, always working? Red was a former engineer for one of the big three automakers, drove every day to Detroit and back, worked all the time. On weekends he worked more, maintain the home, the yard, a boat, and building things in his shop. He never had time for kids. Maybe he never slowed enough to think of having kids. Or maybe they couldn't. Either way, Red now wanted to see Tom's kids.

"I'll bring them over. They want to come. I'll check with Carol, see what their schedules are," Tom said.

"Schedules?" Red huffed. "Kids shouldn't have schedules."

Tom sipped from his tumbler but didn't reply.

The two sat overlooking the river. Bird songs filled the air.

The bow of a freighter appeared from behind the trees framing the view of the river, moving left to right, headed down bound. Only the nose of the gray hull and half of the forward cabin and pilothouse were in view when Red announced, "The Ford. She's the E.M. Ford, Huron Cement boat, 428 feet."

"Right again," Tom replied, knowing Red had nailed another. He was the king of freighter spotting. Tom knew it was a Huron boat by its distinctive cement colored hull, but not which one. Not that quickly.

"She's an old, old boat," Red stated, "built in eighteen something, 1895 or '96."

"But she's still running, still working," Tom said as the ship moved silently by. Both men had seen the Ford many times. From shore, on patio's and porches high above the river; while driving through town on River Road; while leaving the Drug Store; while cutting the grass or raking leaves; from someone's dock; while seated at a restaurant; close up, on the water, while fishing or motoring on the St. Clair. She was a common sight on the river, yet each passing was special, and remembered, for she was an old, classic lake freighter and her kind were disappearing from the lakes, torched and cut by the ship breakers, to be replaced by 1,000 foot behemoths.

The two followed the old ship as it slid silently downstream. As it passed beyond the tree line at the bottom of Red's property a cruiser appeared, headed north. It drew closer, moving slowly along the dock line, Red inquired, "Is that the *Lena*?"

"Sure is" Tom answered.

"So, you boys doing any runnin' lately?"

Tom replied in the affirmative, retelling the adventures of the previous night. Of the rendezvous with Kevin Casey, the run after a full day of boating, taking Kevin along, against Clay's wishes, the anxious moments of the encounter with the fishing boat moments before the handoff.

Red knew of the boys moonlighting. Tom had told him some years back. No one else knew, except, now Kevin Casey knew. At first, Jeff and Clay weren't aware Red knew what the boys were up to, but Whitey gradually broke the news. And despite Red's propensity for storytelling, he never breathed a word of the boy's adventures. They trusted him. So did Clay, grudgingly. He fortified this trust with an occasional bottle of vodka.

As the *Lucky Lena* approached Red's dock and boathouse Tom could make out Jeff and Kevin on board. He couldn't make out the third passenger though. The *Lena* slowed down and Jeff moved from his position at the wheel to the side rail and began waving.

"What are they up to now?" Red inquired.

"Not sure, but it looks like they want us to head down to your dock," Whitey answered.

Red pulled himself out of his chair with a groan, walked the short distance to his driveway and slid into his golf cart. Tom quickly cleaned up his paint gear, hopped into the cart, and they rolled down the hill, tumblers in hand, to the dock.

The *Lena* headed north, up river, the Waterboys' crew grown to five with the addition of Kevin, Renee and Red. Like the day before, when Kevin first boarded, Captain Jeff Waters seemed genuinely excited to welcome additional passengers on board. Now, with Renee sitting on the aft bench seat alongside Kevin, the Waterman was raring to go. Wearing a T-shirt that read 'I'm the Captain and You're Not', he regaled her with a river and home tour from the moment he picked them up at the boat harbor. Kevin sat quietly, he'd already heard much of the travelogue, and though content to be sitting and resting, would have preferred to remain aboard the *Captain Jack*, with Renee. Tom stood at the wheel. Red stood across from Tom, steadying himself with one hand on the cabin top, one on his tumbler.

Just south of Potter's buoy, Tom swung the *Lucky Lena* to starboard, powered up the engine, and headed for the middle of the river, the roar of the motor and rush of wind effectively ending the Waterman's river tour for the moment.

"Too much snot," Tom hollered back to Jeff, who shuffled his feet and grabbed the side rail for support. The river, which the night before was as flat as a tabletop, was becoming a surging, rolling mess. The previous night the *Lena,* and the occasional freighter, were the only boats on the water. Now, it was Saturday. A sunny, hot, summer Saturday, and the weekend warriors were out in force.

Captain Jeff knew by the traffic they encountered in the Pine it would be a busy day. He knew the Martini Fleet and Poodle Navy would be running, roaring up and down the river, too fast and too close, too close to other boats and too close to shore, wakes from their boats crashing into breakwalls, roiling back into the river to collide with other wakes, creating the surging stew known as snot. For calmer water there were two choices. Get off of the river or move to the middle. That's where they headed.

Though things were less choppy as the *Lena* moved toward the Canadian shore, the water dance old Red was trying to maintain was too much for him, so he ducked below into the cabin. The remainder of the crew and passengers rode in silence, watching the passing boats, soaking up the sun and wallowing in the wind.

From bliss to this, Kevin thought. From alone with Renee on the *Captain Jack* to another river run with the Waterboys. He was tired, had more work to do, and again, needed off the *Lucky Lena.* He stumbled forward on the rolling deck and joined Red Holtz in the cabin.

"Rockin' and rollin' out there, eh?" from Red as Kevin flopped down at the table seat across from him.

"Sure is," Kevin replied. He had briefly been introduced when Red came aboard but Kevin knew nothing about Red, other then he appeared to be the oldest member of the ever-expanding crew of the *Lucky Lena,* maybe in his mid-70's.

Red was one of those over busy, overworked executives, always working, and even though now retired, still had a hard time dressing down. Too busy for leisure-ware, maybe a golfing outfit or two, but usually he wore what he had on; older, slightly worn slacks and a dress shirt. The pants with cuffs, the shirt sleeves rolled up, and scuffed-up loafers with no socks.

Another attribute of retirement he wore, and with great pride, was he didn't give a shit about a lot of things, not only his attire. His short, grey hair stood straight up, like he'd just been shocked, too short to comb, and he refused to have a shaved, bald head. His plump face, covered in a three-day old beard, was a constant crimson. Any unfamiliarity with each other had no apparent effect on Red, who began firing off inquiries as soon as Kevin hit the seat.

"So, I hear you were in on a little action with the boy's last night."

"Action?" Kevin feigned.

"Yeah," Red laughed, "You know, the run down to the Flats."

Kevin sat silently.

"Hell, its O.K, I know all about it, Whitey told me," Red stated, then took a long drink from the tumbler. "Sure was more exciting than that boat show at the harbor I bet."

After a short pause Kevin replied, "Well, certainly more exciting, and surprising." And terrifying, he thought to himself. He couldn't believe this guy heard about it, already. How Red mentioned it as a simple matter of fact. How he half expected him to say, as Jeff would, it was no big deal.

"Well, it's really no big deal," Red said. "Not with these guys. It's not too dangerous. They're careful. They know what they're doing. The Waterboys have been moonlighting for a long time."

"How long?" Kevin inquired.

"Oh, I'm not too sure, ever since I've known them."

"Really?"

"Sure, hell, now that I think about it, that's how I met them. Ha, they hooked me up with a couple of cases."

"Man," Kevin exhaled, "I didn't know about it till last night, or this morning, or whenever it was. I don't get why they do it, you know, risk it," he added as he shifted in his seat.

"Well," Red sighed, "Like I said, the risk is minimal if you're smart, and the boys are, and hey, it's always been done in these parts. For river folks around here rumrunning isn't a crime, but a bit of good luck."

"You think?" Kevin inquired.

"Sure, you know, booze maybe bad, for some, but money is good, especially for those who need it. Those who need a little extra to get by. Why shouldn't they get a little extra on the side? Why should the guys who write the rules, the laws, make all the money?"

"You think Jeff and Whitey need the money?" Kevin inquired.

"It doesn't hurt, they aren't getting rich around here," Red replied before taking another drink and carrying on. "You know, there's a natural way to things, and then there's the manmade way, someone's laws, some guy's legal way. If you need a little extra to help get by, why not. Why not go for it if it's there? It's only natural. What's not natural is waiting 'round for someone or some law to tell you, hey, now it's O.K."

"So, you ever run rum," Kevin asked? "Got any of it in your past maybe?"

Red turned to look out the cabin window before answering, "No, I'm one of the haves, never needed to."

Kevin thought he sensed a dash of regret in Red's reply, but it was gone in a moment, as he carried on about the Waterboys.

"Hell, Clay has it in his blood, the Flats, the parties, the booze."

"Yeah?"

"Sure. I think he's the great grandson of Joe Bedore," Red announced, "Something like that. Not sure, maybe his great uncle, something."

"Who?"

"Joe Bedore. You never heard of Joe Bedore, and his hotel?"

"No."

"I thought you grew up around here?" Red asked. "Incredulous that anyone who had been to the Flats didn't know of Joe Bedore."

"I did, but that was long ago, and it's been a while," Kevin stated sheepishly.

Red Holtz needed an audience, he was full of info and stories, experiences and tales, many old, some new, and felt he was running out of time to tell them. He needed someone to indulge him. He needed an audience and he had Kevin in his web, and wasted little time spinning Joe Bedore's tale.

"Joe Bedor was the King of the Flats," Red started. "He was a stocky Frenchman who moved from Quebec and settled in the Flats instead of going to Louisiana with most of the other Cajuns. He was a great outdoors man. Loved to fish and hunt. He opened a hotel in the Flats and it became a landmark and Joe became a legend."

"When was this?" Kevin inquired.

"Oh, late 1800's, turn of the century."

"Yeah?"

"Oh yeah, I guarantee," Red said in his best French Canadian.

"Is it still there?" Kevin inquired.

"No, it's gone now," Red answered with a bit of sadness in his voice. "But I remember it," he added proudly. "I was there a few times as a kid."

"Really?"

"Oh, yeah, my father took me fishing there. I was 10 or 11 then. It was in the mid-20s, I know that because it was during prohibition. Joe and his wife had passed away by then, but everyone on the Flats talked about 'em as if they were still there, running the place."

"Where was it, what was it called?"

"It was called Joe Bedore's Hotel," Red announced as he took a drink from his tumbler. "It was located on the South Channel of Harsons Island, just 'round the bend from what is now the freighter cut off, south of San Souci." Then glancing at the chart Jeff had

65

tossed on the table the night before, "here let me show you." Red unrolled the tattered chart, spun it around, then after moving his head back and forth to focus, pointed out the infamous location.

"My father and I rode the *Tashmoo* up in the morning, the finny crowd, Joe called them, supplied everything for the finny crowd. We would leave Detroit at 8:30 or so in the morning, fish all day and stay for dinner, then take one of the last boats back. But you could stay over, for a day, for the week. At its peak there was a dance pavilion, picnic areas with great willow trees, and the hotel had a great wraparound porch where Joe would spin his fabulous tales. He was known everywhere throughout the Great Lakes. He greeted every guest, every boatload, his place had everything you needed to hunt, fish, row boats, and he knew where to send you to get them, or he'd send his boy out with you. But mostly he was a hell of a story teller and entertainer. He wanted his guests to kick back and have a good time. My father told me his slogan was, 'Give me a call and I'll give you a good time.' He never started out to be a hotel guy. Matter of fact the hotel started out as his house."

"Really?" Kevin inquired.

"Yeah," Red stated. "He was working on a ship passing through the Flats, saw how beautiful it was and moved there. He built a house, which expanded into the hotel when his personality made him the perfect inn keeper."

Red fell silent, exhausted from talking of such memories from his youth. Curtains flapped on a breeze that blew through the open cabin windows. The *Lena* rocked gently. He and Kevin realized they were times gone, never to return. Times Red missed dearly, and times Kevin wished he'd known, when the Flats were wonderful, a paradise of wildlife and wild times, a land of few inhibitions, a centuries old delta yet unchanged by the urban wrath growing around it.

Jeff stuck his head through the open entry way, "Hey, you guys hungry? I think there's an open slip at the Crab, let's get somethin' to eat." After a pause he added, "Come on, I'm buying."

The two joined the others on deck where Red insisted Jeff repeat, to the rest of the crew, what he'd shouted into the cabin. "No, not the lunch part," Red grunted, "the buying part."

"Yeah, yeah, I'm treating."

"Ha, the Captain's treating boys, and my dear," Red exclaimed remembering Renee, "Can't pass that up, eh?"

Kevin, Whitey and Red looked up in a knowing glance. This was a bit unusual. Not that the Waterman was cheap, far from it, he was a generous soul, but the River Crab was not the burgers and beer joint that the Waterboys usually patronized. Not that it was out of their league, but it was a more special occasion place, a happy hour place, when the drinks were cheaper and the finger food free. Not a middle of the summer, Saturday lunch kind of place.

Kevin and Whitey simultaneously turned to look at Renee, at Jeff, and back at each other. That's it, they agreed without saying a word. The Captain was taking Renee to lunch, with the rest of the crew tagging along.

CHAPTER 4

The Water Merchant

The *Lucky Lena* slid slowly towards the River Crab docks, rocking on the roiling waves, Whitey at the wheel waiting for a calmer moment to make an attempt at entering the last open slip. This was no easy task. The *Lena* was heaving in the churning waves they'd tried to avoid earlier.

Whitey stood, feet apart for balance, spinning the spoked wheel to keep the cruisers bow facing up stream. Kevin and Renee sat on the back-bench seat, out of the way. Red stood across from Whitey with both hands on the cabin top and feet spread eagled. Captain Jeff stood on the side rail, looking at the River Crab docks 25 yards away, then at Whitey, then back at the docks.

"Let's go for it Whitey," the captain hollered.

"O.K," Tom White replied, "It's your boat."

The Waterboys and Red knew the only way the *Lena* could sit safely, and avoid being pounded to pieces against the pilings and dock was to pull into an open well and tie off four ways. Two lines from the bow post, through the cleat guides, one port, one starboard, to cleats on the dock, on opposite sides of the slip. Two more lines off the transom cleats to pilings at the end of the dock. Once in the slip, the lines, adjusted for play, the *Lena* could rock and roll in the rough conditions without hitting any dockage.

The Waterboys checked for a calmer set of waves, Whitey putting the *Lena* in and out of gear to keep them parallel to the docks. Kevin watched anxiously. He knew the plan and was happy not to be at the wheel. He also knew to get ready, so he rose to stand at the port side corner off the stern and grabbed the line. This brought a quick look and smile from the Captain.

If it wasn't a tough enough docking, Whitey would be attempting it in front of a large audience. The lunch time crowd at the Crab filled the outdoor tables along the patio and open windows of the restaurant. The real boaters among them stopped to watch, for they knew what was up. The others were unaware, landlubbers, or skippers of the boats bouncing off the docks and break wall, the bumpers placed over the side only partially working.

Whitey took one last glance toward Jeff, who was staring at the docks, then at Red and Kevin. This is a situation the boys would normally avoid. A moment later, after a break in the passing parade of pleasure craft, Whitey made his move.

"Here we go," he yelled, his head spinning on a swivel as he searched the scene in all directions before powering up. He turned the cruiser to enter the passage between docks at a 45-degree angle, adjusting the throttle. The *Lucky Lena* was a single screw, not a twin-engine cruiser that could spin on a dime by opposing engine thrusts, so Whitey diligently worked the brass gear shift, the wheel and throttle to guide the boat toward the slip.

Jeff darted into the cabin, through the front hatch and onto the bow deck. Red moved to the back bench opposite Kevin and grabbed a line. Renee took a spot on the side rail.

It was, quite frankly, a thing of beauty. Whitey maneuvered the *Lena* into the opening between docks, the point of no return or recovery, caught a rolling wave that was pushing up stream, and surfed into the slip, throwing her into reverse at the precise moment to avoid touching any wood. Jeff hopped off with the bow lines while Red and Kevin held off the stern. It must have looked great from the restaurant, the old cruiser slipping into the dock, perfectly, for a few glasses were raised with shouts of acknowledgment as the crew of the *Lena* walked along the dock, through the patio diners and into the restaurant.

"Hey, what are you guys doing here?" the hostess inquired as she greeted them, as surprised to see the Waterboys as they were to be there. "It's not happy hour," she smiled.

"Yeah, I know," Jeff smiled sheepishly, "Special occasion I guess."

"No shit," Whitey mumbled turning to Red.

As the hostess searched for a table, a figure stood before the open windows, backlit by the brightness of the sun splashed river, and began waving. There was no recognition till the voice rose above the restaurant clatter.

"Renee! Over here."

It was Jack LaCroix, Renee's father. The *Lena's* crew snaked through the crowd, behind the hostess, to tables along the open windows. Jack moved from behind the cluttered table to greet Renee with a hug and introduced four or five men as fellow judges of the antique boat show. It was a boisterous group, finishing with lunch and in the process of polishing off a pitcher of beer. The judges began to shuffle and slide chairs, to rise and greet Renee, but she hurriedly requested they remain seated.

A series of rather awkward introductions followed, with everyone speaking in unison while reaching back and forth across the table with darting and stabbing handshakes. Kevin had met Jack that morning, but after the babble of slinging names around, no one appeared to remember anyone else's name.

The Waterboys and judges looked at each other while Jack talked with Renee, the awkwardness broken when one of the judges, a tall, sun tanned, distinguished looking man, rose to congratulate the crew of the *Lena* on a masterful job of docking under adverse conditions. Two pitchers of beer with five more glasses were called for and the waitress took orders from the new arrivals.

The ice may have been broken between the groups but a little frost had built up on Jeff Waters. As the others opened up smiling conversation with tales of dockings, currents, heroic feats and near sinking's, he stood by thinking this is not what he expected. His lunch with Renee was drifting out of control. He could handle being there with her and his crew but now it was becoming a full-blown party, including her father, and he was supposed to be buying, for everyone? He looked past the suddenly boisterous new buddies, out the window to his *Lena*, rolling in the slip, suddenly wishing he could escape with her.

If it wasn't what the Waterman anticipated and hoped for, this accidental meeting didn't bother Kevin. He would have been more than happy to remain at the harbor, aboard the *Captain Jack* with Renee, alone. Then Jeff sailed in, and now his attempt to treat her to lunch wasn't going as planned. He was a bit surprised with Jeff's apparent sudden taking to Renee, but wasn't upset. Who wouldn't be taken by her? Apparently they both were.

She was single and so were they. Both now divorced.

Jeff Waters had what he called a semi-regular companion, also divorced, who enjoyed his occasional companionship but in no way was going to move in with him, or another man again, ever. Kevin was what he called, drifting.

Jeff married too young, in an era when that's what small town kids soon out of high school did. He swooned Karen, the girl of his choice, with wild ideas and tales of brave Ulysses. He was a couple years older and went to the local community college while she finished up high school. Then they were off to Europe where they survived a hallucinogenic summer in which they crammed a century's worth of museums, monuments, music, food, culture and cathedrals into three months. When they returned they moved in together and were married shortly after, against her parent's wishes, but with their eventual consent, realizing the tide they were fighting was too strong.

With help from their parents they opened a book shop which provided Jeff a forum to practice his dream inspired gift-for-gab and laid-back life style, and the young bride an environment in which to shine. They were a power couple who worked by day and continued the blitz-Krieg party pace they'd developed in Europe by night. Their apartment became party central.

However, the shop was a financial disaster. It was small town Michigan, not London or Paris, and they got out, lucky to find a buyer, and bought a party store. For Jeff, it wasn't as romantic, but he soon realized there was much more money in numbing the mind with alcohol than trying to expand it with books.

For Karen, it wasn't what she wanted anymore. She stopped helping around the store, she hated the hours, standing behind the counter ringing up six packs, cigarettes and beef jerky. She began to hang around the house, day after day, after day, partying, alone.

They'd lived an entire lifetime, and more, in the matter of a few years. They'd done it all together, they knew it all, experienced everything, and now they were out of gas, the well was dry, the flame extinguished. It was ending and they both knew it. Eventually she left for the west coast to visit folks they'd met in Spain.

She never returned.

Jeff bought the *Lucky Lena*, returned to life along the river, and still ran the party store, called Pirate Pete's.

Kevin Casey left town when the Waterman was in Europe and rarely came back to visit. Unlike Jeff, he'd married much later, after college, after a few jobs on mid-size newspapers in different mid-size towns around the country. He'd shot pictures of high school sports, local politicians, grand openings of highways, bridges and municipal buildings, leaves in the town square and floods on main street.

At his last job he'd made the fatal mistake of fishing off the company pier, hooking up with an editor, his boss, who was on the rebound from a bad marriage. They were married in a whirlwind, in an acquaintance's living room. She chewed him up and spit him out, but strangely, it really didn't bother him, even as it was happening. Nor now, even though it was a fresh wound. It was an exciting, stimulating experience while occurring but ended suddenly, and cost him his job. He'd been on the road, free-lancing ever since.

These tales of marital implosion were spun early on in the boating bender, with Whitey, the happily married father of two,

73

quietly piloting the *Lucky Lena* up and down the river. Jeff and Kevin both divorced, one a while ago, the other recently, with no kids, both smitten by Renee.

The busboys cleared a just emptied table and slid it alongside that of the judges. The crew of the *Lena* slid up chairs and the two pitchers of beer arrived in short order. Whitey and Red sat along the windows next to the judges. Jack took the empty seat at the head of the table while Jeff and Kevin found themselves on either side of Renee.

As the beer flowed and the *Lena* crew ordered lunch, Jeff was immersed with Jack and Renee LaCroix. Sitting between the two at the end of the table he was as close to a nautical nirvana as he could imagine. Jack, after all was a retired freighter captain who'd spent his working life aboard the ships Jeff followed religiously as they moved up and down the river. Jeff hung on every word as he heard tales of life, with views, from a pilot house. The best was Jack's telling of the power of the Lakes, for he knew like all mariners of big water knew, that while landlubbers sit on beaches, bluffs, and sandy slopes dreaming over waterscape vistas of surf and sunset's, sailors gazed back over those very horizons longing deeply for terra firma, especially when a sudden tempest changed a waterman's existence from decades to days, and each minute could be his last.

"One thing you've got to understand about the Great Lakes, right off the top," Jack said with enough conviction to grab everyone's attention, "They can kill you as quick, if not faster, then an ocean. Shallow water, multiple, rapidly changing weather patterns, waves stacking close and tall, and bang, you're in the shit. Before the days of radar and forecasts, you sailed off from the tranquil shoreline and sandy beaches, and the next thing you knew a squall is racing across the lake, fast, and you're blown over, or swamped, or both, or run aground, and then you are in the water and in the shit, boat sunk, and you're dead."

Seated on Jeff's other side was Renee, who listened to her father attentively and with great admiration, leaving the Waterman turning from one to the other, his mouth slightly open, in wonder.

74

Kevin was occupied by the judges, anxious to give the reporter all they knew about their beloved hobby, antique boats, making sure he'd be there to shoot photos, of their boats of course. He couldn't help notice Renee pressing her bare knee against his under the table. Was it on purpose? She was engaged with the Waterman but rubbing knees with him, did she even know she was doing it? It was like in his dream the night before, when he was in the cabin and the girl was rubbing his leg under the table, he recalled coming out of the dream, the part about the *Bullet* not having a cabin. He sighed at this quick flashback. It reminded him of his current state, beat up and burned out. Too tired, he felt, to muster much emotional energy over this or any possible competition with the Waterman over Renee LaCroix.

While Jeff was immersed in conversation with Renee, her father turned his attention towards the other judges, and during a lull, raised his head from his just arrived fish sandwich and announced, "Say, Duke, tell 'em about your new project."

The distinguished looking guy who'd dominated much of the conversation with Kevin about the boat show was Duke Wilson. The Waterboys had recently learned this guy was a high roller, not minding if all at the table knew it. He owned the yacht taking up much of the breakwall on the Pine River and had entered three classic runabouts in the show. He was in charge of the judging staff, set the prizes and was paying for many of the events expenses. He was also picking up the tab they were currently running up, and Jeff only hoped it included his as well.

All eyes turned toward Duke, who eased back in his chair and folded his arms. Smiling, he looked about the table. His fellow boat judges were aware of his new venture, but he wasn't sure of telling this new group of it. Yet Duke, knowing a reporter was present, couldn't pass up the chance at getting his story out and some possible free P.R.

"Well, boys, and Miss," he added, "I'm now in the water business."

75

His fellow judges gave out a cheer and raised their glasses. Duke grabbed his with a smile. The crew of the *Lena* watched. After a drink, Duke continued.

"I'm in the fresh water business, the drinking water business. I'm collecting some of this plentiful, clear water we see all around us and sending it to places that have none."

"Water will be the new gold. There will come a time when a rainy day will be the happiest day of your life, because if you can't afford to buy it, the only way you'll get water is from the sky. Twenty percent of the world's fresh water is here, in the Great Lakes, and I'm going to be selling it!"

"Hear-hear," from the judges, again raising their glasses. Jack and Renee worked on their sandwiches.

The Waterboys stared at the tycoon in silence. It caught them by surprise. Jeff Waters, wondering if he'd heard it right, said to Duke through the beer drinking merriment, "You're doing what? You're going to sell the water?"

"I've already started, well the process has begun anyway," Duke answered.

"What are you doing, putting it into bottles?" Jeff asked.

"A very big bottle I guess you could say," Duke laughed, looking around the table at the others, then added. "I'm putting it in ships."

"What?" the Waterman asked incredulously.

"I've got a converted freighter, the first of many, I'm going to sail it into the big lakes, open the valves, fill it with fresh water, then sail it to where it's needed, which someday will be almost everywhere. I already have a ship up North on a trial run. I named her the *Grand Venture.*"

Red and Whitey, who'd remained fairly silent through much of the lunch, soaking up the free beer and food, turned to each other in a knowing glance. This was not good. This was a crack in the cosmos, a shape shifter, especially for Jeff Waters, the Waterman.

"You can't do that," Jeff stated. "I mean, what will the state say? What will Michigan and Ontario say? They won't let you do that," Jeff exclaimed, his voice rising in protest.

"They'll get their cut," Duke Wilson stated as a matter of fact, focusing on Jeff, "They will all get there share, and be happy to have it." He finished off his beer then leaned forward on the table. "Listen, times are changing. Everything is changing, business, the natural world, social fabric, everything. The economy here will go down the shitter and this water will be too valuable. It's the new gold and governments will be in on it. Someday someone's going to sell it, so," he said leaning back with self-satisfaction, "it might as well be me."

He didn't reveal any details but felt the demand would be huge, and he'd supply. The need would be so great that any details would be worked out and that politicians would line up at the trough like the pigs they were. He had his business plan, and was going forward.

To say Duke Wilson's idea cast a pall over the group would be only partially correct, but it was at that moment the lunch party broke up. The last pitcher of beer was empty and the food eaten. The boat show judges, stuffed and happy, headed for the courtesy van for a quick trip back to the harbor. Renee joined her father for the ride.

The Waterboys were left wondering what had just happened. They were having a great time, good food, cold beers, boating conversation, then this Duke guy is selling the Great Lakes, and then everyone left.

Jeff Waters was floored by Duke Wilson's plan. He didn't remember climbing aboard the *Lena* and departing the restaurant. He was numbed by the idea. The more he thought of it the more bummed he became. He couldn't even enjoy the fact that Duke had picked up the entire tab. He forgot about the pleasure of sitting between Renee and Jack, the feeling of happiness the two brought, had dissipated. He sat on the back-bench seat of the *Lena,* head down wondering, pondering, pissed.

The rest of the crew wasn't as bothered by Duke Wilson's talk as Jeff. Red, who stayed pretty quiet throughout the lunch, thought the guy was blowing smoke out his ass, showing off. Whitey thought the plan was pretty ingenious, but that it would never work, not by this guy. He may have thought he was a big timer, but for a project of such scale and ramifications, he would become a bit player. His idea taken and he shuffled aside to a minor role.

Kevin went along with Whitey, adding corporate interests would control everything, including governments, as usual, and if it ever happened, the selling off of the Great Lakes, they'd control it all, ruthlessly. He also wondered if it was even logistically possible, or profitable enough to bother with.

The *Lena* crew tried lifting the spirits of their Captain but had little luck. This was a serious blow to the Waterman's cosmos, and just the idea had dropped him like a punch to the gut. The river had become his life and his crew knew it.

Over the years changes in the small river town seemed to follow Jeff Waters, trying to chase him away, always right on his heels. Two of his childhood homes had been torn down. An ill-conceived urban-renewal plan tore the guts out of the waterfront and the soul from the town. The Riverland boat and bait shop was gone, Don's Shrimp Boat restaurant gone, the small boat club gone, and the Library, where he first discovered the world, and the love of books, gone. Painful changes drove him to leave but he always returned, drawn back to the river, the one constant. That's when he learned the only constant in life was change. He spent less time at the store. He purchased a place on the Pine River to dock the *Lucky Lena* and spent much of his time there. The rivers, the water, had mellowed him, now Duke's venture had him worried, scared, and angry. Now his beloved river was threatened.

Red finally got him to accept a beer for the run-down river.

"He'll never do it," Jeff announced, twisting the cap off a Labatt Blue.

"That's right, eh?" Red said looking around. "That's it, you're right. Cheer up Cap, that guy will never do it."

"One way or the other it'll never happen," Jeff stated to his crew, who glanced at each other wondering what he meant, and what was that strange, far off look in his eye.

"I'll drive now," Jeff said as he rose to relieve Whitey at the wheel.

"Don't worry about that guy, or his plan," Red continued. "It would be such a government nightmare it would take years to figure out. It would be a quagmire of rights and rules and who gets what followed by every party suing the shit out of each other. It's not going to happen."

"Probably not," Whitey added as he stepped away from the wheel. "Plus, by the time they get 'round to sellin' off this water it will be too polluted to be worth much."

"Ha," Red exclaimed. "That's right, wait till they suck the toxic blob off the bottom near Sarnia into their precious water ship."

"Yeah," Jeff said, "but that guy's not sucking it out of the river, he's got his ship in the big lakes, north, where it's still clear, clean water. What if he does what he says, just sails into Huron or Superior, fills up and departs?"

"But how much water can that really be," Kevin added? "Wouldn't that be a drop in the bucket?"

"Maybe at first," the Waterman replied, spinning the spoked wheel of the *Lena* to take on a set of waves bow first. "But it would be the start. What if he got 20 ships, what if the next step is to one up him, by someone bigger, to run intake pipes into the lakes and just pump it straight out?"

"By the time that happens, even the big water may be polluted," Whitey stated. "It's not just the factory made toxic stew anymore. It's going to be the farm runoff, the sewage, it's all that shit from 'round the world that will get in through the locks."

"Ha," Red bellowed, "the wonderful St. Lawrence Seaway System, piece of shit. I knew it would be a disaster. I knew it would."

When they connected the lakes to the Atlantic Ocean with locks in 1958 Red was a lone voice around town against it. The Waterboys were kids at the time. They didn't understand what it meant other than different types of ships, not like the long lake freighters, were now passing up and down the river. But Red knew. He knew when they built the lock system to allow passage into the lakes by ships from around the world they'd unlocked the door to hell, a change that could change the natural ways of the Great Lakes. When the Waterboys first got to know Red, it was a story he told them early and often. And again he repeated it.

"It's only a matter of time boys before those salties bring in some shit in their bilges that will alter these waters like we can't even imagine," he paused before adding, "in a way, that water merchant is right."

"What," Jeff exclaimed staring at Red.

"Well, about the coming value of water, he's right. In the big picture the next great war will be the battle over fresh water, drinking water, growing water, water to live on, the basis of life, with every prior conflict to that being small potatoes. The entire world will change. If people can't get guys like Duke to bring it to them, they will pack up and migrate to where the water is. Unless of course, we, mankind, destroys it first, and we're already well on our way, we will be the civilization remembered for destroying the water. Hell, there's pipelines running under the lakes now, there's an old crude oil line that runs under the straights, laid in 1953, what if that thing bursts? Both Huron and Michigan will be screwed. There are pipes under us here on this river."

The crew of the *Lena* stared at Red who took a deep breath and roared on.

"For Christ sake, in prior civilizations water was sacred, with religious significance, they prayed to it because they knew it was the life giver, it came from God. Future generations will look back on the flatlanders of our era, the deniers of the water being destroyed, poisoned, who insist nothing was wrong, like those who felt the world was flat as sailors explored her circumference. In the future people will look back on this period and wonder how could they let this happen, how could they fuck this up for everyone else," Red sighed. "This water will be shit at some point."

"Then they'll rate the water," Jeff said from his place at the wheel. "Low grade, polluted or dirty water will go to third world countries and the cleanest, top grade stuff will go to the richest nations, or the richest individuals, or corporate interests. Either way, it's selling off and drying up the lakes."

"Hell Jeff," that's not going to happen, not today," Whitey stated, rubbing his temples, a headache beginning, agitated that the sunny, summer boat ride was interrupted by such depressing talk. Suddenly he longed for the top of his ladder.

"No kidding, it will not happen." Jeff said as he powered up the *Lucky Lena*, causing the crew to shift positions and hold on. "I won't let it happen."

CHAPTER 5

Reflections on the Water

The Waterman pushed the *Lucky Lena* hard, driving into rollers pushed against the current by an increasing south wind. The crew held firm as waves broke over the bow and sprayed across the windshield. It was uncharacteristic to see him work his boat this way, but no one said anything, he was the Captain, and they weren't.

Kevin, sitting on the back-bench seat, felt trapped again by the Waterboys. He figured he'd spent most of the past 28 hours aboard the *Lena*. That's it? he wondered. It felt more like 28 days, a month's worth of thrills and chills, ups and downs. No, a year's worth, hell, a lifetime of excitement for his normally staid existence, all in a little over a day.

But he knew this river run would end soon, for the Captain had agreed to drop him off at the Inn. At least that was the plan when he and Renee stepped aboard, off the *Captain Jack*, at the harbor, but that was before the run up river, before stopping at Red's, the water tour, lunch at the Crab, before meeting the Duke of Disaster and his plan to sell off the lakes, and before Captain Jeff got a crazed look in his eye and stepped to the wheel.

It wasn't much longer before the Captain throttled back and the Inn appeared off the starboard side. The new North Wing came into view, with a balcony on each second-floor room overlooking the river. On the ground floor, where Kevin was staying, each room featured a sliding door that opened onto a small patio not 50 feet from the water's edge. A wonderful spot, Kevin thought, as he longed to stretch out in the lounger outside his room.

They moved further south and the brick, half-timbered English Tudor, original main section of the Inn, built in 1926, appeared. Large windows, overlooking long porches and the river, ran the length of the building. A second floor of guest rooms sat below a towering roof, peaked at both ends, with tall brick chimneys climbing into the sky.

Jeff spun the wheel hard to starboard, timing the rollers just right, and approached the Inn's wooden boardwalk from the south. Kevin rose from the bench seat in anticipation of going ashore. The excitement of the Waterman sticking to his word was quickly tempered by the rocking of the *Lena.*

"You still want off?" Jeff hollered back at Kevin.

"Sure." Can you dock here?"

"Were not docking here," the Captain stated as he spun the wheel and worked the throttle, "Too much snot."

Whitey and Red concurred with the Captain as the *Lena* rolled in the waves 100 feet off the boardwalk. Guests, sitting on the expansive porch or strolling along the boardwalk, could be seen admiring the classic cruiser.

"Get below and climb through the hatch," Jeff yelled. "I'll nose her in and you jump ashore."

Kevin didn't like this plan and as he stood behind the engine cover, trying to keep his balance, thought of changing his mind. "Are you sure?" He heard himself ask.

"It's the only way off in this stuff," Red acknowledged.

"That's right," Whitey added, "he'll get you close enough."

"Don't worry," Jeff hollered, "it's no big deal."

There it was again from the Captain, Kevin thought. No big deal. But Kevin had little time to change his mind as the *Lena* maneuvered closer and closer to the wooden breakwall.

Jeff hadn't been at the wheel much lately but he surely remembered how to dock at the Inn where the only spot to pull alongside was where the deadheads were, the broken off pilings that lurked below the surface, waiting to puncture unsuspecting hulls. Precision and care was called for.

Over the years the Waterman and his *Lucky Lena* had made regular stops at the popular riverside hotel. Not so much recently, but many unofficial fishing charters by the *Lena* originated from the Inn. Harold, the front desk clerk, whom Jeff Waters knew well, would answer casual inquiries about fishing on the big river with, "I know someone who will take you out if you're interested."

This led to a call to Jeff, who pulled Whitey down from his paint ladder and a rendezvous at the Inn a short time later. The Captain provided the boat, all the gear and bait, and the storytelling, Whitey the fishing expertise, and the clerk stowed aboard the drinks and ice, while the guests provided the cash, distributed equally between Jeff, Whitey and the clerk.

Fish were often caught, and on trips where there was little or no luck the excursions turned into one of the Waterman's guided river tours with histories of the riverside homes, tales of rumrunning and ship wrecks. Should a freighter pass, its story was told, its length, beam, when she was build and where, gross tonnage, how it was powered and name changes. All the while Whitey tended bar, or piloted the cruiser, or both.

These trips weren't limited to fishing. Some were for sightseeing and others for the simple thrill of a boat ride. The Waterboys were always amazed when someone stepped aboard and stated they'd never been on a boat before, ever, especially if they were from Michigan, the Great Lakes State.

One of these charters became river lore, known among the Waterboys as the "Cruise of the Operator Queens." The call from the front desk clerk came to Jeff as usual, but the circumstances were not. It wouldn't be a fishing run, just some ladies that wanted to go out on the river. It was a little early for such a request, around lunch time, before noon, and it came on a Monday, when most people were recovering from a busy weekend in the river town. Jeff was at the store when he got the call and as his day was just getting started. He had opened at ten and hadn't had a customer yet. He was reading the morning *Free Press* and waiting for the beer truck with the week's delivery. It was early in the season, beginning of June and not all that wonderful a day, started out nice but was turning overcast and solemn, reflective of the mood for a Monday.

Jeff flipped over the open sign on the front door, headed out the delivery door in the back, placing a key under the mat for the beer man. He knew it was too early and to grey to find Tom working so he picked him up at his house and headed for the Willows, the boathouse and property on the Pine where the *Lena* moored. There was more money to be had this morning on the water than at the store, or on top of a ladder.

The ride down the Pine River was one the Waterboys made countless times and there'd be hundreds more, but they never tired of it. Rounding each bend of the twisting and turning course brought a new waterscape each time, day or night, foggy or clear, sun or rain, back dropped by seasonal change. The stillness of the water, split by the cruiser into a symmetrical pattern off her stern, the rhythmic clicking of the engine, the spitting of the watered exhaust, induced a spiritual transition from life ashore to the next water adventure.

The big river was fairly calm when they pulled up to the Inn. Their buddy, the front desk clerk, was standing alone on the boardwalk waiting, a cooler and two boxes at his side, with a Cheshire cat grin spreading across his face as the *Lena* got closer.

Jeff and Whitey were beginning to wonder what was up when suddenly, a contingent of women appeared from the Inn and headed for the boardwalk. It didn't take long for the Waterboys to realize this would be no ordinary boat ride. These women were partying, big time, like it was late Saturday night, not Monday noon, laughing and shouting their way towards the *Lena*. There were seven in all, telephone operators with a day off to celebrate one's promotion and subsequent leaving of their office.

Jeff and Whitey glanced at each other, at the drunken crew lining the boardwalk, at the smiling clerk, then back at each other, and immediately began to calculate the ships plan for this trip. How would they even get them on board, without falling in? They were, well, large ladies, and tipsy, and getting louder by the moment.

"What the hell is this?" the Captain inquired of Harold as he maneuvered the boat parallel to the boardwalk.

"These ladies want to go for a boat ride," he replied, rubbing the ends of his fingers against his thumb indicating they were paying big bucks.

As Jeff brought the *Lena* alongside the boardwalk one of the women leaned over and shouted, "This is it? This is what we're going in," and turning to the other girls added, "This clunky old thing will probably sink!" With this the ladies broke into a universal howl.

Captain Jeff Waters initial reaction to this was, screw them, I'm not taking these toads out. They're insulting me, Whitey, my boat! He said nothing. Tom White stood in the rear of the boat holding off, Harold still smiling on the dock above.

"You got life jackets on that tub?" The same lady continued, clearly the leader of the pack, "I don't want to have to swim when that thing sinks," again a chorus of laughs from the others.

Jeff thought of saying something, like there not being enough life jackets in town to keep you from going down, but only turned to give Whitey a nod. With this Tom pulled the only jacket from its bungee strap in the side hull and hoisted it up for the ladies to observe, and called out the number one. He then lowered the jacket below the side hull, out of sight, switched hands and raised it again and announced two. He repeated this till he got to nine, the number of passengers and crew. For the men of the *Lucky Lena* this was a familiar drill. It was used for other charters, sheriff's patrol, and

87

coast guard auxiliary, whomever. Of course they had life jackets; the *Lena* had a dozen or more onboard, stored in the bow lockers, within easy access if needed. When kids were aboard they wore them, but generally they cluttered up the back deck.

As Whitey was working the jacket routine, Jeff was seriously debating bagging the trip. He ran down a pre-cruise captains list; the passengers were fairly out of control, had already hassled the crew, and the ship hadn't even left the dock yet. The weather was gloomy, even though the river was relatively calm, and he wasn't sure how much fuel was aboard. The gas gauge was on the blink so he had been testing levels by dropping a wooden yard stick into the tank to measure levels. He didn't want to perform this in front of the ladies and induce more insults.

He needed to make a decision, the ladies were beginning to maneuver closer to the edge of the boardwalk, he looked up at the clerk who again rubbed his fingers and thumb together.

"How much?" the Captain inquired.

The clerk raised three fingers on his right hand.

"Three hundred?" Jeff asked incredulously.

The clerk nodded. No wonder he was smiling Jeff thought.

"Three hundred, dollars?" Jeff repeated, louder.

"That's right poop-deck-Paul," the chief operator stated, "so let's get this cruise going." With this she began to step down, off the dock, into space. Whitey moved quickly to assist her, get her one foot on the side hull rail, and with a thud she landed upright on the back deck. Jeff left the wheel to assist as the other six women began tumbling aboard the *Lena*.

Three hundred bucks, Jeff kept turning the number over and over, it would be a record haul, especially for a quick river run, but these passengers were going to require maintenance.

"O.K, you get fifty and Whitey and I get the rest," the Captain told the clerk, "you can hit 'em up for a tip when we get back."

The clerk began to negotiate but was quickly interrupted by the chief operator who announced that money wasn't an issue and that the crew needed to "shove off!"

For Captain Jeff, money swayed the day, his take would be nearly a season's worth of fuel. He hadn't made a decision; it had been made for him. The passengers were already aboard, and the *Lena* had drifted away from the boardwalk.

Any trepidation Jeff had about the trip dissipated shortly into the cruise. While he was at the wheel Whitey set up the bar and snacks on the engine cover and the operators sat along the back bench and in deck chairs. Soon after, they were best friends.

The Waterboys discovered the leader of the group was Betty. Boisterous Betty, as she would always be remembered. It didn't take her long to disarm the Waterboys. She had strength, character, and a great sense of humor. She was the ladies boss, the office manager, who watched over her girls and was responsible for throwing the going away party. Her girls worked hard for her and she wanted them to have a good time, no, a freaking great time as she would say, on their last day together. She led the girls in a few verses of "Gilligan's Island," howling each time they got to the three-hour cruise part, and kept interrupting the Captain's historical home tour as they headed north, up the shoreline. Betty never let on that she had been passed over; again, for the job her underling was accepting. It had happened before. That time they'd gone bowling. She'd accepted that the big shots at Bell Telephone felt she'd reached her peak, was too old to go further, even though she deserved it. But Betty was smart. She knew they'd all be out on their asses in a few years. The corporate honchos as well, all victims of a new technological age. Betty knew it, accepted it, and was determined to go down with guns blazing, having some good times while they lasted, at the expense of the company, hence the sea cruise.

Whitey kept the drinks and 'horse divers', as the ladies called them, coming while Jeff remained at the wheel, but he quit the historic home tour and joined in on the laughter. It got to the point where it was hard to tell who was entertaining who. For the ladies, the bar had been open since before noon, and now they'd talked the crew into joining them. They wanted to drive the boat, dance, sing and drink, more and more.

The Captain steered the *Lucky Lena* into the middle of the river and headed for the Canadian side of Stag Island and began telling stories of the many weekend rendezvous on the beaches of the island. Of the 20 boats, many antique woodies, sterns anchored ashore, with over 100 folks staying the day, till a late summer sunset, partying all day, bar-b-qing, with kids splashing in the water. But as with other stories on this cruise, he had a tough time finishing. As soon as he said Stag Island the ladies went a howling. They'd already begun flirting with the crew, asking them to pretend they were pirates and to kidnap them away like in a Harlequin novel, and the mention of Stag really set them off. Take us ashore, they pleaded between howls. Please. Show us why they call it Stag! The party was raging.

At least till the *Lucky Lena* rounded the head of Stag Island. As the Captain swung the wheel to port, to turn south and head back down river, everything changed, quickly. The cruiser got sideways between two rollers and the back deck of the *Lena* became chaos. Everything went flying as the boat rolled 25 degrees. All the drinks, bottles and food slid off the engine cover with a crash. Two of the operators tipped over in their deck chairs with Whitey falling on top of them. Boisterous Betty, who had been standing opposite Jeff, flew across the deck, just missing the spokes of the wheel and slammed into him. The four operators on the back-bench seat remained seated, but doused each other with spilt drinks.

"Holy shit," the Captain exclaimed. His mind racing, suddenly ciphering what had happened and what needed to be done. Whitey and the Waterman hadn't noticed the weather changing. Maybe because they were riding with the wind on the run up river, sheltered by the island, riding the aft waves smoothly, not noticing the increased rollers. Or maybe because they'd been totally distracted by the passengers, and had joined the party and lost track of conditions. Either way, they instantly knew they'd made a fundamental error. What they didn't know was, it was about to get worse.

Jeff pushed Betty away and spun the wheel to get the *Lena's* bow around enough to slice into the next roller and avoid a repeated roll. If Jeff and Whitey where sobered by the event, the ladies' reaction after picking themselves off the deck was to burst out with laughter. Even being doused with spray flying over the port side rail didn't dampen their spirits.

Jeff wrestled the cruiser around to a heading that would take them back down river toward the Inn. Whitey assembled what was left of the food and drinks and stowed them below in the cabin. The comfortable cruise north, riding with the rollers, changed to beating straight into them. Jeff adjusted the *Lena's* speed to keep them from pounding every time they dropped off the top of a wave, but the ride was a rough one. The operators responded with a hoot and holler each time the boat dropped as if on a carnival ride.

As Jeff worked the wheel he noticed the sky to the south had darkened considerably and the wind seemed to be increasing. He and Whitey hurriedly put up the canvas top and snapped it into place. Halfway down the American side of Stag they left the protected leeward side of the island and readjusted the heading. Now the *Lena* was taking the full force of the storm's fury head on, and would be for the rest of the cruise.

The laughter and whooping from the ladies came to an end. No speed adjustment kept the *Lena* from pounding between every set of waves or prevented water from washing over the bow deck and splashing across the wind shield. It was getting very uncomfortable. The ladies began stumbling towards the safety of the cabin, out of the cold, wet spray. The captain realized this caused an entire new set of problems. The cruiser was now way too bow heavy with everyone in the cabin. Whitey was below, still trying to wait on the passengers but they were suddenly not in a partying mood. Below, in the tight, enclosed space of the cabin, the fun ride of the up and down was now beginning to make some of them sick. Jeff tried to convince them that it would be better on deck, but they weren't

91

buying it. All of a sudden they wanted off the boat. Whitey joined Jeff on deck.

The *Lucky Lena* continued her way south, slowly, beating hard into each wave. With the cabin full and all the weight forward her steerage started to become sluggish. They could see the Inn down river in the distance, but it seemed they were sitting still. Jeff checked the shore line to check their progress, and yes they were moving, but barely.

Then Betty hollered up from the cabin entryway, "Hey boys, there's water down here, is that supposed to be in here?"

They looked at each other, Jeff nodded and Whitey went below. His first step found water. He removed the cover from the center floor board, reached into the flooded bilge, and grabbed the bilge pump. There was no vibration. It was dead. Jeff pulled the switch on the console up and down, nothing. The boys were horrified. There was no panic, but both knew they might have reached a point of no return.

"Hey, what's up?" Betty shouted.

"Just checking things out," Whitey said as he returned topside.

"That water isn't supposed to be in here is it?" she yelled after Whitey. "I know that much," and she rose to join the crew on deck.

"No," the Captain replied above the roar of the wind, but not so loud the ladies below could hear. "There should be no water in the cabin."

"What's wrong," she inquired? Then with concern growing across her face, she got right to the point, "are we going to make it back?"

Captain Jeff had figured out the situation quickly. It was early in the season, and although the lower planks of the wooden hull had soaked up in the water, swelling together and closing the openings between each, the top ones had not. Each time the *Lena* drove headlong into a wave, water breached the hull through openings in the upper planks. To make it worse, waves breaking over the bow washed across the front decking boards which were open wider than the hull planks.

"The waves are getting in through the planks, too much water for the pump, burned it out," Jeff answered. "We should be O.K. but we need to get the girls out of the cabin, we need all weight in the back of the boat. Tell them they will feel better out here in the wind and air."

"I told you this thing might sink," she barked before sticking her head through the cabin door and ordering the girls on deck.

When reading sea tales and shipping histories Jeff, the Waterman, always wondered how captains often made what appeared to be such simple, stupid, mistakes that cost them their ship, crew, and often passengers. What would other captains think of him when they read the headline "Seven Lost in Boating Tragedy?" It was early in the season and the river was still cold, a shock to the system. The waves were big. He pictured himself and Whitey trying to keep seven women afloat.

"We'll be O.K.," Jeff shouted to Betty before turning to Whitey, "Get the jackets out."

The Waterman angled the *Lena* toward the shoreline and ran along the docks. If she were to go down there at least they could get the ladies ashore quickly. He thought of tying off a dock, but wanted to try to save the cruiser as well as the passengers, and also save his and whiteys ass' as well. They had no license to charter or inspection stickers, nothing. They needed to get the ladies off. The steering was getting worse. The women huddled around the engine cover, under the protection of the canvas top. Whitey helped get the life jackets on. Crew and passengers grew silent. The floor boards in the cabin were afloat. If the water level engulfed the battery the *Lena* would go dead in the water. Maybe they'd be dead as well.

When they finally reached the Inn they saw Harold pacing frantically, up and down the boardwalk. He could see they were in trouble, he could see the cruiser riding very low, water well above the painted water line. He also knew it was too rough to pull alongside. The *Lena* got as close to the seawall as possible, Whitey took the wheel while Jeff stepped to the side rail and yelled through the wind.

"Get the van and meet us at the mouth. Call the boat harbor and tell them to bring an electric pump to dock one, and tell him to hurry!"

The cruiser limped toward the entrance to the Pine, passed the long boardwalk and park. It began to rain. The woman became animated as they approached the mouth of the Pine, ecstatic that the nightmare was about to end. The Waterboys knew differently. The current was strong at the entrance to the tributary and required proper angling and speed on a good day. For this entry the *Lena* would have no speed, very sloppy steering, and would be caught sideways in the rollers before entering the safety of the Pine.

Tom White was glad to be back at the wheel. When the Waterman was steering down river, Whitey was left trying to console the women, huddled under the canvas, stumbling around the rolling deck, their party cruise gone wrong. He didn't have much to say when they looked him in the eye. He forced a smile and a not too convincing, "We'll be fine, we're almost there," but couldn't stand the waiting. He grabbed a bucket and went below to start bailing. Betty was quick to help. Whitey scooped and filled, passed the bucket to Betty who poured over the side rail. Whitey started tallying. One gallon bucket, 10 to 15 seconds per repetition, six or seven a minute, six or seven gallons a minute. Good enough? Probably not.

The *Lena* finally reached the entrance to the Pine. Whitey swung the wheel hard to starboard and pushed the throttle full forward, giving the cruiser everything she had. The *Lena* responded, barely. She swung slowly but gained little power. The Waterboys ordered the ladies to line the side rails for balance, four on one side three on the other, as the *Lena* got sideways in the rollers. The next moments were the worst, the *Lena* left rocking heavily in the rollers, and held from entering the mouth of the Pine by the huge backwash from the waves hitting the breakwall and rolling back at the cruiser, straight on her bow. The wind and rain began pushing the cruiser north of the entrance. Whitey fought the change, frantically working the wheel. Miraculously, when it seemed the *Lena* wasn't going to have the power to make the entry, the wind dropped dramatically, and the boat edged forward into the Pine River.

Whitey steered the drifting *Lena* to the north breakwall where the desk clerk was waiting with the shuttle van from the Inn. The passengers fairly leaped from the boat with only Betty looking back and with a smile crossing her face, yelled "Thanks boys, for not killing my girls," then disappeared into the van.

For Jeff and Whitey the job was only half finished. Now they had to save the boat. They pushed off the wall and inched further into the Pine, crawling under the lift bridge, where the tender leaned from the window to check if the crew were O.K. Jeff responded with a shrug. They finally moved into much calmer water, past the Rocky Dock Restaurant and the park. They rounded a bend in the river and headed for an empty slip in the first dock at the harbor. As they approached the slip the engine died. The cruiser drifted slowly, quietly, the last 20 yards, straight into the empty slip, the bow bumping gently against the dock, a perfect landing. A dock boy arrived with a large, electric pump, plugged in the extension, and whitey placed it in the flooded cabin while Jeff dropped the outtake hose over the boats side rail. Water began pouring overboard. The cruiser was saved from going down. They'd made it, barely. Had the engine died five minutes earlier the *Lena* would have floundered. Fifteen minutes earlier the ladies would have been in the water.

A half-hour later, as the crew were moping the cabin floor and back deck, Harold pulled up in the van, waved Captain Jeff over, and handed him the crew's cut of the money. They couldn't believe they got paid, after almost losing the girls at sea. That day, the *Lena* became the *Lucky Lena*.

There wasn't a time since, when the Waterboys approached the Inn that the voyage of the operator queens didn't flash before their eyes. They imagined at least one of the ladies who took the cruise that day, still telling the yarn at a cocktail party somewhere, or regaling her kids, spinning it over and over in her mind, where she longed back to her only water adventure, one with pirates and storms, and rum and fun, and a near death experience, off an island named Stag. Probably boisterous Betty, they figured.

"Get on the bow," the Waterman yelled, "and don't forget your camera bag." The Captain gave the order and Kevin Casey obeyed.

Kevin balanced on the bow deck, hand on the cabin top for stability, as Jeff nosed the *Lena* closer and closer to the breakwall. At the precise moment, as the bow rose on a wave, Kevin took two steps forward and leapt off the cruiser to the boardwalk as Jeff backed the *Lena* away. He walked across the lawn to his room and plopped down in the lounger. Kevin waved good bye to the *Lena* as she swung round and headed south.

He had work to do, there was probably a message from his editor, but he was exhausted. He put his head back on the lounge chair and closed his eyes. A soothing breeze rolled off the water and across his face. A blend of sounds reflecting life along a river walk filled his ears, laughter from happy partiers on the Inn's deck, waves splashing along the boardwalk, seagulls crying from atop spiles, various boat engines passing by, kids calling out as they ran, all mixed into white noise by bursts of wind. He began drifting off, he thought of the water merchant, and last night's adventure with the Waterboys, of the kids running and shouting along the docks, and of Renee.

CHAPTER 6

Big River Run

"Hey mister," a voice called above the others, a boy's voice, looking to make a delivery from room service, or a message from the front desk, Kevin wondered, or a warning to an old gentleman strolling along the boardwalk to avoid a bait bucket? Another breeze cooled Kevin's body and rustled his hair.

"Hey mister," he heard again, this time louder and closer.

"Me?" Kevin heard himself answer. Me, he thought, mister? He wasn't used to being called mister.

He opened his eyes, squinting against the bright light. A boy stood next to the lounger. Kevin lifted an arm to his forehead, shielding the light. The boy looked out across the river, then back at Kevin. "Yeah, you, here," and handed him a beer bottle with a rolled up note in its mouth. Kevin pulled it from the bottle and looked at the kid who pointed towards the river before dashing off.

Kevin pulled himself into a sitting position, tugged his ball cap back on, and looked toward the river. He was staring but couldn't see. He was waking up. He'd fallen asleep. For how long, and who was that kid, and what is this, he thought as he looked at the note? He sat there, straddling the lounger, confused. As he fumbled with the paper he became aware of a stiff neck, and a dry mouth. He unrolled the note, focusing on its hand-written contents.

"Hey Kevin......... wake up! Did you forget about your dinner date with us, down on the island?" It was signed by Renee and included a stick figure cartoon of two smiling characters on the back deck of a boat.

He searched the boardwalk and scanned the occupants of the Inn's deck for the boy, now disappeared. The river, Kevin recalled, the boy had pointed towards the water, where Kevin found, as he focused for the first time since awakening, the white hulled *Captain Jack* holding steady off the break wall. On the back deck he saw Renee waving as she stood along the side rail. Two short blasts from the cruisers horns filled the air, bounced off the Inn's brick façade behind Kevin and rolled back across the river towards Canada. A figure stepped from under the cabin top and waved. It was Jack LaCroix.

Kevin staggered to his feet, his mind reeling. It was the *Captain Jack* with Renee and her father aboard. How long had they been there? What time was it? How long had he knocked off in the lounger? The sun was over the roof of the Inn, casting the lawn in shade but shining brightly on the river. The white side hull of the old Chris-Craft shone brightly against the turquoise water that surrounded her. He remembered the invitation, delivered by Renee on board the cruiser at the harbor, just before the Waterman arrived in the *Lucky Lena*. But he'd forgotten. He'd passed out in the lounge chair on the lawn, outside his room and now, they were here to pick him up. He wasn't ready. He wasn't anything. He sat there staring out at the *Captain Jack.*

By the time Kevin fully awoke he was once again on the river, about to make another big river run, but not on the *Lena,* not with the Waterboys. He was aboard the magnificent *Captain Jack* with Renee and her father, and he soon discovered, Duke Wilson and his wife. He hopped aboard, ruffled and groggy, like earlier that morning at the boat show. Renee greeted him with a hug and took the rolled-up note from his hand.

"So, you like my message in a bottle?" she smiled.

This brought laughter from her father and the Wilson's.

"We were sure that was you," Renee said, "knocked off in the recliner but we couldn't get your attention. So we put this note in a beer bottle, came alongside the boardwalk and Duke tossed it to that boy, and pointed him in your direction."

"He also waved a fiver at the lad and placed it in the bottle with the note," Jack added with a laugh from his position at the steering console.

"Well," Kevin paused as words fumbled around in his head, "It surely worked," he lifted his arms upward with open palms, "'cause here I am."

He was introduced to Duke's wife, Mary Lou, as Jack put the cruiser in gear and pulled away from the boardwalk.

Mary Lou was a lovely lady, tall and tanned. She had wavy, blond hair, wore white rimmed sunglasses, a summer dress splashed with red and orange flowers, and sandals with white ankle-straps. She reminded Kevin of Marilyn Monroe. Duke was a perfect match, taller, distinguished, tan, expensive shades, sported a once-a-week haircut with well-proportioned hints of grey. He was nattily dressed in a short-sleeved sport shirt, pleated shorts and top of the line Docksiders. Together, they reminded Kevin of Ken and Barbie.

Duke announced they had a pitcher of Gin and Tonics made as he turned to the bar and Renee inquired if Kevin would like to go below and freshen up. He followed her down the steps wondering if he looked that bad.

Below deck the living quarters of the *Captain Jack* were warm and inviting, wonderful red brown varnished mahogany, matching cushion fabric and curtains, bright white interior cabin top, and fully appointed brass fixtures, weather instruments, clocks, lamps, even the navigation instruments lying on the cabin table-top. They turned and went down two more steps into the aft cabin where Renee pointed out the rear head.

Kevin stared into the mirror above the sink and scared himself. He looked as bad as he felt. He needed a shave, his eyes were blood shot. At least his cap covered his grungy hair.

"Use whatever you need," Renee stated from beyond the door. "My dad said to help yourself. Take a shower if you want."

Kevin turned to notice the shower stall, "O.K, thanks."

He could tell it was Jacks cabin and head by the shaving gear and bottles of after shave on the rack. He passed on the shower but washed his hands and face, shaved and splashed on a lot of Old Spice. He found a few unopened tooth brushes in a drawer and used one. All of a sudden, he felt good, and a moment later he felt better, even great, for as he left the cabin he collided with Renee rounding the corner of the steps. The tight quarters brought them together. She grabbed his arms.

"You feel better?" she smiled. "You sure smell nice," she added and leaned forward and kissed him on the lips, then grabbed him by the hand and led him up the steps.

Duke Wilson paced around the sun splashed back deck of the *Captain Jack*, drink in hand espousing the finer points of his Great Lakes water plan. Jack piloted the cruiser while Mary Lou flipped through pages of a magazine she'd retrieved from an overstuffed beach bag. Like many other of her husband's wild ideas, she'd heard this story before. Kevin and Renee were the audience.

"I already have the first ship," Duke announced. "She's up north right now on a shakedown cruise. We've converted two of the storage tanks, one in the bow, one astern, to keep her balanced and built valves to let the water in. I named her the *Grand Venture*, you like that," he inquired as he paused to take a drink of his gin-and-tonic.

Renee, sitting at the table next to Kevin, and facing Duke, smiled and nodded. Kevin, hiding behind his sunglasses didn't reply. He was only half listening. He was lost in the moment. He wasn't worried about much beyond the next five minutes. He was sitting with Renee, now dressed in a light sweater over a summer button down shirt, her tanned, angular legs dark against the white deck, stretching all the way to her tennies. And now he'd received that kiss he'd imagined. He had his feet outstretched with cool refreshments on the table before him. Behind Duke, the expanding view of the Michigan and Canadian shorelines passed by as the *Captain Jack* cruised down river. Now he knew why they called them cruisers. For he was totally, and truly, cruising. "What if the Lakes begin to run dry?" Renee inquired, paying more attention than Kevin thought she was. "Isn't that the big fear that the water will begin to disappear, drained for farming, or down the Mississippi, or evaporated by heat waves due to changes in the climate? Then you drain the water, and others start pumping it out and piping it to the southwest, and other places?"

Smart girl Kevin thought.

"Well, good question," Duke stated. "It could happen, it would take a creative plan to prevent the water from declining, but remember, necessity is the mother of invention and solutions would be had. Like expanding the Lakes by adding more water from Lake Nipigon, make it a sixth Great Lake, drain more water from the far north, open the dams, and let all that water in Northern Canada into the lakes."

"Nipigon?" Renee broke in, "as in *Paddle to the Sea?*" she inquired leaning forward in her seat.

"Not sure of that," Duke replied, "but I know Lake Nipigon."

"Dad," Renee fairly shouted as she jumped from her seat. "Do you have *Paddle* aboard?"

"I think so honey, try the rack in the salon," Jack replied turning to Renee who was already heading down the cabin steps.

When Duke went forward to the bar, his story interrupted by Renee's sudden departure, Kevin leaned over to ask Mary Lou Wilson what she thought of her husband's grand scheme. He found she was a pretty smart cookie also. Not only had she married the wealthy guy, she had a good handle on what made him tick.

She leaned back in her deck chair and looked at Kevin, "Duke is full of big ideas. He moves from one to the other and, how should I say, loves the attention. But," she paused, "he's always very serious about them. As far as this water thing goes, it might not go as planned but he knows it will happen, somehow, someway, someday, and he wants in on it. He'll use his water ship to get his name out there and then collect the incoming venture capital."

Renee bounded up the cabin steps with a book in hand, "Here it is," she exclaimed as she placed it on the table and began paging through its contents.

"Oh, look at these beautiful pictures," she cooed. "This was my first favorite book."

"That's nice dear," Mary Lou stated, not really knowing what she was looking at as Renee displayed one of the full page colored renderings.

Kevin knew. It was *Paddle-to-the Sea* written and illustrated by Holling Clancy Holling, the story of a small canoe carved by an Indian boy and the journey it makes from Lake Superior all the way to the Atlantic Ocean. A story every kid of his generation who was raised on the Great Lakes knew. There were two tales children of the lakes learned; Paddle's, and the opening to the Song of Hiawatha,

"By the shores of Gitche Gumme,
"By the shining Big-Sea-Water..."

The Indian name for Lake Superior.

"Here it is," Renee said as she turned the pages, "second paragraph of chapter two," she began reading.

"Now I will tell you something!" said the boy to the little figure in the canoe. "I have learned in school that when this snow in our Nipigon country melts, the water flows to that river. The river flows into the Great Lakes, the biggest lakes in the world. They are set like bowls on a gentle slope. The water from our river flows into the top one, drops into the next, and on to the others. Then it makes a river again, a river that flows to the Big Salt Water."

102

"There," she said looking up with a smile while pointing to the page, "This Nipigon country."

While Duke and Mary Lou listened politely Jack stared at Renee with deep admiration. Suddenly, all the feelings that had been building since their trip began came flooding to the forefront. He was so proud of her and so happy to have her around, finally. So proud of everything he'd learned about her, her strength of character, sense of humor, her love of books, and her mental and physical toughness. How she had the knowledge and skill in all aspects of running the *Captain Jack*, or the willingness and ability to learn it in a hurry. How she took charge, with no hesitation, when a situation arose on board. Like the time early in their voyage when she dressed down, in no certain terms, the crew of middle aged men in a pleasure boat who were berating her father, when Jack was attempting to dock the big cruiser in a tight spot, in a stiff wind, in plenty of boat traffic. Renee was on the bow, lines ready while guiding her dad into a slip, when a small pleasure boat filled with yahoo's kept yelling at Jack for being in their way. She stepped to the side rail and announced firmly, without yelling, that if they didn't shut the fuck up she was going to drop the *Captain Jack's* anchor thru the bottom of their little piece of shit boat. Nothing else was said. Jack never heard. He knew she was strong. He was full of pride for her, and realizing for the first time, how glad he was to have her around after so many years. He stepped from the wheel, with tears welling in his eyes to enwrap his daughter in his arms.

"Hear-hear," Duke saluted the pair as they stepped apart grasping each other's hands.

Kevin was falling harder.

Duke forged on without missing a beat, "If handled right, there would be enough water. Like I said, bring it down from the north, your Nipigon Country," he said waving his glass in Renee's direction.

"Everyone's freaked out about draining their beloved lakes. Hell, so am I, but, I think we can do both. Distribute it, and replenish it, and keep enough here."

"You mean sell it, right." Renee interjected.

"Of course," Duke added, "as a matter of fact, such an operation is very costly, and of course there's supply and demand. Anyhow, he added, "the amount of water won't be the issue, hell, twenty percent of the world's fresh water is here, the issue will be how clean it will be."

"You mean polluted," Renee asked as she returned to her seat at the table and Jack to the wheel.

"Oh yeah, it's already becoming polluted down here, that's why I'm starting up North, but wait till the oil and gas men get in here, and start drilling. That's when it will get messy, that's when it will start to go to hell. That's why we need to get to the water while it's still usable," he said as he took a drink from his glass before adding, "While it's still worth something!"

"O.K dear, that's enough shop talk," Mary Lou interrupted without looking up from her magazine, sensing exactly when, and how, to slow the growing wave of her husband's mounting rant. She'd done it many times before, enough that Duke took his cue with good nature, stepped from under the canvas top into the bright sun and pronounced, "Oh yes, what a magnificent day."

Kevin was happy Mary Lou pounced. Like at lunch, Duke's plan weighed on most who heard it. They really didn't have anything against him, well, maybe Jeff Waters did, or disbelieve in what he was saying; they just didn't want to hear about it, not now, on a glorious summer weekend. The tale he spun was a buzz kill and could be addressed later.

Kevin was happy for a change in the conversation, or for that matter, no conversation at all. He was cruising. He took Renee's book from the table and paged through its contents. He remembered the first time he came by *Paddle-to-the-Sea*. He was a kid, and it was at the old St. Clair Library that sat on the water side of Riverside Avenue downtown, in the old town, before urban renewal bulldozed it away. The Library, a onetime retail store had wood floors, a high tin ceiling, and large front windows that overlooked the movie house, restaurant with soda bar, and clothing store across the main drag.

Passed the rows of books and Liberian's desk, through a door in the back was the children's reading room, a small space lined by low bookshelves and a child's size table and chairs in the center. Another door led to a short hallway. At the end of the hallway a screen door opened onto steps overlooking the river.

Paging through picture books at the table was always special. Surrounded by all the knowledge a youngster needed. The silence was righteous, entering the quiet world from a warm summer day full of shouts and laughter, baseball cards humming in bike spokes, cars rumbling by.

There was the draw of knowledge in all those books, the curiosity and mystery of the unknown. Yet even greater was the lure of that screen door at the end of the hallway, for beyond the door, only feet away, lay the river, deep and blue, moving past, towards all the knowledge of the world. It's there Kevin discovered *Paddle*. The Librarian saw him peering through the screen door and handed him the book. Again he paged through its pages, this time on the back deck of the *Captain Jack*.

"As the motorboat chugged lazily down the St. Clair River, with Michigan on one bank facing Canada on the other, it passed farms and summer cottages and came to marshy little Lake St. Clair. Here the water was so shallow the buoys with lights and clanging bells had to mark out a course for ships...."

He looked up at the wake disappearing into the blue distance, then back at the sketches that adorned the page. The wood cruiser, the map of the river and the delta it formed as it drained into the Flats. He was travelling full circle, to connect again, thanks to Holling and Renee. Same place, same feeling, timeless.

105

The *Captain Jack* made one more stop on its way down bound for Brown's Restaurant in the Flats. Duke Wilson had called ahead from the boat harbor and ordered something to eat from a little marina in Marine City. As they reached the sleepy river town Jack motored past the lighthouse, a proud sentinel of the past, when the river was full of merchant ships, many built in the small towns along the waterway. The *Captain Jack* ran past the small beach, the park, and backs of stores and homes with comfortable looking porches overlooking the water. Just past Catholic Point he spun the wheel hard to bring the cruiser around, near 180 degrees, to point the bow north, at the entrance of the Belle River.

"Not much room here," from Duke who had joined Jack at the wheel.

"Yeah, she's pretty tight. It can be tricky at times, especially at night," Jack replied.

Jack maneuvered the Chris-Craft out of the fast-moving current of the big river into the quieter water of the narrow entrance. Fisherman looked up, waved and nodded, then returned to bob or cast.

"It's hard to believe this little river could have been such a busy place onetime," Jack stated.

"Yeah, back in the day, eh?" Duke wondered.

"It was a hub of activity, boom days."

"When was that?" Duke inquired.

"Mid-1800's, to the start of the nineteen's. Between St. Clair and Marine City they built hundreds of merchant ships, passenger ships too, you can't forget them" Jack stated. "Right here at the mouth of the Belle, same with the Pine."

"You remember it well, I'm sure," Duke smiled.

"Huh," Jack huffed before a grin crossed his face. "Not quite, but my granddad did. He told me of the ship building at places like the

McLouth and Langell boat yards. When he was a boy the sounds and smells of boat building filled these towns."

"Big ships," Duke asked?

"Oh, hell ya, some of 'em were up to 200 feet, or more," Jack answered.

"Really?" Duke replied, looking about, noticing the *Captain Jack* occupied most of the Belle River, "No way."

"Oh sure, the big ship yards and saw mills were located on the big river, mouth of the Pine, or Belle. The smaller yards and supply business's ran up and down the shores of the small rivers. The big river was a calmer one in those days. Sand beaches and woods came to the water's edge. There were no breakwalls. Waves and currents washed ashore smoothly. There wasn't much rough water back then, unless a storm came up."

"First they built the wooden schooners, mostly 'round 100 feet I guess. Then came the steamboats," Jack said as he steered the cruiser up the Belle. "It was natural for the boat industry to boom here. Michigan was one big forest. So they had the trees and the water, and the need, the need to move goods and people through the lakes. In those days they clear cut the forests inland from the river 50 miles," Jack exclaimed. "The supply business went up on the smaller rivers and the industry boomed. A person could walk across these small rivers on the decks of the moored ships," he said turning towards Duke for emphasis.

"Then the big steel boats, more like the lake freighters, round turn of the century, I suppose," Jack said, returning his attention to the river to pilot past large covered boat wells on one side and back yard docks on the other. "Everyone in these river towns was involved in ship building."

One of those was Mary who Duke spotted waving from ashore as they reached her little marina on the west side of the Belle. Her family had worked along the Belle for three generations; husbands, grandfathers, brothers, sons and uncles. Some in the saw mills and shipyards, some in the supply stores and bars in town and later on, at the Chris-Craft plant down river in Algonac. All of them were fisherman.

Her small four dock marina, squeezed between a boatel and large covered wells, had become more fish store and gas stop than marina over the years. Mary's house was located on the property. She'd sit in the shade of the porch waiting patiently for customers. A rusting metal barn, full of boats in various states of disintegration sat next to her house. Her boys tried to keep the place up and running but the boat business wasn't what it was in Mary and Warren's day. The boys moved away in search of bigger and better. Warren was gone and now Mary pumped gas and sold fish caught by local anglers.

Duke knew Mary. He'd found a few runabouts in the barn, paid too much for them, paying the cost of nostalgia, and had them restored. He was showing one of them at the boat show.

Just off the docks Jack spun the cruiser on a dime, facing back towards the rivers mouth, and laid against the gas dock. The big cruiser filled much of the river with this maneuver and several small boats gave way to wait. The setting so intimate friendly conversations broke out between the crew of the *Captain Jack* and happy, sun splashed occupants of the pleasure craft and folks ashore.

Duke Wilson stepped off the cruiser to greet Mary with a hug as she joined him on the dock. "I hope you folks are hungry," she announced with a laugh.

"You know we are," Duke replied, "Especially for one of your splendid meals," and with this Duke introduced Mary to all on board.

Like all of her orders, this was a carry out, so Jack kept the cruiser idling at the dock, grasping a spile to keep in place. Kevin hopped off and followed Duke and Mary down the dock, passed a grill sizzling with foil packs of walleye and into the small store. Inside, it appeared time had stopped. A musky smell filled the only room even though the windows were open. An ad for outboard motors, an old Red Wings schedule, an outdated motor oil calendar, and charts of the river and Flats filled two walls. Black and white photos of unlimited hydroplanes, *Gale V, Such Crust* and one of *Miss Detroit* autographed by driver Chuck Thompson, occupied another. An electric Vernor's clock hung behind a display case full of fishing lures and reels. Stacks of canned foods and boxes of boat supplies lined shelving behind the display. A stack of rods leaned in a corner. A small layer of dust collected on everything except the food display where fresh fillets glowed enticingly under lights. Mary finished packing a box of condiments, then pulled a large bowl of shrimp on ice from the refrigerated display and handed them to Kevin. Duke paid her twice what he owed. Outside she removed the walleye packs, placed them in a basket, handed them to Duke, and sent them on their way.

By the time the *Captain Jack* reached the Flats the post-eating-lulls had set in on the crew, and aided by the gentle roll of the boat and a soundtrack provided by the constant drone of the engines, they rode quietly, absorbing the waterscape. Jack headed southwest down the middle channel, lower into the Flats, the stillness of the scene hypnotizing. The ever-changing angle of light, the sun playing visual tricks on the bayou, where islands floated in the air and solitary trees rose from the water. Wind patterns changed the shimmer on the still waters that melted together with the sky. On the horizon cottages appeared from nowhere to sit atop the water. Lower they cruised, deeper into the Flats, where an orange oriental sun hung low in the sky.

CHAPTER 7

The Six Bottle Boys

The tranquility of the Flats abruptly ended when Jack LaCroix wheeled the Chris-Craft off the middle channel into the docking area at Brown's. Joyous voices, reflective of a scintillating, summer Saturday evening, had the place buzzing. People, partying people, were everywhere. They filled picnic tables and overflowed the docks. Merry crew members occupied decks and cabin tops of boats filling the wells. Laughter and shouts spilled from the open windows of the waterside roadhouse.

Like earlier that morning, Kevin and Renee stood together at the side rail of the *Captain Jack,* and like earlier that morning, the Waterman suddenly came into view. Renee spotted him waving from the end of a dock.

"Hey, there's Jeff," she shouted waving in his direction.

"Yeah, there he is," Kevin replied, feigning excitement. He wondered how she picked him out of the crowd so quickly.

As they moved closer, Jeff signaled for Jack to continue along the channel to an open slip further down. Duke climbed around the cabin top to man the bow deck as they drifted along the dock line, past Sea Rays, a runabout, a couple of Rinker's, a small sail boat, pontoon power porches, a Bassmaster, and the *Lucky Lena*, into the last open well. The Waterman greeted them as Duke tossed the bow lines. Moments later Tom White joined Jeff on the dock.

"I can't believe they got a spot," Whitey smiled as the cruiser slid into the slip. "What happened to the guy who was just here?" Whitey inquired of Jeff. "The guy with the *Commander*, he was here 15 minutes ago?"

111

"Oh, he was travelin', moving on," the Waterman replied. "He said he was headed for the North Channel I think, and wanted to take advantage of the good conditions, cover some miles."

"And I think he foresaw the coming bender," Whitey grinned. "I think he was gettin' while the gettin' was good."

"Smart Captain," Jeff agreed. "Once this party hits nightfall, and a few more beers, he'd be spending the night, that's for sure."

"Good choice," Whitey said, half to himself, his imagination flirting with the image of running up river, sun setting over the Michigan shoreline to the west, under the Blue Water Bridge and into Lake Huron, where a star-spangled night sky guided the way north, across 225 miles of open water, north to Georgian Bay. "Yes, good choice."

"This is great," Jeff beamed as he addressed Renee from the dock. He hadn't taken his eyes off her since the cruiser arrived. He wasn't thrilled to see the Duke of Disaster but Renee's presence surpassed any bad vibes he had towards the water merchant. "I didn't know you guys were comin' down here," he exclaimed. Kevin thought the same thing of running into the Waterboys.

"Sure, where else would we go for a perch dinner, on an evening like this," she replied with a smile as she swung her arm around to encompass the surrounding scene.

"That's right," Duke added as he stepped off the cruiser onto the dock, "Best perch dinner on the Flats, wouldn't you say Jack?"

"Oh, sure Duke," he replied over his shoulder, busy securing lines on the transom. "But I'm still stuffed from Mary's," he added with a laugh. "I couldn't eat another thing."

"No problem," Duke announced, "The night is young, we'll have a few drinks, do a little dancing and eat later if we want." And with that Duke ordered one and all into Brown's. He was good at that, ordering people around, telling them what to do. Making sure everything was coordinated. He had a way of proceeding politely, convincing people it would be in their best interest, practically guaranteeing a good time would be had by all. He had a presence and a way of doing so in a friendly, simple command. It was easy for most to comply, as he usually finished such invitations with the hook, "I'm buying."

"Should I get Red up?" Whitey inquired of the Waterman as they worked their way down the crowded dock, past the *Lucky Lena*, docked a few boats away.

"Na, let him be, it's been a long day," Jeff replied.

Sometime after Red and Whitey were picked up off his dock, the river tour, lunch at the Crab, and the long, hot run down river to the Flats, Red had gone below to mix another drink, and not returned. He was still knocked out in the V-bunk of the *Lena*.

Inside, the restaurant was half empty. Stools along the bar were full of patrons watching the Tigers game, but most revelers were outside taking in the remaining glories of the summer twilight, including members of the band, who had set up, but on evenings like this, waited till sunset.

The party, Duke and Mary Lou, Jack and Renee, Kevin, and the Waterboys, Jeff and Whitey, pulled together two tables, and Duke ordered the first round of pitchers. Jack ordered coffee. Kevin and Jeff maneuvered to assure a seat next to Renee, one on each side. Kevin sat back with legs out stretched and arms folded, confident with his situation. After all, he'd gotten the kiss. Meanwhile, the Waterman was playing hard for Renee's attention, laughing at everything she said, engaging her dad in freighter talk, espousing the coolness of their present trip together, and drinking Dukes beer while completely ignoring him. Duke rambled on about who he thought would win what at the boat show's award ceremony in the morning. Mary Lou lit a cigarette and read over the menu.

"How many you goin' to win?" Whitey inquired of Duke."

"Well," Duke paused, reading the intent of Tom's question, "I don't know. We'll see tomorrow."

"Oh, come on now," Whitey said with a disarming smile, "You gotta win something, right? I mean how many boats you got there, at the show?"

"Three, but we'll see what the judges come up with."

Everyone around the weekend boat show knew it was pretty much Duke's baby. He was the main sponsor and made sure everything was organized, and always brought the best of his antique collection. He thoroughly enjoyed the camaraderie of fellow wood boaters, took pride in the restoration and preservation of such American craftsmanship, but above all, liked to win.

"What you enter this year?" Whitey pressed on.

"Well," Duke hesitated again.

"Did you bring the Cobra?" Whitey inquired, remembering the classic craft from one of Duke's previous visits to the boat show.

"Yes, I have her on a display trailer near the marina office."

"Oh, man, aren't you going to splash her? Aren't you going to run her up and down the river?" Whitey asked.

"No, not this year, I might run her at Hessel later this summer."

Whitey remembered the summer Duke ran *Duke's Delite* at the boat show. He had never seen one before, Cobras were very rare. Chris-Craft built fewer than a hundred and for one season only, 1955. The futuristic looking 18' runabout, with its tail fin, which gave it a truly race-boat look, was the hit of the show and swept the awards that year. While the hull and front deck were made of Mahogany, the rear deck and tail fin assembly was fiberglass. It was the first-time glass was used in a Chris-Craft and was a portent of things to come, as Chris-Craft moved onto fiberglass and left Michigan for Florida.

Whitey refilled his glass from the pitcher of beer. "Let's splash it, what do you say?" he asked. "I'd love to drive it. Maybe tomorrow after the show's over, eh?"

"Well, sorry Tom," Duke laughed, "No can do, not this year, plus there are a lot of people who'd like to take her for a spin."

Whitey wondered why he was pursuing this conversation with Duke. Why he was even engaging him in conversation. Something about Duke was gnawing at him, had been since they first ran into him at the Crab. Like a flashback, something about Duke kept pushing from the recesses of his mind. But he couldn't grasp it. Maybe it was that rich man, poor man thing, that so few with so much, and so many with so little thing. He was an alright guy but operated in a different world, one of having it all and not wanting to lose it, to anything or anyone. A world of I got mine, get your own, where the wealthy were always right in everything and the rest reduced to merely a market share, or the working poor, where more and more simply disappeared as untouchables, while in Duke's life it was so easy to be righteous when rich. He took another draw on his beer. He knew about Duke but Duke didn't know him. That he was drafted into the Vietnam war for having a low lottery number when Duke was learning to expand the family wealth while away at business school on college deferment, where contributing to a military industrial complex had contributed to Whitey and his buddies being shot at. Now, while Duke dabbled in venture capital Tom daubed atop paint ladders and ran rum to pay the rent and feed the family. But that wasn't it. He didn't dislike the guy. He seemed a good man. Yet there was something he couldn't grasp about this dude. He sat back, peered out the open windows at the boat cabins and masts silhouetted against the burnt orange backdrop with a sigh, too much sun, too much beer, not enough sleep, too many thoughts.

"I also brought a '39 barrel back and a '47 Utility. I have those in the water," Duke continued.

"Nice boats," Whitey stated without turning.

"Especially the twin seat barrel back," Duke added, happy to talk boats, his boats. "Some feel it was the sleekest runabout ever made. I know it's one of my favorites. You know, 1939 was a banner year for Chris-Craft."

"Yeah," Whitey replied, "I've heard that." He knew all about the barrel backs, Clay had one, but Whitey preferred the utilities. The runabouts were the more stylish but the utilities more versatile, and got the most use, more of a working boat. One could move around the engine cover, could walk about when underway, not confined to the seating of the runabouts. Utilities were ideal for fishing as well as pleasure seeking.

"Yes, 1939 was a special year for Chris Craft," Jack stated, now following the boating conversation as Jeff and Kevin chatted up Renee.

"Not only is '39 considered to be the zenith of the company's designing, that was the year Christopher Columbus Smith passed away."

"Really," Duke inquired after an extended pause, "How about that. I didn't know that, I guess he went out on top then."

"Quite a man," Jack added.

The three sat through an impromptu moment of silence until Whitey raised his glass, "Here's to Chris Smith and all his boats."

"Hear, hear." They toasted in unison.

As darkness settled over the Flats the lights at Browns came on. Members of the band wandered in and began fiddling with the equipment. Two of the players strolled over to the table to greet Jeff Waters and Tom White. The Waterboys introduced Gord Petrochenko and Billy Greenmeadow to the rest of the table. It appeared Jeff and Whitey knew them well.

The two returned to the small stage to join two other members and began to tune up, adjust microphone-stands, and uncoil cords. The room filled with electric sounds of tuning E-strings, P.A. feedback, the buzz of a Fender twin reverb coming alive, rim shots on a snare drum, and the thud of the bass drum with the band's name, Six Bottle Boys, scrawled across the front. There was no apparent rush to get going and no one seemed to mind as the musicians laughed and joked with the waitresses. Jack drank his coffee, Duke and Mary Lou scanned a menu, while Kevin and the Waterman remained mesmerized by Renee. Whitey continued to stare out the windows.

It was nightfall by the time Gord stepped to the microphone to count off, "One-two, a one-two-three-four," and the room exploded into a blues shuffle that charged the atmosphere and changed momentum for the night. All conversation came to a halt, fingers on tables and toes on the floor found the pace to keep time. Partiers along the dock headed for the bar, servers shouted orders to bartenders, and it was party on.

Kevin turned his chair around to better view the players, and it didn't take long for him to observe that these guys could play. Gord was front man and leader, who scratched out a simple but accurate rhythm guitar and handled the vocals and crowd chatter with a commanding confidence. He sported curly, mop top hair, wore cut offs, a Maple Leafs T-shirt that hung over a slightly protruding belly and flip flops.

Billy played lead guitar from the back of the stage. He was a First Nation Canadian who wore his long, black hair in a ponytail with a small beaded head band, black jeans and T-shirt. He looked considerably younger than the others, and didn't move much and said little. He just played the shit out of his Stratocaster, so tasty, with great dynamics and feel. When he played his leads the other boys in the band turned to watch with admiration. At times people dancing stopped to watch.

The full, rich cords of a Hammond B-3 organ provided background for the guitars. It was more massaged than played by a big man who wore a cowboy hat and sported a scruffy beard. He pushed big, sweeping cords out of the wooden monster, then softer rhythms that filled the room with a gospel feel. But mostly, the dude danced across the bass pedals with a booted left foot that drove one to look for a bass player, for there must be one, to have such an accurate, beat bopping walking bass.

The big sound was held together by the drummer, who in contrast to the other three, appeared to have stopped in on his way home from the office, which he had, still wearing a white dress shirt, sleeves rolled, top button open, sporting a loosened tie, clean shaven and close cropped hair. He worked a simple drum kit, much smaller than the monster double bass drum sets that were in vogue, played it with great command, the precision of a metronome and accents perfectly timed. He moved effortlessly, all wrists.

During his newspaper career Kevin had reviewed many bands and it took only half a song to figure out this bar band, playing a Saturday night gig at an island roadhouse, floating in a vast delta, had it. He would learn that Gord was from nearby Wallaceburg, the biggest town near the Flats on the Canadian side. He'd made his way down the Chenal Ecarte and around Walpole Island to Harsens Island, where he hooked up with fellow party boys and music aficionados who led him across the river to Detroit and the exploding rock scene. He'd sat on the floor of the Grande and East Town Ballrooms soaking it up and in. Gord bought a guitar, a twice owned Les Paul, moved onto Toronto, slept on a friend's couch, waited tables in clubs and met a string of musicians as they played their way through. He got some gigs, went broke and returned to Wallaceburg, where one rainy, summer night, while walking down the street, he heard amazing guitar licks emanating from an open window of a small house. He couldn't resist, knocked on the door, and waited for someone to appear, it was Billy. It took Gord six months or more to convince the shy boy to play with him in public, but the wait was worth it.

After convincing his widowed mother things would be O.K. he headed back to Toronto with Billy in tow. Gord's onstage abilities combined with Billy's raw talent got the two plenty of gigs with local players and they earned enough to stay alive in the big T.O. One was Otis, the B-3 player, a Canadian Cowboy from Calgary, who took lessons as a kid on a smaller Hammond in his parents living room, played in church on Sunday mornings, then went back evenings with a key from the pastor to practice and proceeded to pump out country swing and blues from the alter before running off to Toronto during the rock revolution to ply his trade.

When the next spring came around Billy became homesick for the quite life and simple pleasures of the Canadian Bayou and returned home. Gord followed, got a day job as a mechanic. Otis became music director at a Toronto church by day and played lounge gigs by night around the metropolitan area. During the summer the three hooked up on weekends to play in Southern Ontario bars, weddings and parties, but especially enjoyed Browns, where they became the house band. The music wasn't the only thing that brought them together each spring, for in their hearts, they were Waterboys, constantly drawn back to the wonders of the Flats. Even Dave, the current drummer, was a boatman, having discovered the boys and the band on a trip to Browns by boat, along the well-traveled route from the Clinton River in Mount Clemens, Michigan, across Anchor Bay. Members of the Six Bottle Boys made it a habit of spending Sunday's following gigs, sitting on a dock or drifting quietly in a fishing boat somewhere in the Flats.

The locals knew them and loved them and by the time the band ripped into the second song the dance floor had filled. Duke and Mary Lou were some of the first and Jeff wasted little time in asking Renee to join him. The crowd hooted and hollered at songs end and the band blistered on. Kevin turned to see Red now sitting at the table, apparently awoken by the booming sound emanating from the bar. Whitey watched the dancers. Jack sipped another coffee.

After three or four tunes Duke needed a break and headed for the restroom and suddenly, Kevin found himself being pulled to his feet by a smiling Mary Lou. She was revved up and proceeded to drag him around the floor. At one point they ended up next to Jeff and Renee where Kevin couldn't take his eyes from the beautifully flowing Renee. When the Six Bottle Boys slowed the pace to their specialty, a blues tune, it was slow dance time. Mary Lou snagged Kevin as he turned towards the tables and pulled him into her arms and held him closely, pressing her body firmly against his, with each step of the meandering blues beat her right leg pressed between his. The reverberation of the beat filled the room, flowed through the wood floor, traveled through Mary Lou's body and into his. From across the floor he saw Renee watching him over Jeff's shoulder. When the song ended Gord announced the band's first break and Mary Lou smiled at Kevin, squeezing his hand before letting go. The dancers stumbled to the tables, sliding and shuffling chairs around before collapsing, exhausted.

"Hey, you move pretty good there," Red said to Kevin.

"Yeah, you think so?" Kevin replied, wondering what had just happened.

"Sure," Red smiled, elbowing him playfully in the ribs for emphasis after looking across the table at Mary Lou.

"Yeah?" Kevin mumbled his heart beginning to pound. He snuck a peek at Mary Lou as she dug a pack of smokes from her bag, then searched the table and around the bar for Duke. He caught a glimpse of him and Jack through the haze and crowd at the pool table near the far end of the bar. Duke was holding court with the young, boisterous beer crowd, playing all comers and apparently winning.

Jeff and Renee returned from the bar with fresh drinks and joined them at the table. Renee sat next to Mary Lou and smiled at Kevin who returned the gesture. He glanced over at Mary Lou who lit a cigarette, exhaled smoke across the table towards him, then smiled seductively through the haze. He blinked and coughed on the smoke. Renee and Jeff laughed.

Kevin's brain snapped, suddenly pissed. He didn't mind the laughs from the women, but not from Jeff. He quickly became confused; what was happening, what was Mary Lou up to? He was sad; was Renee really pairing off with the Waterman. He was frightened; would Duke knock him out. And suddenly overwhelmed; he was tired, sweating. He grabbed a glass from the many on the table and took a quick swig. It was warm and tasted like shit. The sound from the band still roared in his head, the room swayed and rolled, he felt like he was still aboard the *Captain Jack*. When Clayton suddenly appeared at the table Kevin's mind raced faster, what was he doing here, remembering the previous nights smuggling, why was Clay here now, what was up, something wrong, the cops? Kevin spiraled into a paranoid mish-mash of losing Renee and smuggling gone wrong which led to flashes of missed stories, interviews, photos, editors, deadlines, boats and endless river runs.

The Waterboys rose to greet Clay, not only Jeff Waters and Tom White, but Gord and Billy as well. They moved away from the tables, across the dance floor to huddle briefly by the stage.

"I need some air," Kevin managed to announce to the rest at the table as he stood and exited the bar stage right. His angst began to dissipate with his first breath of clear night air. Moments later sweet aromas of the bayou replaced the stale stuffiness of smoke and bar essence. He caught his breath, his racing pulse slowed, he began to relax.

"Say, you all right there?" Red inquired as he joined Kevin.

"Yeah sure," Kevin stammered. "Just catching a break, I needed some air."

"Ha, you were really cutting a rug there, eh?"

"Guess so," Kevin smiled a little embarrassed. He couldn't remember the last time he danced like that, or did anything that strenuous. No wonder he was gassed. The pair sauntered the short distance to the dock where each boat was occupied with revelers, enjoying the magic of the summer night.

"These folks got it right," Kevin thought out loud.

"Come again," from Red.

"Oh, I was just thinking that these people sitting on their boats, backed into the wells here, got a good thing going. Sitting under the stars, close enough to hear all the tunes but not inside where it's too loud to even talk…"

"Or breathe," Red added with a laugh.

"Yeah," Kevin said turning to Red with a smile.

"Looks like the boys are out for some fresh air too." Red stated looking over Kevin's shoulder. Kevin turned to see members of the band and the Waterboys round the corner of the building and head down the dock.

"Where they headed?" Kevin inquired.

"Oh, to the *Lena* probably," Red answered.

"Yeah, what's up you suppose?"

"Well, knowin' them, probably to burn one. They are the band you know." Red laughed, "That's what bands do, eh?"

"Ha, yeah," Kevin agreed. "That's what bands do."

"You know about that I'm sure?" Red asked with a smirk.

"Oh yes, I lived through those times," Kevin replied as he watched the boys disappear down the dock. He not only lived it, but survived it.

"Or maybe they have some business to discuss," Red stated.

"Business?" Kevin inquired.

"Sure, maybe they have another run, something like that."

"What?"

"That might explain why Clay showed up."

"They'd discuss that in front of the band?" Kevin asked a bit surprised.

"Well, at least Gord and Billy," Red replied. "And I'm sure the others know what's going on."

"Going on?"

"Didn't you know?" Red inquired turning to Kevin.

"Know what?"

"That Gord and Billy are partners with the Waterboys."

"They are?" Kevin responded with surprise.

"Sure," Red stated. "They're the Canadian connection. That's who meets the *Lena* when they come ashore."

"Those are the guys who came out of the thickets last night?"

"Sure, that's them. I thought you probably knew."

"No, I didn't know," Kevin said as he began to rerun the previous night's adventure, but before he put it all together Renee suddenly appeared at his side.

"Hey you guys, what's up," Then turning to Kevin, "Mary Lou's inside looking for you."

"Oh, I….." he stammered before Renee spared him.

"Hey, I'm only kidding," she added with a large, illuminating smile.

By the time the boys, the six bottle version from the band and the Waterboys, the bayou pirates, returned from igniting imaginations and expanding the boundaries the night would take, Kevin had stolen a few moments alone with Renee in the bar. Red had strolled down the dock towards the *Lena*, to 'sort of keep an eye on the boys,' they were after all, his crew. He didn't have boys of his own, so these were his, and Whitey's sons were his grandkids. Jack and Duke were still hanging around the pool table and Mary Lou had gone to powder her nose. As she sashayed her way back towards the table, smiling at Kevin as she approached, Gord stepped to the mike and announced it was time for everyone's favorite, Brown's bayou medley. Kevin looked at Renee sitting across from him, at Mary Lou closing in from behind her, and back at Renee. At the precise moment the band started, on the down beat, Kevin leaned across the table, grasped Renee's hand and said, "Let's dance." If Jeff had Renee the first set, he was going to dance with her the second.

The floor filled quickly as the boys broke into a hard pounding version of CCR's "Born on the Bayou" with Gord barking out the vocals, Billy sticking the raunchy guitar part perfectly, Dave driving nails with rim shots. At song's end the place erupted into cheers and calls for more and that's what the boys gave them, as they broke into a boogie version of "Jambalaya." The lid was about to blow. The entire place became the dance floor. People eating at tables in the back were up, pool players stopped and played air guitar on cue sticks. Folks on bar stools swung to face the band, arms over heads, clapping, partiers outside at picnic tables were up, dancing under strings of lights running along the docks, boats in slips rocked as crews bounced on back decks. It was the bar's theme song. When the Six Bottle Boys sang out, 'have big fun on the bayou,' the entire crowd joined in, and after the next verse the band repeated the line over and over till the place turned full frenzy. On the floor Kevin and Renee bounced around off each other and fellow revelers. It was fever pitch till the band stopped from exhaustion and the crowd cheered itself out. A moment of transcendence emanated from the glowing, little roadhouse, up, out and over the bayou.

The band started a long, slow, organ driven intro and a waitress joined them on stage to help finish the medley, belting out a soulful version of "Blue Bayou." Patrons swayed to the rhythms and dancers held on tightly as love filled the room. A love fueled by a serendipitous moment, fueled by spirits, food and dance, a feast built on friendship and common cause of condition, a cosmic clarity, when all was right with their world, a shared base connection with, and celebration of the one true mother to all habitants of the bayou, Mother Nature.

Renee was certainly feeling the love. She hadn't felt this way for a while, a long while. Love for deciding to make the trip, love for her father, loving the release of debilitating worry, love of the sun and water, and love for these Waterboys, who managed to retain a life of adventure in otherwise mundane existences, and the attention they brought her way. She liked them all, Jeff Waters and Kevin Casey especially, and had no intention of playing one against the other, but was a little excited when she first noticed the competition. She had no intention of picking one over the other, but at that moment in time and place, with all spinning in cosmic order around the dance floor of her world, it just happened.

Renee drew Kevin close as they moved slowly around the floor and before the song ended, during Otis's flowing organ solo, she held Kevin's hand and lead him from the bar. It was a magical stroll down the dock for both but only Kevin talked, rambling on about the crisp night air, striving to put into words what his mind's lens was capturing in a rapid stream of conscious; strings of lights from boats and docks reflecting off still water, crowds of partiers in various states of inebriation, aware that on this night, they were reaching their peak, flashing smiles for imaginary party portraits, flickering fires from torches, silhouettes of folks around a campfire burning across the inlet, the moon appearing from behind drifting clouds casting a supernatural glow across the bayou. Renee just smiled.

The band was still playing by the time they reached the *Captain Jack* and headed below deck. Kevin never stopped talking until Renee leaned against the bulkhead, pulled him to her, placed a finger on his lips to silence him and followed with a long kiss. The beat from the next song reverberated deep in the water and through the hull as the two fell upon the bunk.

"Do you have a condom?" Renee whispered into Kevin's ear.

"No, I can't afford one," he said, "I live in an apartment."

CHAPTER 8

The Waterman's Prize

The Six Bottle Boys were exhausted and in dire need of their second break when it arrived. Sweat ran down their faces and soaked their shirts as they left the stage to applause, shouts and catcalls of admiration.

"That's it the *Smarty*, you're the Captain of the *Smarty* aren't you, the owner?" Whitey suddenly shouted out as Duke and Jack wound through the crowded bar toward the table.

"Yeah," Duke replied with surprise after looking around to make sure Tom White was actually addressing him. "Well, at least I was. I sold it a while back."

"The *Smarty*, the Mackinac winner, you won the Mackinac Race with her didn't you?"

"Yes, we won one year," Duke answered, still wondering what was up. "I mean I had a crew, an experienced team. I was part of a very good crew."

"But you owned her, right?" Whitey shouted, pointing at Duke.

"Yeah?"

"That's it," Whitey laughed turning towards Jeff, "The *Smarty* man, remember? We towed her ass off the sandbar. It was the freakin' *Smarty*," he announced falling back in his chair thrilled to have finally figured out what it was that had been bugging him about Duke.

"What are you talking about?" Duke inquired as he sat down at the table and poured a beer from a fresh pitcher. "When was that? I don't remember that."

"Well, I do," Jeff said, a smile growing across his face as he leaned forward, "And I imagine you don't, because I'm guessing your kid never told you about it."

"About what?"

"About towing his ass off the sandbar in your *Smarty*, on the way back from wining the Mackinac Race," Whitey said with a laugh.

"What the hell are you talking about?" Duke inquired, looking annoyed for the first time all day.

Captain Jeff certainly remembered the *Smarty* incident from a few years back, for it nearly cost him his beloved *Lena*, but unlike Whitey, hadn't made the connection of the giant sloop with Duke. Anytime he'd spent thinking about Duke had been about his dreaded plan to sell off the Great Lakes water, which he didn't want to think about, which lead to blocking Duke from his mind. Jeff had been occupied by more pleasant thoughts, namely Renee. Now reminded, he proceeded to spin the yarn for Duke, Mary Lou, Jack and others who had joined the party at the table, some who had heard some version before including Red, Clayton and members of the band.

Like other river stories and shipping tales, the Waterman could spin a yarn with the best of them and he transitioned into this one with ease. He told of a quiet July morning on the river, he and Whitey drifting on the current, fishing from the *Lucky Lena*. The water lay still and a soon to be hot sun rose over Canada, burning off the last of an early fog. A summer morning similar to many others till, out of the haze a sailboat appeared from the north, sails down, under power, its single mast with spreaders towering skyward, tallest they'd ever seen. Dead on, it resembled a giant cross moving down stream. The *Lena* drifted in the freighter channel at the north end of the shifting middle ground, that season located just north of the Inn. As it approached they recognized the long, sleek hull of a racing sloop, most likely returning from the Port Huron to Mackinac Island sailboat race, an annual 250 mile run across the deep blue waters of Lake Huron. They also recognized she was not only headed very close to a channel buoy, but actually passed on the wrong side, placing her on a course headed straight for the sand and mud of the middle ground.

The Waterboys exchanged glances of, did you see that? This giant sloop is coming from the race, its daylight, and a crew of that class sailing machine couldn't make that kind of mistake, could they? Those questions quickly became the Waterboys wondering if the sloop spotted the *Lena* or were they about to be run over. Their confusion answered shortly after as the sloop passed by quickly, too fast, off the *Lena's* port side, the wrong side. They saw the crew consisted of a dozen or so college age kids, laughing and partying, having the time of their lives, driving the Mackinac winner home with pride, music blaring, catching rays, beer flowing, probably the son of the owner and a bunch of his frat boy buddies accompanied by hot looking co-eds in bikinis and halter tops.

The Waterboys moved to the side rail of the *Lena* and waved their arms, and pointed downstream in the direction of the sandbar, then back and forth between buoys, and shouted out warnings of the impending peril, but either the music was too loud or they were being ignored, it turned out to be the latter.

At first the Waterboys' waves were greeted as salutes of recognition of the great racing sloop and its cool crew and deck full of sea nymphs, not gestures of warning. Only a few returned a wave, the rest glanced away, or ignored them completely. The guy at the wheel actually raised his head, and therefore his nose, in the air. A crewman hanging on the stern rigging, above the name *Smarty* painted on the transom, caught a glance of the *Lena* as the sloop passed by. He looked down on the old Chris-Craft, its decks and side hull in need of paint, and its two crusty crew members and laughed, then with a beer in one hand, flipped them off with the other.

"No, he didn't," Jack interjected. "He did that?"

The Waterboys confirmed so, in unison, and then Jeff continued his tale.

Again, the Waterboys exchanged looks of disbelief, then outrage, then anticipation of what was about to happen. They didn't say much other then, "Fuck 'em," and, "this is going to be great."

As the sloop moved away downstream, straight for disaster, music trailed behind her, across the still water, a soundtrack for impending doom.

When they hit, she struck the bar harder than even the Waterboys expected, her towering mast diving forward 45 degrees and her bow sprint plunging into the water as she plowed into the middle ground. There was no great rush aboard the *Lena* as Whitey opened the engine box in preparation of firing up the engine. A quick scan of the river confirmed they and the *Smarty* were the only boats on the water and the boys knew this may be more salvage then rescue.

The *Lena* moved downstream the short distance to the imbedded sloop, Whitey at the wheel and Jeff standing along the side rail. The first person they saw was the guy who flipped them off, just now pulling himself up by the stern rigging. He wasn't laughing at the old cruiser now, or its crew. The *Lena* drew little attention as she slowly passed the stricken sloop. The kid at the wheel was ramming the gear shift forward and roaring the engine, then pulling it back in reverse and revving the engine, back and forth, back and forth, with no success. The Waterboys knew he was just driving the sloop's keel deeper and deeper into the middle ground. A few of the *Smarty's* crew looked dazed and bruised but no one appeared truly injured, unless one counted the owners kid who was completely spent, in the midst of what appeared to be a full melt down. Everyone knew what he knew - his father was going to kill him.

The *Lena* took a very long time circling the sloop, her engine backfiring as she moved, announcing her presence, the Waterboys savoring every minute of the *Smarty's* distress.

After one complete lap of the sloop Whitey maneuvered the *Lena* alongside and floated there for a while. The crew of the *Smarty* ignored them till Jeff shouted, "Say, need some help?"

"No, I don't think so," one of the frat boys replied.

"Well, I think you do," Jeff shot back. "You better tell daddy's boy there that he's only making it worse."

"We'll call for help if we have to, besides, what can you do with that?" the kid asked pointing at the *Lena*.

With this Whitey hollered, "Hey asshole, you're the one stuck in the mud, we can motor away anytime."

This brought no reply as the panicked crew of the marooned sloop raced around the deck, some hurrying to the bow to stare overboard while the distressed one kept running the motor back and forth in vain. The *Lena* continued to bob alongside.

Finally, one of the co-eds took charge, "Can you really help us?"

"Sure," Jeff replied.

"How, what do we need to do?" she asked as she moved to the side rail, leaned against a stanchion and peered down at the boys with a desperate yet commanding voice. The Waterboys stared up at the bikini-clad co-ed, at each other, and back at the girl, a damsel in distress.

"Well," Jeff paused, taken back by her near naked beauty. "Well, for starters tell the boy captain there to stop racing the engine, he's going to blow it up. Then everyone needs to calm down."

All on board the sloop heard the Waterman but the frat boys did not like the idea of taking orders from two river rats in a dumpy old cruiser, what could they do, and repeated their plan of radioing ashore for help.

"Listen kid," Jeff stated, knowing that could piss 'em off even more, "There is no one around this part of the river who's coming out here to help you. If you call the harbor, they'd probably call us anyway, no one else is around. Plus," he added after pausing, "If you radio in for a salvage tug or the Coast Guard, your old man will surely hear about it."

This got his attention. He stopped racing the engine, but wouldn't look the Waterboys in the eye, while some of the other frat boys looked like all they wanted to do was fight.

The two boats sat alongside each other for an uncomfortable amount of time, no one speaking. Whitey, who was working the *Lena* against the current to keep her in place, turned to Jeff and said, "Hell with them, let's just leave 'em."

"No, don't leave us," the girl shouted, and turned to the boy captain first, then the rest of the frat brothers and laid down the law. If the sloop was going to be rescued it would be by the crew of the *Lucky Lena* and that was that. The other girls aboard quickly agreed. Whitey and Jeff smiled. They had just witnessed a mutiny. The co-eds had just taken command of the *Smarty*.

"Hey, that's great," Mary Lou laughed and turning to Duke added, "good for them."

Duke didn't respond and stared straight ahead as Jeff continued the story.

The frat boys leered down at them with contempt as the Waterboys began giving instructions on what needed to be done. They addressed the girl, who Whitey latter dubbed the Mermaid. The *Smarty* was ordered to take the halyard from the jenny sail and hand it to Jeff on board the *Lena*. Jeff tied the strongest line he could find off his two transom cleats and clipped the halyard to it, forming a tow line that ran all the way to the mast head of the *Smarty*. The plan was for the *Lena* to line up perpendicular with the sloop, at the mast, and pull away from her at a 90-degree angle, in essence tipping the Smarty over sideways so the keel would rise up, out of the sand. As the *Lena* was pulling the sloop over, the boy captain would be ordered to put the sloop in gear, thus pushing the *Smarty* off, over the bar instead of trying to plow through and deeper into it.

The plan was perfect, the execution wasn't. The crew aboard the sloop made the proper preparations but it became quickly apparent the *Lena* might not have the power, especially considering her mechanical condition. This was before Jeff converted her engine to a V8. She was running with her original straight six-cylinder motor and under stress only about four-and-a-half of those seemed to be working. She labored heavily as she pulled away from the sloop, backfiring and smoking as she went. Whitey fought to keep the *Lena* at a right angle to the sloop as both the current and weight of the *Smarty* fought against her. The giant sailboat began to lean, started to power up, but only moved a few feet.

"More, give her more," Jeff hollered at Whitey. "She needs to lay over further!"

"I don't know man," Whitey replied from the wheel as a loud back fire report bounced off the sloops hull and reverberated back across the open deck of the *Lena.*

"Come on man, just a little more," Jeff pleaded as he turned back toward the sailboat, temporarily blinded by a large cloud of dark smoke emanating from the cruisers exhaust.

"No way, it's too much for her," Whitey shouted as he pulled back on the throttle.

"She can do it," The Waterman stated.

"Hey, Jeff, you going to blow her up for these assholes? It's not worth it."

As the smoke cleared the Waterman saw the beautiful mermaid, hair blowing in the breeze, body glowing in the sun, standing at the side rail, staring at him with pleading eyes.

"Hit it Whitey," he ordered without taking his eyes off her.

"What, are you crazy, I'm telling ya, you'll blow her up," Whitey yelled.

"Just freakin' do it!" The Waterman shouted back. The *Smarty* was his prize and he wasn't letting her go. For him this was the 1800's, when if a British captain and his ship captured, defeated or salvaged another ship, it and everything on board belonged to the conqueror and was sold to pay off the crew so the Royal Navy didn't have too. The Navy authorized privateers to take prizes as well and although in Jeff's mind he was more a pirate than privateer, because he'd keep the spoils instead of giving it to any government, either way he was the Captain, this was war and the *Smarty* was his prize.

Everyone around the table was glued on the story teller now, straining to hear every word above the noise of bar patrons as Jeff continued the story.

The Waterman was the Captain, so Whitey again brought the nose of the cruiser around to 90 degrees off the sailboat and ran the engine up slowly till it reached full throttle. The *Lena* stopped moving, the tow line from the mast head pulled taught, the engine of the cruiser roared, missed, backfired, and smoked as the entire boat shook and vibrated under the stress. This was crazy Whitey thought. If the *Lena's* engine didn't blow and go right through the bottom, the tow line would rip the transom out of the stern, either way sending them to the bottom.

Jeff stood firm. He stared only at the girl, she at him. Suddenly the sloop started sliding slowly forward and, to everyone's surprise, miraculously slid off the bar.

The intoxicating joy of the moment was short lived. To the horror of the Waterboys the moment the sloop escaped the middle ground the boy captain began to swing south in preparation of taking off. Fortunately, Whitey quickly noticed what was up and threw the *Lena* in reverse, backing toward the sloop in an attempt to put slack back in the tow line, still attached to the *Smarty's* masthead.

"What the hell's he doing?" Jeff shouted.

What the boy captain was doing was panicking, again, and running, running away, as fast as he could, as far from this mess as he could get, running from any consequences. His terror packed mind didn't know, or care, that his father's sloop was still attached to the *Lena* and his actions could surely destroy the boat that rescued him and possibly snap the mast off the *Smarty*.

The Waterboys didn't notice the chaos aboard the sloop, where the mermaid and others were screaming at the boy captain, for they had only moments to act. The sloop began moving downstream and Whitey had to full throttle, in reverse to gain a few precious moments so Jeff could run below in search of a knife to cut the tow line. Waves of water began breaking against and over the transom, onto the back deck of the *Lena*. In seconds the line from the sloop would snap tight, pulling the stern of the *Lena* down and into the river, sinking the Chris-Craft. Whitey watched as the tow line danced across the river and begin to rise out of the water just as the Waterman burst from the cabin. He cut the line off the port cleat but didn't have to cut the starboard side, for the line snapped taught and ripped the cleat form the deck. It just missed Jeff's arm and rifled toward the sloop, entangling in her rigging before hitting someone in the head, possibly killing them.

"That son of a bitch," Jeff snapped. "Follow 'em'" he barked towards Whitey.

Tom White spun the wheel on the *Lena*, jammed the throttle full forward and chased the sloop down river. Because of Whitey's superior piloting skills and the preoccupation of the *Smarty's* crew with hauling the halyard line aboard, the *Lena* was able to gain on the sloop. They pulled even with the sailboat's stern where the mermaid stood against the rigging staring at the Waterman, he back at her.

Whitey was irate, not transfixed as his captain was, and shouted at the boy captain, "Hey, pay up you bastard." It was customary, not to mention common courtesy on the Great Lakes to reimburse the captain of a boat who comes to the aid of another in distress, a little money here, for gas, or a few beers there, for all knew someday, they would be in a similar situation, only reversed.

No reply from anyone aboard. The mermaid took her eyes off of Jeff only long enough to turn and scream something at the boy captain, then turned her eyes back towards Jeff, who stood silently at the side rail, gazing back at her.

"Where's the money?" you bastard, "Pay up!" Whitey shouted. He couldn't believe they had saved a million-dollar sailing machine and were not only about to be stiffed by these assholes, but had a cleat ripped out and were full of water, while freakin' Jeff, the captain, was playing goo-goo eyes with the near-naked sea nymph.

Just before the *Lena* began losing ground one of the frat boys emerged at the side rail of the *Smarty* and tossed a plastic ring top six-pack of beer cans at them that landed on the back deck of the *Lena* with a thud. Whitey turned to see only four beers remained. Four cans of beer was their reward. Furious, he stepped from behind the wheel, retrieved the beers and fired them with purpose back toward the sloop, to no avail. The *Lena*, her engine tired and bilge full of water had lost ground and the beer bomb fell short of its target.

The *Smarty* pulled further away. The sea-nymph, standing at the sloops stern, waved farewell for a long, long time, till finally the Waterman replied with a salute and just like that, it was over.

"Christ Jeff, let's report 'em," Whitey said as he slowed the *Lena* to a crawl and turned on the bilge pump."

"For what, being assholes?"

The two fell silent. Whitey turned to starboard heading the *Lena* up river and moved to the back to check the decking where the cleat had been ripped off. Jeff continued to follow the *Smarty* as she moved away in the distance, till the mermaid disappeared from view, his prize gone. "I think she liked me," he muttered.

All at the table turned towards Duke awaiting his reaction to the Waterman's tale. Silence grew more uncomfortable the longer it went. Bar noises filled the void. He took a drink of his beer and set his glass down on the table, hard.

"You're right fella's, I never heard that one. I've heard a few in my time but never that one."

"True story," Jeff stated.

"Oh yea, every word," Whitey chimed in.

Duke looked around the table, paused a few seconds on Jeff and Whitey and stopped at Mary Lou.

"Hey," she shrugged taking a drag on her cigarette "Don't look at me, he's not my kid."

"Four beers that's it?" Duke asked Whitey.

"Cans," Whitey responded with disgust.

"Boy, that's not good." Duke said.

"No it wasn't," from Whitey.

Duke paused before adding, "That was a while ago."

"It was," Whitey answered. More silence.

"Well, fella's," Duke said looking at Whitey then Jeff, "You guys still feeling owed?"

Before either could respond Red suddenly blurted, "Duke you've been pickin' up the tabs all day, so I'd say you've caught up on any kind of restitution," Then turning to the Waterboys asked, "Wouldn't you say boys?"

The Waterboys glanced at each other, caught off guard by Red's interjection and sudden decision to make everything hunky-dory.

"Right boys?" Red repeated.

"Sure, that's fine with me," Jeff stated after taking a drink of beer to wash his parched throat from storytelling. For Jeff it was all about the story and his being able to tell it again, with feeling, in Dukes presence.

Apparently it wasn't fine with Whitey, still annoyed by the *Smarty* incident and having heard Jeff retell the tale, with Duke present, put him on edge. He couldn't believe Duke took it all in so calmly, his apparent lack of interest in the story or any outrage toward the inept captain and crew of his champion sloop. He either didn't believe much of it, or didn't care or both. Maybe this was just one of a long list of antics by his son, and he was used to hearing about them. And now Duke was willing to pay up, without a fight, until Red butted in.

"Christ Red," Whitey finally snarled in response, "You sail boaters were always a pain in the ass."

"What?" Red asked. "What are you talking about?"

"I'm saying you blow-boaters are all the same, sticking together," Whitey complained with little thought to letting things pass, then added, "A pain in the ass."

"You think?" Red snapped back, taking the bait.

"Sure do," Whitey said. "You're always in the damn way, always crossing my bow, always blocking the damn bridge entrance and," he added with emphasis, "so freakin' slow. And sail boat races," he said turning towards Duke. "What kind of race is it when sometimes you can walk faster than some of these boats, with their sails floppin' around and shit?"

After this salvo folks on the periphery of the story telling turned argument, began walking away towards the bar. None of the others at the table responded, those familiar with Whitey knew he had crossed into "Whitey Mode" which might escalate into a rant if anyone played the next card by speaking. Duke and Mary Lou said nothing, they appeared ready to go. Only Red, predictably, dove in, head first.

"You know Whitey, the problems with stink-boaters are many, but your biggest is your total lack of understanding and total disconnect with the timeless connection of the sail with the wind, the sea, the water, ageless, the wind, trying to catch that wind, and anyway, what does that have to do with Duke here?"

"You blow boaters always sticking together." Whitey answered.

"Well," Red hesitated, "Duke has a power boat now, a cruiser, hell-of-a-yacht."

"An ugly one," Whitey stated.

With this Clayton and the boys in the band turned and headed for the stage, they'd heard it all before, a few times. Red and Whitey often ended long day into night benders with debates and arguments, some feigned, on various topics, and the blow-boat sailor versus stink-boat captain was a common one and not the first to emerge from a Great Lakes tavern.

Too many drinks followed by too much bluster led to the inevitable confrontations. Unlike Red and Whitey's arguments, which were mostly theater, battles of eras gone by were real. Sailors felt threatened, jobs were at stake, a way of life disappearing. Crews of the new iron boats knew the ships they worked were bigger, stronger, and faster which would bring them more money. The future was on their side. But sailors stood firm, they still had a lot going for them, especially on schooners. The wind was free and a schooner could be sailed by a crew of only five or six. Steam boats required skilled mechanics to keep the temperamental engines running and coal was expensive, and sailors always had good karma on their side, descendants of the ancient mariner, sailing on God's wind. The transition divided families, crews and friends, and the battleground for the debates was often the saloons that lined the water's edge of harbor towns.

By the turn of the century iron and steel replaced wood as the prime shipbuilding material and it was over for sail power. By the 1920's schooners, and their proud sailors, were gone from the Great Lakes. Red carried on for them.

After Whitey's ugly boat comment and general unwillingness to let things go quietly those remaining around the table began to shuffle about, rise if seated and began working their way towards the door. Duke lead the way, with Mary Lou in tow, she having a good time and wanting more, appeared not to happy with suddenly having to leave.

"Nice goin Whitey," Red snapped.

"What?" Whitey inquired with a smirk.

"You insulted the guy and now they're leaving."

"So."

"He was the host. He bought for us, for you, he was picking it up for everyone, now what?" From Red.

"The party, it appears, is over," Captain Jeff stated.

"He owed us," Whitey added.

"And it looks like he knows it," Jeff said as he watched the Water Merchant move across the floor, "Because he just stopped our waitress and handed her a wad of cash. And you know what else, now that I think of it, he's going to owe us for a long time coming."

"What do you mean?" Red inquired turning to the Waterman.

"If he starts selling off our water he'll owe big time, he'll owe us and everybody in this place, for freakin ever."

139

"Shit," Whitey spit, "That's right, I forgot about that. What a dick."

"Christ," Red groaned, then added emphatically, "That's not going to happen. It's a pipe dream, no way, not by this guy."

"We'd better hope you're right," Jeff stated.

As Jack, Red and the Waterboys rose and moved towards the door, waving so long to the band and Clayton as they went, Jeff announced. "You know, I can still see that mermaid on the *Smarty*, vividly. I still think of her, she was a beauty, eh?"

And, speaking of beauties, he thought of Renee, and as he looked about, where was she? And Kevin, where was he, where was Kevin?

They were aboard the *Captain Jack*, scrambling off the bunk, Renee laughing freely, when they heard Jack, Duke, and Mary Lou step aboard.

CHAPTER 9

River of Vapors

Within steps of leaving Brown's the night changed from the rowdy sounds of a waterfront roadhouse to the quiet, mysterious darkness of the Flats. Each step along the dock removed them further from the laughs, music, and smoke of camaraderie. The previous hours of storytelling, some true, most exaggerated, the dancing, the games of pool, the hopeful flirting, the baseball talk and hockey bragging was fading. Down the dock passed boats backed into wells – their crews quieter now as the night wore on. As Duke, Mary Lou, and Jack climbed aboard the *Captain Jack* they met a flustered Kevin Casey exiting the cabin followed by giggling Renee.

"But I thought you said condo," Kevin repeated turning back towards her.

"What's up?" Renee inquired with a smile noticing the boarding party.

"Time to go love," her father replied.

"It sure is," Duke stated then turning towards Kevin added, "Those partners of yours were getting annoying."

Kevin, confused, didn't respond or even look at Duke.

Mary Lou did, "Oh, it was no big deal honey," she said, "One of 'em told a funny story, one got a little lippy and the big fella here got all pissy."

"Funny? You thought it was funny?" Duke blurted at Mary Lou.

"Well, it wasn't enough to end a fun time."

"Well," Duke huffed and headed below, "I gotta take a leak."

Jack worked switches at the steering console, lights came on and turning to Renee said, "Let's go honey. You and Kevin handle the lines."

This was fine with Kevin who suddenly wanted off the *Captain Jack*. Renee headed forward to handle the bow lines while Kevin hopped on the dock to tend to the stern lines. Jack fired up the cruisers twin engines, the loud roar and exhaust water splashed off the break wall at Kevin's feet. He tossed lines over the *Jack's* stern railing and walked out the dock to undo the spring line. Renee met him there.

"I'm not sure what's up," she said, "but I'm going with Dad to make sure everything is O.K."

"Want me to go with you?" Kevin inquired just as Duke returned topside and barked something inaudible above the engine noise at Mary Lou.

"No, I don't think so," she said grasping his hands.

"You sure?" He asked suddenly realizing this wild, magic night with Renee was about to end.

"Yes," she smiled. "I need to be with dad," and with that she rose on her toes to kiss him softly. "I'll see you tomorrow," she inquired, then added with a laugh, "I guess, I mean latter today?"

"I hope so," he exhaled as she stepped aboard the cruiser.

Kevin turned and headed down the dock, crushed to be leaving Renee behind but relieved to be away from Duke and Mary Lou. Before he covered the short distance to the *Lena's* slip the *Captain Jack* slid out of the well and idled down the canal. He waved but no one aboard was visible. As he reached the *Lucky Lena* the boisterous trio of the Waterboys and Red were headed down the dock towards him. One moment it appeared they were arguing the next laughing and back slapping. When they reached him Red and Whitey spewed bits of incoherent replays of what he missed, of which Kevin understood very little. Jeff only stared at him. As Jeff, Whitey and Red fell aboard the *Lucky Lena* Kevin found himself on the dock alone, near the bow of the cruiser, untying more lines. The past two days on the river had returned his confidence as an able-bodied boatman and he was happy to contribute what he could to running the ship. The engine roared to life, drowning out the voices of the crew, and with a wave of the hand from Whitey behind the windshield, Kevin unwrapped the bow line from the dock cleat and hopped onto the bow. Balancing on the deck, wet with dew, he was at the ready to fend off if needed, but Whitey backed the Chris-Craft out of the well and swung around into the canal with his usual precision.

Kevin coiled the bow and spring lines, laid them on the deck and took a seat on the cabin top. As the *Lena* slid down the narrow canal and into the channel the voices from Brown's were gone, but the Six Bottle Boys had started another set, and the bass notes and low-end chords of the Hammond B-3 organ still reverberated through the night. Two proud wooden icons pushing through the summer darkness; the Chris-Craft cruiser sliding through the water, her engine clicking rhythmically along, and the wooden B-3, Leslie speaker horn spinning like a prop, her magic sound pushing out of Brown's, across the water, till it dissipated far away in the unknown.

Whitey put the *Lena* at a comfortable cruising speed for the run up the Middle Channel. Kevin felt the cool night air against his face as he sat on the bow unprotected from the wind. It was quiet, sounds of engine and wake left behind, with only the hiss of the *Lena's* bow cutting through the water in his ears. Thank God he was alone, he thought. He didn't have to talk to the Waterboys, especially Jeff and his inevitable questions about Renee. He knew they would come eventually, he could tell by that stare he'd shot at him on the dock. But not now, now he was left with the joy of riding through the night on the bow of the *Lucky Lena,* seated on the cabin top, leaning back, rocking gently in rhythm with small waves and occasional wakes. The moon and a bounty of stars appeared as clouds parted in the night sky. Moving across the open water chilled his bones, a huge difference from the sticky heat of roadhouse dancing, but he embraced the chill of the night. It awoke him, snapped him out of the haze of the 36-hour bender that engulfed him. The Waterboys had kidnapped him and dragged him through the adventures, partially against his will, but now he felt invigorated. The cool night air a wake up slap in the face. The wind, the open water, the darkness, the mysteries of the winding channel, and thoughts of Renee had him pumping and alive.

Ahead he saw the white stern lights of another boat, or was it more than one boat, or lights from ashore. Was it the *Captain Jack* with Renee on board? Visions of her filled his head, her hair, her eyes and that smile, and that laugh, her touch, and her smell. He could still smell her.

The *Lena* continued up the channel, passed drifting fishing boats, overtaken by speeding power boats moving too fast at night, as they weaved through blinking white stern lights and oncoming red and green running lights. Whitey swung to starboard as they met the North Channel and shortly after boats seemed to be everywhere. The channel narrowed just west of Algonac and the *Lena* found herself heading on a collision course with one of the Harsens Island ferry boats. Kevin pointed at the lights approaching starboard side and turned to peer into the darkness behind the windshield. Whether Whitey heeded Kevin or not, he funneled into a row of traffic passing astern the ferry, continued on around Pointe aux Chenes, and passed downtown Algonac. As they reached the confluence of the North and South Channels the small boat traffic began to dwindle, and shortly after they entered the expanse of the St. Clair where the river widened and the power of the current pushed back against the cruiser.

Kevin was shaken from his cosmic cruise by the simultaneous sound of rushing water and the sight of a freighter's massive bow in his peripheral vision. Suddenly a ship was next to him off the starboard side. The *Lena* and ship, pushing hard out of the South Channel, merged together at the same point just past the buoy north of Russell Island. All of a sudden Kevin felt uncomfortable on the open bow. Again he turned to look into the *Lena's* cabin and back at the freighter moving past, now close enough to read the name, the *Arthur M. Anderson* of the USS Great Lakes Fleet.

He turned the name over again in his head before repeating it, out loud this time, the *Arthur M. Anderson*? Holy shit, he thought, turning to look at the monstrous ship next to him, then back through the *Lena's* windshield where the glow of a lit smoke appeared. He knew that as soon as Red saw the ship he would fill the Waterboys in on her details, which they already knew. Even Kevin was well aware of the significance of the freighter pushing upstream next to them. She was the last ship to have contact with the *Edmund Fitzgerald* on the night of November 10, 1975, when the *Fitz* went down in a gale off Whitefish Point in Lake Superior. Red would be telling the tale, the 767-footer, built in 1952, carrying a load of taconite pellets, 26,116 tons worth, not 26,000 Red would say, but 26,116 tons, loaded at Superior, Wisconsin. How she followed the *Fitzgerald* into the Bay, just short of safe haven, before disappearing, and how to this day, and forever, she was memorialized in a song whose chilling lyrics where universally known around the Lakes. And now here she was, running up river with the *Lena*. Red and the Waterboys saw her often and each time it brought a moment of pause, of reflection, of remembrance and respect, and for Kevin, it was another alignment of all things great and wondrous on his Great Lakes weekend.

Kevin felt the *Lena* throttle back and the ship begin to pass by faster. As usual, Whitey made the right decision, and quickly. They would not try to speed up to race across the bow of the freighter, or move to port along the dock line where a field of white lights of fishing boats dotted the river. Whitey slowed the *Lena* and let the ship pass, tucked in under her stern and moved into the expanse of mid-river. Like the night before he peered into a ships engine room through an open window low in the side hull. When they slipped into the whirlpool action of her wake he observed well-lit stern cabins, open doors and life stations. One sailor emerged, waved and moved away into the darkness. Kevin returned the wave, recalling a story he and the Waterboys exchanged the day before, on one of their river runs. The time years ago, when they slid up behind a Russian freighter whose crew began waving and gesturing excitedly. They wanted beers, American beers, which the Waterboys began tossing. Most fell short but several were caught. In return the joyous Russkies tossed over a round, flat-top sailor hat. The boys fished it out of the river with a pike pole and waved it back and forth, in a gesture of thanks as the ship pulled away down river. They remembered it as a warm exchange of friendship on a hot summer's day, during a cold war. Jeff Waters said he still had it, with its CCCP head band, hanging on the wall at the boathouse.

With open water ahead Whitey ran up the rpm and the *Lena* churned up river. In moments they left the *Anderson* behind. As they cleared the freighter Kevin spotted the lights of the *Captain Jack* off the *Lena's* port bow a quarter mile away, moving up river, slower and closer to shore. His thoughts returned to Renee and her dad. She'd told him about her father. She hadn't told Kevin her story, not yet, but she'd proudly spun the tale of her father.

When Jack LaCroix was young, learning his trade aboard the freighter *S.T. Crapo*, he sailed off Lake Michigan, through the channel, across Muskegon Lake, and into the arms of Peggy. Neither expected it, was looking for it, or even saw it coming, but the connection was instant, powerful and overwhelming. Jack had gone ashore to explore a new port city as the *Crapo* off loaded her cargo of cement at the Huron Portland Cement Dock on Lake Shore Drive. Other members of the crew stayed aboard. For veterans of the Lakes, if they weren't involved with the offload, there was nothing for them ashore. If a wife, or family, or girlfriend awaited that was different, otherwise, catching up on sleep or a decent meal held more appeal then a stroll around the docks of a sleepy, empty harbor town.

Not for young Jack LaCroix. His father and grandfather had sailed the lakes and their tales of ports visited fueled his imagination. Places with wonderful names like Duluth, the Soo, Alpena, Thunder Bay, Ashtabula, Escanaba, Manitowoc and Humberstone. He still carried the post card his father wrote on May 11, 1937 and mailed from Sault Sainte Marie on May 15.

> *S.S. Price McKinney*
> *To Mrs. LaCroix and Jack,*
> *It's raining, snowing and also the sun shines now and then, a sunny day today. Coming across Lake Superior it rained and brought down the dust and sand from the Sand Storm from North Dakota. The boat is a mess, plenty of work washing off the sand and dust. I'll send you some pictures soon. Missing and loving you two,*
> *Louis LaCroix*

Jack would come to know everything about the Price McKinney, a typical lake boat of her era, built in 1908 and 432 feet long. He spent the winter off-seasons, when the lakes and rivers were clogged with ice, listening to his father and grandfather describe the boats they sailed and the tales that emanated from time spent aboard them. Hours, days, weeks, months of quiet, but never boredom, interspersed with intense moments brought on by storms, near collisions, equipment failures, or fires. The quiet moments filled with nature's bounty; sky and waterscapes filled with sunsets, moon rises, carpets of stars and other mystic wonders, experienced only by those who spent time on open waters. One of Jacks favorites was the story of his great grandfather running ahead from lock to lock on the Welland Canal, carrying bribes from his captain to encourage lock keepers to let them pass in the night, to increase speed of delivery and impress the ship's owner.

Jack was two or three when his mother slid the postcard into the corner of a frame holding a picture of his dad that sat on the head board of his bed. Jack spent the next 16 years staring at the picture

147

on the card, three bulkers lined up in the Soo Locks, wondering when his time would come to go to sea.

It was his fourth or fifth trip of the summer on the *Crapo*, the venerable cement carrier built in 1927 and well known to longboat spotters around the lakes, the last of the hand fired coal-burners, known to lake men as a fast boat, a powerful sucker, and traditionally one of the first on the water in the Spring thaw. And no, not the Crap-o, he'd remind his buddies on shore who laughed and called it the crapper. It's the Crapo, with a long "a" like crayfish. Each stop that summer resulted with an offload at the same dock on the south shore of Muskegon Lake. One day, when the panel truck from the supply store arrived at dockside it was discovered part of the *Crapo's* order had been left behind. Jack jumped at the chance to go ashore and rode with the delivery man to Puhalski's Food Store on the corner of Sherman and McCracken.

That's where Jack first met Peggy, racing around behind the counter of the store, filling boxes with cans and sacks of food and other dry goods. She was sparkling, a bubbling blur of activity, smiling and laughing as she worked, slowing only to answer the phone. Jack followed her every move as he and his shipmate waited quietly, next in line. He was transfixed. And in moments, so was she, for Jack appeared in her life from nowhere, suddenly standing before her, young, strikingly handsome, tanned from hours on the open water, his cap tilted loosely on his dark hair. For years the two recalled and recanted the story of that first meeting, how magic it was, how electric, and how each knew at that moment, that they were meant for each other.

On return trips to Puhalski's Jack would learn Peggy was the daughter of a lumberman who worked in the mills that surrounded Muskegon Lake and grew up in a small frame house at the base of the dunes that butted up against Lake Michigan. Her great-great-grandfather was a Scottish immigrant and mill operator who built the first boat used for towing logs and vessels on Muskegon Lake, a small side-wheel steamer called *Peggy.*

That first summer their relationship grew deep and strong through the endless exchange of letters, for young Jack was constantly away, on the water. He spent what little down time he had lying in his bunk writing her, thinking long and hard on how to express in words what was in his heart. The arrival of the pilot boat, which also brought mail, became a moment of great anticipation as he awaited her return letters, which she faithfully sent. He'd waited 18 years to go to sea and now he counted every minute till the *Crapo* would slip through the Muskegon Channel for another off-load, so he could jump ship for a chance at a few short moments with Peggy. The kindness of his Captain, earned by taking on extra duties and shifts that summer, allowed him to visit Puhalski's on occasion. On one glorious late summer day the young lover's prayers for a chance to be together were answered when equipment malfunctions at the docks halted the offload, and with the Captain's permission, the two young lovers stole away.

She led him to the wonderful sand dunes that towered above Lake Michigan. He remembered seeing them from the ship on runs up the coast, with the sun in the west, the dunes a white string of pearls running the length of the horizon in the east, highlighted by towering pine and hemlock trees. On the way they walked through the quiet waterside neighborhoods of Bluffton and Edgewater, sleepy enclaves sheltered from the late afternoon heat by luscious trees and cooled by a refreshing on shore breeze. As they passed the small houses and summer cottages set in the shade she told him of the actor's colony that once thrived there, the members drawn by the ever-present cooling breeze. Of the pavilion built right on the beach at Lake Michigan to attract touring vaudeville acts and how they enjoyed the place so much some stayed the summer, and returned the following, including Joe and Myra Keaton and their son Joe Jr. better known as Buster.

Beyond the homes the street ended at the base of sand dunes that rose skyward and towered above the tip of the peninsula. They climbed, laughing and stumbling, and crawling in the deep, hot sand, till they reached a summit that provided a spectacular view of

Lake Michigan, its expanse disappearing over the horizon in the west, and Muskegon Lake to the east, encircled by the city, highlighted with smoke stacks amongst the greenery. They rolled out a blanket and enjoyed a snack Peggy had packed. Jack observed this girl of seemingly boundless joy, this child of the dunes, who glowed the brightest in the outdoors, in the sun and sand, this nature's girl. They stayed till the sun approached the horizon, and blasts from the *Crapo's* horn filled the air signaling Jack had to run, which they did, literally. They raced down the dune launching and tumbling, rolling and laughing, like they did as children, like anyone did who spent time on the dunes, racing down till one's legs could no longer keep up, then plummeting head over heels down the warm sand face of the dune. They ran all the way to the dock's main gate where they said goodbye till next time, when the *Crapo* returned. It was the greatest summer of their lives. Renee was born nine months later. They were married in the fall. It was the summer Jack thought about the most, now she was gone.

By the time the *Lucky Lena* rounded a bend that put them in the widest expanse of the river off Marine City Kevin Casey was chilled to the bone and ready to get off the bow and go below. A quick glance into the darkness behind the windshield, disturbed only by a sudden orange glow from a smoke the boys were huddled around, indicated they would probably not slow for a walk along the cabin side, tip-toeing along the side rail while grasping the hand rail. A much safer route was through the bow hatch cover, if unlocked, and thankfully, it was.

He balanced on the undulating deck, pulled open the wooden hatch, and lowered himself into the bow cabin. He placed one foot each on a forward V-bunk and stood in the open hatch, the bow deck waist high. He paused to catch one more look at the riverscape unraveling before him. He felt safer, standing half in the cabin, almost detached. He lingered there, unable to lower himself the rest of the way. It was too picturesque, there was too much magic in the air, the many sensations he'd forgotten about, left behind with his youth, began to bubble forth. He closed his eyes, suddenly, for the first time on this adventure, he felt himself letting go, completely, finally, face in the wind, totally released into the arms of the river, his spirit rising, engulfed with total freedom from daily drudgery, with heart and mind vibrating along with the cruiser, in unison, in one, long, spiritual hum.

When Kevin opened his eyes the *Lena* was closing in on another ship in the channel. What happened next unfolded like an old film noir he so loved. The black and white scene already set with a nightscape over the dark river, lights from the ship provided contrast, reflections on the water adding accents, and the moon and clouds above a touch of texture. The *Lena* passed through a small pocket of fog that settled over the river. In moments they were back in the open air, closer to the ship which appeared similar to the old tramp steamer they'd seen the night before.

As they closed on the ship's stern, port side, Kevin saw a crewman appear from a cabin and walk along the deck, then stop and walk back. The figure stopped to lean on the side rail. The *Lena* was very close now and began to rise and roll as it entered the ships wake. Close enough where Kevin again waved at a crewman plying the lakes, who this time did not return the wave. Instead, the sailor looked to his right, up the ship's side rail, then to the left, then hopped up on the railing and without hesitation dropped overboard into the water.

Kevin watched the scene before him unfold with no feelings, no emotions. He wasn't sure it even happened. He turned quickly and looked around the open hatch cover into the darkness behind the windshield and yelled, "hey, you guys see that?" hoping for a fellow witness. No response, his voice lost in the night breeze that blew across the open bow. He turned to frantically search the surging wake running quickly away off the stern of the freighter. He saw nothing.

He turned back towards the closed cabin of the *Lena* and yelled again before dropping into the bow cabin and busting up the steps, "You guys see that?"

"What?" mumbled Whitey from behind the wheel, "see what?"

"Somebody just jumped off that ship into the water," Kevin blurted, sounding more frantic as the meaning of what he just said began to sink in.

"What?" Whitey repeated as he turned to peer out the side window, "when?"

"Just now."

Red dozed in the seat opposite the steering station while the Waterman stretched out on the back bench.

"Are you sure? I didn't see anything." Whitey repeated.

"Hell yes I'm sure," Kevin barked, not completely convinced.

"Somebody jumped off that boat?" Whitey asked as if repeating it would make it seem more real.

"Stop this fucking boat!" Kevin blurted. "We have to look! We have to do something!"

Whitey looked hard at Kevin then grabbed the throttle and pulled it back, fast enough that Kevin lurched forward, off balance, and causing Red to tip forward against the bulkhead, waking him.

Without hesitation Whitey spun the spoked wheel and the *Lena* began a sudden and sloppy turn to port, getting partially caught sideways in the wake of the freighter.

"Get back on the freakin' bow and keep your eyes open," Whitey ordered Kevin.

The Waterman, rolled off the bench seat by the sudden turn, was now standing behind Whitey. Red was occupied trying to keep from falling off the seat.

"What's up?" Jeff Waters inquired. "Almost hit something, a log?"

"Casey says he saw somebody jump off that tramper," Whitey answered.

"What?"

"That's what I said. He was standing in the bow hatch as we came up on this tub and the next second he's running back here saying someone jumped."

"You see anything?" the Waterman inquired.

"Hell no, but Kev seems convinced."

"We have to look," the Captain calmly stated.

Red hopped down out of the seat and bounced off the boys before inquiring, "A man overboard, is that what I heard?"

"Appears to be," the Waterman said then ordered Red to the port rail while he moved to the starboard side behind Whitey at the wheel. Kevin manned the bow.

Lights from the ships stern cabins lit the wake directly behind the freighter but it was pulling away, upstream, and the river was rapidly returning to blackness. Whitey slowed the *Lena* to a speed just above the pace of the current to maintain steerage.

"Anybody see anything?" Red hollered.

No one replied. They all saw a lot of things with every ripple of every wave, their minds creating a head, or body bobbing in the water with every reflection of light or shadow on the deep, dark water, but nothing for sure. In moments, the churning wake dissipated as the ship moved away to the north.

"Better start to zigzag," Jeff said to Whitey.

The *Lena* began to weave back and forth across the width of the shipping channel as the crew stared in silence across the river. Lights from shore played tricks on their eyes and minds. The moment turned slowly, stretching time, their minds raced with possible scenarios. Was there someone in the water and if so, could they find him, and if so in time? And each thought what every sailor who'd spent any time on any body of water thought and felt at least once during their experiences; drowning. Sinking, helplessly,

153

flailing away gulping for air that turned to water, sinking below the surface, the last shades of light from above, till sinking into darkness, or succumbing quietly to the silence and peacefulness of the deep, the only way to go for some men of the sea. Either way, it usually came in an instant, from nowhere, that moment of knowing it was over, as water claimed another spirit back to where it all began, unless, like this poor soul, it was time for him to finish off his life, here, on the St. Clair, in front of the Waterboys, who scanned the river for a sign.

"There," Red hollered.

"Where?" Whitey and Jeff answered in unison.

"Over there, ten o'clock," Red replied as he pointed over the port rail of the *Lena*.

Jeff rushed to join Red as Tom swung the cruiser to port and all three stared intensely over the water.

Nothing.

"Where Red, where?" Tom yelled from the steering station.

"Over there, straight ahead now. I saw something."

"You sure?" Tom barked.

"I saw something," Red replied, then added "I think."

"Shit Red," Tom sighed.

"Sorry Whitey, I'm sure I saw something."

Jeff said nothing as he moved around the engine box back to the starboard side. Kevin, hidden behind the open hatch cover on the bow maintained his watch.

"There it is again," Red yelled. "Eight o'clock now."

As Tom and Jeff turned they also spotted something in the water. Tom spun the wheel and punched up the rpm to close the distance. Their hearts raced in anticipation, especially when Kevin turned toward the cabin waving his arms and pointed in the same direction.

There was something floating in the water, bobbing along, in and out of reflected light, on small waves. Tom slowed the cruiser as they approached on the port side. When they closed to within 20 yards the object suddenly rose from the water.

"Shit," Red moaned, as a sea gull disappeared into the night sky."

Tom White spun the *Lena* around and headed upstream, moving slowly against the current. The crew scanned the water for a moment then looked at each other.

"One more run, then we got to make the call," Captain Jeff said after a pause then repeated, "If Kevin saw someone jump overboard we gotta make that call."

"Do we?" Tom stated.

"Sure Whitey," Jeff answered. "Don't you think?"

"I guess, but that will sure make things busy for us, if you know what I mean?"

"Hell Whitey, there's some poor bastard out there in the water."

"Is there?" Tom asked turning toward Jeff. "I don't know. We didn't see anyone jump."

"Let's talk with Casey." Jeff suggested.

There was no need. Just as the Captain was about to duck into the cabin and head for the bow hatch he noticed through the windshield Kevin waving and pointing off the starboard bow. Whitey turned the wheel and Jeff and Red returned to the side rails. Shortly after Kevin waved and pointed to an area just off the bow.

"What is it?" Whitey asked.

"I think it's a tree trunk, or big limb. Yeah, it looks like a log-a-gator." Jeff said.

On the bow deck Kevin quickly placed two hands atop his head in disbelief, as he noticed a second before Jeff that it was indeed not a log drifting in the river with a limb sticking up, but a man, floating on his back, slowly raising an arm when he noticed the *Lena* pull alongside.

In an instant the crew went to work with silent precision. Whitey jerked the gear shift into reverse to halt the cruiser. Jeff leaned over the side rail as far as possible, grasping for the guy. Red yanked the pike pole from its brackets and hurried to the Waterman's side. Kevin dropped through the hatch and joined the others on the back deck. Captain Jeff caught part of the man's wet shirt but couldn't hold on as the body began drifting away from the backing *Lena*. Red lunged with the pike pole, bouncing it of the sailor's head.

"Shit Red, be careful," Whitey barked.

Jeff pulled a line that released the collapsible wood ladder from the interior of the hull side, jerked it open and hooked it in place over the *Lena's* starboard side just ahead of the transom. Tom worked the throttle and gear shift to keep the cruiser close.

"Don't run him over," Red hollered, as he lunged again with the pike pole, missing with a splash.

"Give me that thing," Captain Jeff shouted as he grabbed the pole away from Red. "You're o-for-two and we've got one more shot before we have to come about."

"You think he's all right? He's not moving anymore," Kevin inquired anxiously.

"Hell, I don't know, how would I know," Jeff replied with growing agitation. "If he is, he won't be much longer if we keep pissing around," and with that lunged again with the pike pole. It landed on the body's chest and with a quick twist Jeff latched onto the man's shirt with the hook at the end of the pole. Kevin also took hold of the pole and Red grabbed Jeff and the three pulled in unison with all they had to move the body toward the cruiser. As they pulled, the body suddenly rolled over on its front putting the man's face underwater.

"Damn it," Jeff hollered, and in an instant was on the *Lena's* side rail then in the water. He surfaced next to the body, floating on its front, head now turned to the side. Jeff shook water from his face, wiped his eyes, and found himself staring into the face of the jumper, not a foot away. It was indeed a man, an Asian man, young, with black hair, eyes closed. The Captain struggled to roll him on his side with one arm while grabbing for the ladder with the other. He couldn't roll him onto his back but he got an arm under him and kept him afloat. Jeff swung his head to yell orders to the crew on board and when he turned back found he was looking into the open eyes of the young sailor staring directly at him. There was no panic only a deep, faraway look. Jeff said nothing, only nodded his head toward the ladder and the *Lena*. The sailor struggled to turn his head then caught glimpse of the hull. Seeing this he swung his right arm out of the water, over Jeff's head and grabbed firmly onto the ladder and pulled himself toward safety.

Within moments and with help of the crew the jumper was aboard the *Lena*, sitting on the back-bench seat. Jeff, Whitey, Red and Kevin stood around the shivering sailor huddled before them. There was an unspoken communal 'what now.' The sailor stared down at the wet, back deck.

"Let's get him below, before he freakin' freezes to death," the Captain ordered.

"Same for you dude," Whitey added as he grabbed the arm of his shaking Captain, "You O.K.?"

"I'm good," Jeff replied as he leaned over and put a hand on the sailor's shoulder. There was no response so he placed a hand under one arm and began to lift while Whitey moved to do the same with the other and they pulled the young man to his feet. Red scrambled to open the cabin door and Kevin raced below to clear the bench seat and dig for blankets.

In the cabin they lowered the limp, soaked sailor onto the bench, supported with life jackets tucked behind. For the first time he raised his head to look at his rescuers, moving his thankful eyes slowly from one crew member to the next.

"We have to get him out of those wet clothes," Whitey said to Jeff.

"Same with you," Red added turning to Jeff.

"Don't worry about me," Jeff stated. "Where are some blankets? "We got any dry clothes down here?"

As Kevin moved to the forward cabin to search the bunks Red squeezed past the Waterboys and addressed the sailor. "You speak English son? Are you all right? Did you jump or fall overboard?"

"Christ Red….," Whitey started but was cut off by the sailor who quietly responded in a language unrecognizable to the crew.

"Well, I guess that answers that, no English," Red stated.

"Sounds like Chinese, or Japanese, I don't know." Jeff said. "I didn't hear enough, something oriental. This guy is obviously Asian."

"Well, not English," from Red. "So, what do we do now?"

The crew looked around at each other waiting for an answer. Kevin emerged from the forward berth with a blanket and sweatshirt. No one spoke. Over the years the Waterboys had seen it all, and done most of what they'd seen aboard the *Lena*. Their voyages on the water, as well as much of life, were guided by a relentless spirit and philosophy of damn the torpedoes and full speed ahead, determined to make sure good times would be had by all. Life was a laugh a minute, with a goof or a gag around every corner, or bend in the river. Even the smuggling and rumrunning had become a bit of a lark, but this was different, much different and it dawned on them, all at once, this was some serious shit. This was new. They looked down at the sailor, so young, so vulnerable, his life so perilously close to ending, and now his fate hung by a thread on the decisions of the crew of the *Lena*.

The sailor again lifted his head to look at his rescuers. Jeff mimed unbuttoning his shirt as Kevin stepped forward to hand him the sweatshirt. The sailor complied partially un-tucking the soaked shirt from his pants. He worked on a button with his numb fingers, opened his shirt to reveal a small plastic bag tucked into his pants. He removed it and handed it to Jeff. The Captain took it, turned it over a few times in his hands, and looked about at the crew.

"Well," Red blurted. "Open it, see what's in it. Looks like some kind of papers."

Red was right. When Jeff opened the zip locked bag he discovered a folded, ragged newspaper article, a tattered photo and a wrinkled section of a map.

"Let's see those," from Red as he took the article and picture from the captain. He found a black and white photo of a family of four or five people. The sailor slowly raised an arm and pointed to a figure in the photo, then touched the middle of his chest. It was him in the photo and it appeared these were his people. Again he pointed at the photo, and then the paper, a clipping about a restaurant or market, a review or story, and then at the photo. And then back at the newspaper, nodding and pointing and saying something they couldn't understand. Before long the crew of the *Lena* figured out the sailor was attempting to find the folks in the photo, who were connected with the market or restaurant. When Jeff opened the map, a map of Ontario, the sailor pointed to Toronto. He leaned forward to search the map closer till he found the Welland Canal and began talking excitedly, running his finger back and forth on the map, tracing a line from the Canal around the Western end of Lake Ontario at Hamilton to Toronto and back.

"He was going to Toronto to hook up with these people," Red stated.

"Probably family or relatives," Whitey said.

"He keeps pointing at the Welland," Jeff said. "He was probably planning on stepping off the ship in the canal, there's only a foot or two of clearance on either side of a ship, and stretches of it are pretty desolate. Maybe that was the plan, step off there, probably the rendezvous point, then on to Toronto. Something must have gone wrong."

"Or maybe he thinks this is the Welland," From Whitey.

Jeff looked at Whitey and then sat down next to the sailor. He placed the map on his lap and pointed to the Welland Canal, then out the porthole to the river, gesturing back and forth from map to river, shrugging his shoulders.

No response from the sailor so the captain repeated the process. The young man lowered his head for an extended pause then his eyes rose towards Jeff, then around to each of the crew. He pointed to the Welland and shook his head back and forth and mumbled something low and guttural. He continued to shake his head in the negative and lifted both hands with palms upward as if to emphasize the no. Then he pointed to the Detroit and St. Clair Rivers on the map and made a circling rotation around a large section of the map, Lake Huron, and again shook his head in the negative.

"That's it," Red proclaimed. "He was jumping ship to join his relatives, it was supposed to happen on the Welland but something went wrong, so he continued on to here, where he went for it. What do you think?" he added looking around.

"Yeah," Whitey added. "Something like that, and he jumped here before they hit the lake. It was his last chance before the big water."

"Why was he trying to sneak into Canada?" Kevin inquired. "Why did he have to jump?"

"Who knows?" from Jeff. Could be lots of reasons, folks are smuggled all the time. Couldn't get a visa, didn't have a passport, escaping a repressive government, a cruel past, having nothing else to lose, searching for work, a criminal, maybe he was a slave on that ship, held against his will, or as it appears here, looking for one's family. But whatever the reason we have to figure out what we're going to do with him, and fast."

"That's right," Whitey added. We should get the hell out of here in case the ship was onto him and saw us scoop him up."

"Or someone fishing or someone ashore saw us," Red stated.

"What are we going to do?" Kevin inquired anxiously as he realized his weekend voyage had yet again taken a bizarre twist.

"Not sure, but let's get out of here," the Captain ordered.

The crew handed the sweatshirt and a pair of jeans to the sailor and headed for the back deck.

"This guy wasn't ending it all," Whitey said as he turned to Red, "He was escaping."

"That's right," Red said, "to freedom," then turned back toward the sailor and smiled, "you're lucky son, very lucky," then added as he headed up the steps, "That's why they call her the *Lucky Lena*."

160

CHAPTER 10

The Willows

"Upus Pineus," the Waterboys called out with laughter as they motored up the Pine River shortly after pulling the sailor from the big water. The approaching sun brightened the sky over the Canadian shore in the east as they passed by the tranquil harbor, boat show partiers still asleep, beyond the painted boat houses, around the golf course bend and back marina, by the rocks at Coop's Bend, passed Cajun Corners to the Willows, home of the *Lucky Lena*. The Willows, is what they called the wooden boathouse on the banks of the Pine, tucked away beneath three giant willow trees. In days gone by every boy, and most girls, growing up along the river had swung on ropes hanging from the majestic willows, and dropped happily into the water, once they got over thoughts of mudpuppies, snapping turtles or muskrats nibbling on toes. It was always warmer than the big river. Various docks had come and gone, recycled by high water. Or, the occasional seiche, when shifting lake waters pushed by wind and storms emptied the Pine in a tsunami like flood. An assortment of boathouses had occupied the shore, from small shed like buildings tucked under the willows to a boat house set atop the water. For years rickety pilings and planks stuck in the mud served as docks. Now, a wooden boathouse transported from a rotting dock on the big river and set on shore served as shelter at the Willows.

At first the property was a community spot, out of the way. No one really knew who owned it. In their minds nobody really owned it. It was the river, it belonged to everyone. In their teenage years the Waterboys partied on the spot with fellow pranksters, one with an uncle who once owned it. Over the years Jeff eventually tracked down the title holder. The year he purchased the party store he made sure he financed enough for the *Lucky Lena* and the property along the Pine River. He paid too much for the land, nothing more than a wedge overgrown with bushes, a twin rutted path through the grass served as a drive, mud banks, and the Willow trees. No one else envisioned what the Waterman had planned.

By the time the *Lucky Lena* reached the Willows the Waterboys had formulated a plan to help the sailor and already set the wheels in motion. They would contact Clayton and have him get a hold of Gord and Billy who had numerous friends in the Asian community in Toronto from their playing days; fellow musicians, club owners, fans, bartenders, chefs, waiters, students, teachers, landlords, girlfriends, dealers, shop keepers. Someone the sailor could talk to and tell his story, someone who could, hopefully, help him, and in a hurry, someone to show the picture to. Whitey had already hopped off the *Lena* at the back marina and put in a call to Clayton on the pay phone, got no answer and left a message.

The Waterboys would meet their rumrunning partners at the usual spot and drop the sailor with them. What else could they do, turn him over to the authorities? Ah, no, the crew of the *Lena* agreed unanimously, that was not an option. He'd be taken to Billy's or Gord's near Wallaceburg till a ride took him to Toronto. To the boy's it was a simple plan, same as dropping off cases of scotch and smokes. So similar that Captain Jeff stated at the end of the planning, "Really, this is no big deal." Little did he know.

After docking at the Willows, the crew stepped ashore and shuffled around the fire pit for a while not sure what to do next. Red plopped down in a chair exhausted from the action packed, tension filled all-nighter. The sailor remained in the cabin of the *Lena*. The boys had time to kill waiting for Clay to get in touch. Everyone was hungry and tired and standing on shore made the seriousness of the night's action weigh heavier. Ashore, everything seemed more perilous. In the back of everyone's exhausted mind was the thought, had anyone seen them haul this guy out of the water, and followed them up the Pine, or made a call. There was a sense of I'd rather not be doing this, floating around. They were wasted. Nerves were fried, stomachs empty and heads ached.

It was the Captain who eventually moved the crew forward. After scanning the area, up, down and across the river at the storage buildings of the back marina, and seeing no one, he hustled the sailor off the *Lena* and into the boathouse, out of sight. Whitey and Kevin followed shortly after.

The interior of the boathouse was a museum to Great Lakes shipping and boating, the walls a menagerie of pictures, postcards and photos, old and new, of freighters, cruisers and runabouts. Banners, flags, pennants, and name plaques hung everywhere, block and tackle, lights and lines were strung across the interior. Over time the Willows had become a shrine to all things nautical in the river town and the people who inhabited it, past and present. A book shelf piled with boat and fishing magazines, plus a few copies of "Know Your Ships" freighter guides sat in one corner, a fridge in another. A round wooden table filled the center of the room, cluttered with beer bottles, ashtrays, an open tool box, and old newspapers.

While the Waterboys' attention was focused on making the young sailor comfortable, Kevin was drawn, like his earlier visit to the Old Club, to the photos that cluttered the walls, of life in the old river town, those of the waterside establishments no longer there. Like the Shrimp Boat diner and the Riverland, especially a place like Riverland, the bait and boat rental business, a large boathouse that sat on a dock right atop the big river. Inside, half the building served as a gear and bait shop. The other half a large open space divided into wells where small fishing boats, fitted with outboard motors, splashed about.

Kevin remembered the excitement as a kid of entering Riverland and venturing onto the narrow docks that crossed the open wells, where water from the river, the big, deep river, splashed below. The reward for the successful adventure out the dock and safely back was a cold Coke from the large, red cooler with the flip up lid, squeezed into the store side. He and his pals would take their Cokes through the screen door onto the porch that sat over the water on the river side of the boathouse. They could see the water running past between planks in the deck. The expansive view up and down the vast body of water breathtaking, and if windy, or stormy, they held firmly to the railing. Large sliding doors on the boat well side of the building opened onto the river, one side to the shallow, clear water shore side, where row boats and rafts were pulled up on the sand, the other side onto the expanse of the big river, deep, dark blue, and moving. When he was a kid he thought working at Riverland must be the best job in the world. A place to spend the day on the water, even when you were inside, you were still on the water, surrounded by the sounds and scents of the river and entertained by the passing parade of ships and boats, and the unique characters who hung around the river all day, the boaters, the fisherman, the mechanics, the customers, the deliverymen, the old timers, all with stories. If the place was there today, he thought, it would still be the coolest place in the world to work. If the Riverland was there today, he told himself, he would move back just to work there, or at least, to just hang out there.

Another picture drew his attention, one of Palmer Park, located north of Riverland. It showed boys swimming off the cement break wall, sitting on the railing and standing on the steps that led into the water, others leaping off a diving board into the wake of the departing ferry boat the *Marlynn M,* the park monument and two civil war cannons in the background, shaded by large trees, the park full of bikes. Kevin looked closer at the photo to see if he recognized any of the boys, or if that was himself, staring back, mugging for the camera, for he surely spent many a day doing just that.

Captain Jeff snapped Kevin from his flashbacks when he announced, "We need something to eat."

Kevin turned to see Jeff and Whitey standing over the sailor seated at the table. For the first time since they pulled him aboard the *Lucky Lena* the young man looked in some duress. The

Waterboys had been trying to explain to him, with the aid of charts, maps, pictures, watches and lots of pointing, what their plan was for getting him to where they thought he wanted to go.

"We gotta get some food into this guy," Jeff said. "He's not looking too good."

"Hungry, are you hungry?" Whitey asked of the sailor as he motioned putting something into his mouth while circling his hand around his stomach a few times.

The sailor watched Whitey's mime then weakly nodded in the affirmative.

"We need something to eat," the Captain repeated then gave the orders.

"Whitey, take my car and make a food run. Can you bring anything from home," then added as an afterthought, "I could give you the key to the store but I don't have anything but crap there."

Whitey wasn't sure but replied in the affirmative. The town grocery store wasn't open yet, plus he had no money on him, so home was probably the best shot.

"O.K., good, and where's Red?" Jeff said looking around. "You might as well give him a ride home, I think he's pretty burnt out."

"And, I'll take a lift too," Kevin quickly added. "I got shit to do. I need to get prepped for the boat show."

Jeff seemed preoccupied when he responded, "O.K., we'll try to keep you updated."

And with that Whitey and Kevin dragged Red out of the chair, hopped into Jeff's car and bounced down the rutted drive and headed toward town. Jeff stayed behind with the sailor. On the ride to town Kevin, riding in back, leaned forward with his elbows resting on the top of the front seats and told the others of reading the newspaper article while hanging in the cabin of the *Lena,* with the sailor, on the run to the Willows. It was a short piece, not much more than a photo with caption. It appeared to be about a Vietnamese establishment but there was no indication of a location. The information Kevin related shot a dart straight through the soul of Tom White.

Whitey dropped Kevin at the Inn and Red at his house before heading home to see his family and pick up food to take back to the Willows. When he arrived home he was greeted by his happy, flying around boys, Tom Jr. and Leon, who had just gotten out of bed rested and ready for the new day. He reached down to scoop them up, one at a time, and raise them high above his head which brought shouts of glee from the boys and a steady glare from his wife.

"You won't believe it," Tom said to her as he rubbed the boys mop toped heads after setting them down, both talking a mile a minute as they circled him.

"Probably not," Carol answered. She hadn't seen nor heard from him since the day before, when he headed for Red's to paint.

"Where's your truck Daddy?" little Leon inquired as he looked out the screen door at Jeff's car.

"Yes," Carol inquired. "Where is the truck Tom?"

"Still at Red's," he stated as he began rehashing the long and winding tale that had gotten him to that point.

It's not that Carol didn't believe what her husband was telling, the boat stories, the fishing, the runs down river, the beer, seeing the band at Brown's, the Flat's, it was all familiar territory. She was married to a Waterboy and knew going in that his life upon the water was part of the deal. The part about them running into an old townie, Kevin Casey, was new and the part about rescuing the jumper certainly had never happened before, but he told the story with such conviction she found any annoyance she had toward him rapidly fading.

The only thing that bothered her, however, was he'd forgotten, or worse yet, blown off his promise to take the boys to the Willows the night before. He had promised them an evening of fishing and a fire. She knew he adored them, and was always good to his word when he told them something, so it must have been quite a night for him to have forgotten the boys. She knew he would never snub them on purpose. He took them often to the Willows and onto the water, including numerous boat rides on the *Lucky Lena*. No, she thought again, he hadn't blown them off.

"Are we going down to the boat dad, are we?" Tom Jr. asked excitedly.

"Yes, are we, are we?" little Leon yelled as he bounced around the room, "Are we goin' down to the pillows?"

"Ha, ha, it's not the pillows," Tom Jr. howled, "It's the Willows you dummy."

"Mom," Leon protested as he ran over to cling to his mother's leg.

"Now, now, that's O.K. sweetie," she replied as she rubbed his head and looked to Tom for an answer to their question.

Tom thought for a moment, pondering the situation, the young ship jumper at the boat and all its ramifications, but one look into the pleading eyes of his boys and there was only one answer he could give, "Sure we are boys, get your things together and put them in Captain Jeff's car." Carol smiled at her husband who shrugged his shoulders and added, "What else was I gonna say?"

With that the front room exploded into a blur of activity, the boys running in all directions, shouting out with joy, as Carol called after them items not to forget.

Tom and Carol walked into the kitchen where he opened the fridge, pulled out a carton of milk and took a swig. She protested and set about searching for things to eat, placing them in a large canvas boat bag. Tom wanted to tell her about the sailor being from Vietnam, or at least might be from there, and how he felt a chill down his spine when Kevin mentioned it. He hadn't felt that way in a long while, but all of sudden, for some reason, it gave him the creeps, not really a flashback, like he used to have, with visuals and all, just a clammy feeling. Not really a bad, ominous sense, for deep down, he wanted to help this guy, but he couldn't help wondering if the sailor was related to someone he met, fought alongside, or fought against, or shot at, or shot at him, or killed one of his buddies. Now years later, he was pulling this guy by the collar from the river, not the Mekong, but the St. Clair. He didn't want any revenge, for that passed before he left Asia, maybe it was a redemption thing, him wanting to help, or a closure of sorts. He tried to remember a few words; maybe he could talk with him, then quickly didn't want to. Whatever, he thought of mentioning it, but didn't, he wasn't ready to talk to Carol about it.

While waiting in Jeff's car for his boys, who'd run back for items forgotten in all the excitement, Tom watched the screen door swing open behind them, waited for it to reach the end of its long arc before swinging back to slam shut, loudly. That banging of a screen door is what he thought about, over and over, while in Nam; on the flight over, in Saigon, while walking the rice paddies, on a patrol in the Mekong, in a Saigon Bar. That banging screen door took him back to his home as a kid. That kitchen door, how after a meal was finished and he was excused, how far could he run before he heard it slam behind him? At first he made the bottom step, then leaping them all and running hard he'd make the edge of the yard, and eventually, to the start of the grumpy trail, the dog poop path in the field between houses on Sixth Street, running into the brightness of day or a fading evening light, running towards freedom and adventure. Carol wanted him to fix the door, but he couldn't, and never would.

When Kevin walked into the Inn he stopped at the front desk to pick up a message from his editor, but didn't read it. He walked into his room and collapsed on the bed. He was exhausted but inspired by the jumper. As he lay there he put together a battle plan. There would be no more whining. He was on a new mission, a new course. He had been reenergized by the courage of the young sailor. He would shower, rest for a few hours then go to the boat show, do his interviews, finish shooting pictures and send everything off to his editor. He would search out, then hook up with Renee and be done with the Waterboys and all their crazy shit, once and for all. He noticed at the Willows they seemed distracted with the plot of delivering the sailor and appeared to have already forgotten about him and the two-day voyage they'd taken him on.

When Red staggered into the front door of his home on River Road he moved directly to the back room overlooking the river, fell onto the couch, and by the time Rose arrived, was sound asleep. He dreamt of the sailor.

Jeff remained at the Willows with the sailor. He thought about an interpreter but no time and, really, who? As Jeff relaxed more, he looked out the window, across the river at the backside of the marina storage buildings, and still, no one was around. It was too early on a Sunday morning. The summer sun rose further to wash the shoreline and docks at the Willows in light and warmth. Jeff took the sailor from the chilly confines of the boat house into the brightness of the morning. They sat on the repainted metal lawn furniture overlooking the Pine River. Lilly pads filled the shallows just off the stern of the *Lucky Lena*. Birds sang and darted across the water top. Turtles poked their heads from among the reeds and lilies, looked about, then climbed onto half submerged logs to warm in the sun. A morning breeze drifted across the water to rustle the long arms of the willows that draped the shore and hung in the water just beyond the *Lena's* bow.

Despite the language barrier the sailor and the Waterman broke the moments of uncomfortable silence with bursts of short sentences, with inflections of questions, pauses, shrugged shoulders, and lots of pointing. In the rare moments of understanding a mutual exasperation of glee punctuated the morning air. Captain Jeff again rehashed the plan and the jumper appeared to understand, as he bobbed his head along as Jeff mimed, or he was just too tired to play charades any longer and was agreeing to anything.

All was pretty much going to plan by early Sunday afternoon when Whitey returned to the Willows with food and supplies, and his family. The weather had switched some, the clear, bright sun of the previous few days replaced by a warm wind blowing from the south-south west, which brought a haze of humidity with it.

At first Jeff was surprised to see Whitey arrive with his entire brood. What was Whitey thinking, the Captain wondered, as he hustled toward the drive to greet them? After a hug for Carol and a few jabbing attempts at tickling the boys, he pulled Tom to the far side of the car and inquired, "What's up man, are you nuts? What are you thinking?"

"What?" from Whitey.

"What?" Jeff repeated incredulously, "You brought everyone with you. With this guy sitting here, and with what we're about to do?"

"Relax man, it's O.K."

"Relax, everything is O.K?"

"Sure," Tom said confidently, "Come on, what's the big deal? Carol's going to rat this guy out? No way, and the boys will be on the float boat, they won't care about this guy. They'll just think he's one of the crew."

The Captain remained silent, mulling over what his first mate had said.

Whitey grabbed the moment to add, "Like you always say man, this is no big deal."

To this the Captain could only add, "I hope you're right."

"And hey, I got the food," Whitey added, "And, what else was I going to do with the family, ditch 'em again today? That wasn't going to happen."

'Yea, I guess so," Captain Jeff said.

"Plus, if they didn't come here now, I was spending the day with them, at home," Whitey stated, then added with emphasis, "And not going with you tonight."

"O.K," the Captain mumbled before adding, "Did you talk to Clayton, did he call?" the Waterman inquired.

"Yeah, he called."

"What did he say?"

"He said, don't worry, we'll get that Chinaman to Spandia and Dundas before ya know it."

That came as no real surprise to the Waterboys, they knew that was in the heart of Toronto's Chinatown, and they also knew that Chinese, as well as other Asian immigrants, legal or not, had been coming across the border for some time. Most not as dramatic as the young man they pulled from the river, at least that they knew of. Clayton had told them of a character who ran a few Chinese Restaurants across the river in the Sarnia area, and also ran the occasional group of illegal's. The Waterboys remembered eating there as kids on family outings. It was always a big thrill crossing the big bridge from Port Huron into a foreign country, where the people talked different and the money looked funny. For small town folks it was the closest they got to ethnic food. Coming from fishing villages along the river they had plenty of perch and pickerel dinners, fried smelt, burgers, fries, hot dogs and meat loaf, but not much more variety. At the Chinese places you could eat with the funny sticks and have mini corn on the cobs.

"Where are we supposed to meet him?" Jeff inquired.

"Usual spot," Tom replied, "after sunset."

"Good," Jeff said looking at his watch, "we have a little time before we have to take off, we should be good to go."

For Jeff Waters, the smuggling of folks across borders was nothing more than another chapter in the evolving history of the Great Lakes and the movement of goods on and over her waters. In 1679 LaSalle sailed the *Griffin* through the Flats and, with strong head winds blowing and the current to battle, ordered her crew to drop the two square sails, and go ashore to tow the 60' boat, the first ship on the Great Lakes, up the St. Clair River into Lake Huron. Voyageurs and trappers, the early water merchants of the French River, which emptied into Georgian Bay from Lake Nippising and the Ottawa River, had been traversing the Indian routes for years but now a ship had entered the lakes, and the evolution of trade began in earnest. But not by the Griffin who made it as far as Lake Michigan where she sank becoming not only the first ship on the lakes, but also the first to sink.

The furs, pelts and skins came first, transported across the lakes and her tributaries, then the lumber, wheat and grains followed by coal and iron. All in vast quantities and all moved further and faster across the waters of the inland seas. And the fish, the always vast abundance of fish caught and shipped to the growing number of cities emerging around the lakes. At times so much fish one could shovel them out of the fresh, clear water. And always the people, from early explorers, to the first courageous pioneers, to the swelling tide of immigrants, many transported across and around the Lakes on the burgeoning fleet of passenger ships. And with them the cornucopia of goods needed to sustain a people on the move as they filled up the wilderness in the name of civilization. And people brought with them their views and beliefs, religions and traditions, while still others brought opposing ideas and feelings.

Over time all types of goods moved across the waters in all types of ships and not always legal; booze during prohibition, opium, later cigarettes and weed, and always people; on the underground railroad and immigrants without papers, all seeking freedom, escape, or a new beginning by any means. Everything had been transported over the water of the Great Lakes. Every item of commerce imaginable had been bought, sold and moved across the water, including people. And now, Jeff thought, with the arrival of Duke Wilson, the water itself was to be sold and transported.

Whitey had been right about his boys meeting the sailor. They barely paid attention upon being introduced before running off to climb aboard the pontoon boat tied at the far end of the property. If the Waterboys were river rats, then Whitey's boys were river runts. The sailor, confused, just nodded with a smile. Carol also smiled, held out her hand, and bowed a little when introduced. Anything uncomfortable about the meeting passed as soon as she opened the canvas bag full of food. They moved to the wood picnic table and chairs on the water's edge to eat. Carol had loaded up on apples, oranges, cheeses, bread and a jug of lemonade and the jumper began to devour them as quickly, and politely as possible, pausing to nod thank you all around.

At home Whitey had taken a quick shower, and while rummaging for clean clothes, grabbed some for the sailor as well, who changed in the boat house after eating and emerged dressed in a blue T-shirt, a pair of old Bermuda shorts and flip-flops, looking like he just walked out of a campus bookstore.

It almost felt like a normal afternoon at the Willows, the young boys playing on the boats and docks, watched by Carol, while Jeff and Whitey sat along the shore with the sailor, now just one of the many watermen who showed up at the venerable Willows at all times, day or night, to immerse their souls in the life dockside. Those who came to have a beer or two, a smoke, a laugh, build a fire, talk boats, fix boats, or just sit and watch the river. To BBQ yardbird, to sit on the banks of a river, to make the cosmic connection with the ancients, the remaining contact to men of the water from millennia gone by, the fire, the sky, the moon, the water, the Ulyssian tales. The Willows had that special feel.

It was quiet and almost bearable, whiling away the time, waiting for departure on the big adventure. At least until one of these rivermen suddenly appeared, accompanied by a sudden gust of warm wind that caused the willow trees along the banks to sway and bend in the burst. It was Beau Duchene, a marine cowboy, who kept his work boats and barges on the Pine and motored over, or walked the shore line many a time to visit the Waterboys. He was a pile driving, salvage diving waterman who was born a century too late, the son of a shipyard worker who was always searching for a riverside tavern, a place to sing dock yard sea shanties and spin tales.

"Hey fellas," he hollered out with a wave as he appeared from around the trees lining the bank.

"Hello Beau," from Whitey. "How are you?"

"Absolutely average." Beau replied.

"Beau, what's up man?" Jeff followed, somewhat startled.

All but Tom's sons were surprised and a little uncomfortable with the sudden arrival of Beau. The boys shouted out and waved as they scampered through the reeds along the shore.

"Got any cold ones?"

"Sure, inside, in the fridge." Jeff answered.

"Anyone else?" Beau inquired.

As he entered the building a few people mumbled no thanks followed by glances all-around of what now? The few seconds gave the Captain much needed time to think of what to say about the presence of the sailor. He came up with nothing.

Beau returned with a can of beer, snapped it open and looked about. He hugged, then exchanged pleasant catch ups with Carol, laughed about not wanting to hug the Waterboys, and called out to Tom Jr. and Leon with a wave.

Beau was a short, stumpy character, loud and brash, always laughing, friends with all. He was always working, Sunday's included, thus the short sleeve, sweat stained, brown work shirt, cut off jean shorts and ankle high work boots. A red, plaid do-rag, hung loosely on one side of his head.

"What's up Beau?" Jeff inquired again.

"Oh, we were tryin' to pump water out of a half-sunk barge, but the pump crapped out, came back for another," he replied as he looked about, settling a gaze on the sailor.

Jeff noticed and after a long pause stated. "Hey, this is Johnny, he's an exchange student, ah, visiting for a few days," then added, "Johnny Chang."

The long, unsettling silence that followed was broken by Beau who said, "O.K., hello there Johnny," as he stuck out a hand to greet the sailor then took a seat amongst the others, and added as he fell into a lawn chair with a grunt, "Johnny Chang."

"Yeah, and he doesn't speak English," the Captain added. "He's just learning."

"O.K. boys, no problem," and added with a smile, "As you all know, I do."

This brought smiles from all, a chuckle or two from the Waterboys and broke any uneasiness that hovered over the group, at least for the moment.

Beau took a slug on his beer and lit a cigarette then asked. "So, busy night on the river last night, eh?"

No one answered.

"Were you guys out?" Beau carried on. "I seen the *Lena* was gone."

More silence from the Waterboys.

"Well, I heard on the scanner this morning," Beau said then took a drink of beer, "I heard some salty callin' in from up in Lake Huron, may have lost one last night, a crewman fell over, or jumped, or whatever."

"I didn't hear that," Jeff stated.

"Me neither," Whitey added.

Beau took a drag on his smoke, put a steady gaze on the sailor, and carried on, "And that's not all." He shifted in his seat and chugged on his beer. He didn't really care if that was the jumper or not, probably was, if so, so what. He knew the Waterboys for the pirates they were at times, and if this was the guy he heard about on

175

the scanner, he didn't want to know, and he didn't give a shit. He had his own story to tell.

"And that's not all," he repeated then paused as he shifted in his seat again.

"What else?" Jeff inquired.

"Last night, me and the boys was pushin' a barge, with the big tug, up Lake St. Clair, and just as we enter the Flats, you won't believe what happened."

After another short pause Jeff asked, "What happened man?" For he knew Beau wouldn't continue if someone didn't pick up on the cue.

"Well, I'm glad you asked," Beau stated. "We was all on the bridge of the tug, the three of us, pushin' this barge, payin' attention ya know, it was a dark night, eh, and we had patches of fog, ya, we were runnin' through patches of fog, and like I said, we were all on the bridge, I was at the wheel, when someone said something funny, I can't remember what, and we looked at each other with a laugh, and when we looked back, what do you think we saw?"

"Don't know Beau, what did you see?" from Jeff.

"Well, something that I'll never forget, even in a million years. Man, I'm still shaking a little," and he paused to look around the group before continuing.

"Well, what I saw I couldn't believe, none of us could, for we saw Jesus walking down the barge straight towards us, from the front of the barge, out of the dark and fog, straight for the bow of the tug."

He had everyone's attention now, even the Waterboys, who had heard many a Beau tale, and were waiting for him to get on with it, especially now. They needed him to end his story and leave, to get going back to work, but the marine cowboy commanded all attention around the fire pit, and knew it.

"What?" Whitey asked, turning to see if his boys were close enough to hear this crazy talk. They were out of earshot, climbing aboard the float boat.

"We saw Jesus walk on the barge we were pushin'."

176

"You saw Jesus?" Carol asked incredulously.

The Waterboys wondered if he had finally lost his mind and drifted over the edge.

"Yup, we sure as hell did. It was him, long hair, beard, wearing a long white robe thing and sandals. Well, as you can imagine we were shocked. I mean here was Jesus walking towards us," he stated with the emphasis on us. "We all saw him, we all looked at that bottle of rum, at each other, and back at him. I'll swear boys," he said turning to the Waterboys, "At that moment we sure got religion in a hurry." Now even Johnny Chang was paying attention.

"Well, what then?" From Captain Jeff.

Beau took a drag on his smoke, leaned forward and announced, "Well, he got closer, hopped off the barge onto the tug, and headed for the pilot house, and ....."

"And what?"From Whitey.

"Well, it turns out, it wasn't Jesus."

"Really?" from Whitey.

It wasn't Jesus?" Carol asked quietly.

"No, it wasn't," Beau repeated as he sat back and took a pull on his beer then a drag on his cigarette.

"What?" everyone asked together.

"It wasn't Jesus," Beau repeated.

"Really Beau," from Jeff, "well then who was it?"

"Well," it appears it was a fisherman."

"A fisherman, you ran over a fisherman, you ran over some guy fishin?" from Captain Jeff."

"We sure did. It was an accident, a freak accident, a freakin' accident," Beau stated.

"Jesus was a fisherman," Carol said with a smile.

"He was a carpenter honey," Whitey said turning towards his wife.

"Well, he was a fisher of men," she quickly replied.

"Well we surely thought it was Jesus, at first," Beau continued. "I mean there he was walking towards us on the barge, out of nowhere. To us, at that moment, it was him. It looked like him, the hair, the beard, the robe, but it wasn't. The robe was his wet, stretched out T-shirt, and they weren't sandals, just flip-flops, man…"

"And," Beau quickly added, "yes it was an accident and, a miracle as well."

"How so?" Jeff asked.

"Well, it appears we didn't see this guy, he was in a small boat, outboard, it's foggy as hell, and dark man, and he said he didn't see us either, could hear the push water coming on, but couldn't see us, till the end. Just one of those things, I guess. Anyway, we were about to run him over when at the last moment he jumped, and climbed up and onto the bow of the barge."

Everyone waited for more.

"Well, good thing we were running so slow, I guess he hung there, swinging for a bit, before pulling himself up. And he comes marching down the barge towards us, pissed."

"Pissed eh, ya think?" Whitey asked.

"Sure, but we kept tellin' him he was O.K., nothing had happened, he made it, he wasn't hurt, it ended up not even a scratch. We told him it was a miracle."

"The miracle was he didn't kick your asses," Jeff stated.

Beau pushed on with his tale, "So we tell him over and over, it was an accident, he survived, and to us, for a minute he looked like Jesus coming out of the dark. We apologized a hundred times or more, he was going to be alright, it was an accident, one of those things."

"What happened to his boat?" Tom asked.

"Well, nothing."

"What?"

"Nothin' happened to his boat. As soon as we saw this guy I'd slammed her into reverse, and we were goin' so slow to start, I guess we just pushed his boat aside. We found it just off the port side, its fine."

"Really?" from Whitey.

"Like I said, it was a miracle."

178

"So, what's up? It happened last night? So what happened to the guy?" Captain Jeff inquired.

"Yes, what happened to Jesus?" Carol smiled.

"Well, we put him in his boat and waved goodbye. He said he was headed for home."

"That's it?"

"Ya, that's it. Like I said, we apologized a bunch of times, had a few beers, and rehashed what had happened more than once."

"Had a few beers?" Jeff asked, not too surprised.

"Sure," Beau laughed. "Had a few, we needed to calm down man, hell, this guy did too. We told him it was a miracle, and he finally agreed, and we toasted our good fortune. I also told him next time I was down his way I'd drop a couple spiles in for him, help shore up his dock, for nothin'."

"Who was the guy?"

"I don't know, I can't remember," Beau said, "some fisherman."

"It was Jesus," Carol said.

"Christ Beau, man, I don't know." Captain Jeff said tailing off.

"Told ya it was a busy night on the river last night," Beau stated, proud of his tale. He paused, looked around, waiting for the Waterboys to pick-up on the opportunity to talk about their night. But they didn't. Just a, "I guess so," from Jeff.

Beau wondered, but didn't push it, he'd hear later, or nothing happened, he didn't care either way, he had work to do.

"Well, I got to get back and get that pump fixed up, I'm sure the boys are lookin for me," and with that he pushed himself out of the chair with a groan, bid farewell to all, waved and shouted to the boys, now poling the pontoon boat in the middle of the Pine, and headed toward the path along the shore. As he reached the willows he turned back to holler above the wind, "Hey, Johnny Chang, good luck to you. Hope for a miracle."

CHAPTER 11

Watermen

When guitarist William "Billy" Greenmeadows' ancestors stood on the sandy shores of what is now Walpole Island they could watch fish swim and pick out a shiny stone in water ten feet deep. They knelt down and drank the crystal-clear water from cupped hands. That was ages ago, a time when elsewhere white men in Europe were ravaging the land and each other, setting out to conquer the world in the name of their god in search of a Garden of Eden, a place where the first Native American's, who would become the Algonquin tribe, had been living peacefully, without invasion, for centuries in what would become a Canadian Bayou.

The Algonquin people were made up of many tribes, including the Chippewa, Potawatomi, and Ottawa bands. Billy was a Chippewa, son of Joseph Greenmeadows, who was the son of Joshua Greenmeadows, an elected chief of the Chippewas. Billy had three heroes in his life, first and foremost his father Joseph, second Tecumseh, and third, Kichiwiski, a Chippewa Chief.

Billy's father told him of Kichiwiski and the journey he made, in the early 1800's, an adventure that boggled Billy's mind when he first heard it. Could it be true he wondered? It was, and he implored his father to tell it again and again when he was growing up. The Chief left from a place near Duluth, on the Western tip of Lake Superior, pushed his canoe into the big, cold water and began to paddle. He didn't stop till he got to Buffalo. Across Mother Superior, around the Keweenaw Peninsula, into Whitefish Bay, down the St. Mary's River, the length of Lake Huron, the St. Clair River, through the Flats, past where Billy now stood, across Lake

St. Clair, down the Detroit and east across the extent of Lake Erie. It was a journey of 988 miles, but he wasn't finished. When the Chief reached the Buffalo area, he climbed out of his canoe and walked to Washington, the young nation's capital, for a Congressional conference on Indian affairs. At the conclusion of the meetings Kichiwiski walked back to Buffalo, hopped back in his canoe and paddled back to Duluth.

Billy was in awe, to this day he thought of Kichiwiski's journey, what it would be like to travel across the Great Lakes, along the coast lines, the sunrise, the sunsets, glorious days with majestic clouds marching across distant horizons, night skies overflowing with a blanket of stars, a sudden, mighty storm, the hours alone, in the virgin territory of the inland seas. He imagined pulling a canoe ashore, tipping it on its side to protect from the wind, searching for wood, starting a fire, preparing a meal of berries and fruits picked from trees, and fish harvested that day from the sparkling, fresh water. He could never do that, could he, he often wondered, who could? He had never even been to Lake Superior. Billy knew of boaters who made the trip in the comfort of a cabin cruiser, or worked a sailboat around the lakes, but not many had travelled the route of the Chippewa Chief, let alone paddling a canoe. Billy, like his father, felt Kichiwiki's feat was the epitome of the Indian spirit, being one with nature, for he didn't just travel across the water and land, he moved through it, with it, part of nature in spirit and soul.

He thought of Kichiwiski as he walked along the shoreline, skipping a few stones across the narrow cut, the same Flats he walked as a youth with his dad, on a similar windy, late summer afternoon, when his father told him of another Indian legend, Tecumseh, the Shawnee Chief, a leader of a First Nations Confederacy in the times after the white man arrived, bringing their crusade with them. He fought for the survival of an Indian way of life, eventually allying with the British and locals, who would become Canadians, to fight the Americans in battles over territory. His father loved that he took on the Americans. He had a right to, his father thought, for Tecumseh grew up fighting Longknives, as the Indians called white invaders, for they had taken their land, killed his father and destroyed their villages. He believed deeply in his brother Tenskwatawa, the more spiritual of the two, who after suffering from the ravages of alcohol, recovered to become known as the Shawnee Prophet for his visions of an Indian way of life that rejected the white man's world. He preached giving up the firearms, the liquor, the clothes, and most importantly, to stop giving up their ancestral lands. Tecumseh's first concern was also the plight of his people and how to unite them, but he believed in fighting for the survival of his people, even if that met forming uncomfortable alliances. According to his father and grandfather, anyone who fought the Americans was all right by him. If not for Tecumseh, the Flats and much of Southwestern Ontario would be part of America. He loved the warrior in Tecumseh. That he had the fight in him, a fight that ended at the battle of the Thames, not far away near Chatham, but his spirit lived on, and near.

Billy knew the legend of Tecumseh being buried on Walpole Island, had seen the monument many times, his father told him the chief's remains were there, others said no, Billy believed his father. He rode by the monument often; when he needed strength and courage, when he thought of his father, before he went to Toronto for the first time, before he went on runs with Gord and the boys, at times when he didn't know what to do next.

Tecumseh and Kichiwiski were great men, Indian legends, but to a young Billy, the greatest man he knew was his father, who passed these stories on and shared his love for the Flats with him. He took Billy whenever possible to the islands, canals, and marshes to hunt and fish, during all seasons. It was while on these trips that his father related the stories to Billy, just as his father Joshua had told him while sitting quietly waiting for a fish to strike, or a pheasant to fly.

In the good years Joseph worked across the river in Algonac, on the U.S. side. Through word of mouth and good fortune, Joseph landed a job at the expanding Chris-Craft plant. He crossed the river each day, year-round, in a row boat. If he had a little extra cash he took the ferry. As a Native North American he could cross the border unrestricted, so Joseph and others made the shorter trip to Michigan to work and shop, instead of traveling the further distance to the Canadian mainland. Each morning he rowed around Russell Island, down the South Channel to the Middle Channel and the plant. In the winter he and his fellow travelers walked across the ice, the way marked by fir trees. If openings appeared in the shifting ice they left small boats along the way to complete the trip. At the plant he learned a trade, cutting and stacking the volumes of wood, much of it exotic, needed to build the runabouts and cruisers of the burgeoning boat business. He probably handled the wood that built the *Lucky Lena,* the *Captain Jack* and the *Bullet.*

He learned something else after he got off work, when he went with his fellow workers to the bars, how to drink, or as it ended up, how not to, for he couldn't, but he couldn't resist going out with the guys. He had grudgingly earned their respect, not only as an excellent worker, but he could play baseball and hockey better than just about anybody at the plant, so he joined their teams, and the after-game benders that followed, but he couldn't drink, because he couldn't stop, and he spiraled down, into a life of drunken days, attempted recoveries, and broken promises. Jobs were hard to come by and he lost the few he found. He tried to hide it all from his family. He never raised his voice or hand toward them, but instead disappeared for long stretches at a time. One fall day, he showed up sober, and took Billy duck hunting in the Flats. It was a magnificent day with glorious autumn colors, and they bagged a dozen birds. They carried them home to present to Billy's mom, who prepared them for a succulent, late night, family dinner, like in days almost forgotten. His father stayed the night, the first in a long while, but was gone when Billy awoke the following morning. He never saw him again. His mother got a call from the Provincial Police one night. They found him along a canal at the edge of the Flats. After that, like his father, Billy spent many nights in bars, but not drinking, he didn't drink and never would, but playing guitar, mostly the blues.

He thought of these three men as he shuffled along the shore of Walpole, winding in out of tall grass, waiting for Gord, who in his own way was, if not a hero to Billy, his best friend, who taught him most of what he knew of the modern life he drifted in and out of, and how to survive in it.

Kevin Casey was back on the crowded docks of the harbor for the final day of the boat show. He was there with a sense of purpose, a check list, and a get it done attitude. He was inspired by the events of the night before, inspired by the jumper, by the Waterboys, and even by Red, but especially by the young sailor, who had taken the giant step.

He collected a few quick quotes and facts from proud runabout owners, adding to the many he'd acquired from Jack LaCroix over the weekend, fired off some more photos of watercraft and panoramas of the harbor. He stopped by the *Captain Jack* but neither the Captain nor Renee was around, probably off judging, or at the all-you-can-eat pancake breakfast. He would head back to the cruiser later. He acknowledged greetings from a few boaters who recognized him as the guy doing a story on the show, then wandered to the end of a dock to take one more shot of the colorful boathouses lining the opposite shore. As he raised the camera and peered through the viewfinder it became apparent the shot would be a good one. Like many best shots it just happened, right place-right time, available light, framing, angle, shading, reflection of light, and subject matter. This, if it came out, would be the cover shot. He zoomed in, half way across the river to a grouping of multi colored wood boathouses, partially shaded by overhanging tree branches, hectic with family activities, the foreground busy with boats moving past in both directions. He lowered the camera to see a gorgeous runabout sliding upstream, just the right touch to finish the story, the

185

money shot. He waited for it to idle into the frame of the picture, perfectly, and fired off five or six shots.

At that exact moment the driver of the runabout turned in Kevin's direction, raised an arm and waved. Kevin looked about to see if anyone responded, then back at the craft now stopped, idling in the Pine River. The driver waved again as he began backing the boat with short bursts of reverse gear, which combined with the increasing west wind, pushed it closer to the docks.

Kevin used his camera to zoom in on the boat, identified the driver, and heard his name shouted simultaneously. It was Clay Bedore, his head tucked into a Tigers ball cap sporting the old English "D." When an opening appeared in the passing boat traffic Clay revved the engine, filling the air with the distinctive Chris-Craft sound, and put the boat in gear. As the runabout slowly turned away from the dock Kevin squinted against the sudden glare of sunlight reflected off the varnished barrelback stern. As the boat circled, out of the shine, he read the name painted in gold leaf on the boats transom, *Bullet.*

Moments later Kevin was aboard the runabout and heading under the Pine River Bridge, back into the St. Clair River, again. He wasn't certain how it happened, but was pretty sure it was when his mind went blank as he fell into a trance, realizing he was stepping off the dock into not only the *Bullet*, but his past, once again. He wasn't sure, but he thinks the conversation went something like;

"Come aboard, eh?

"Well."

"Oh sure, come on. Let's take a quick spin."

"Yeah?"

"Sure, hop in, tell me about last night. What a night, eh?"

"Well, I was."

"Get in."

"Is this the *Bullet*, the same *Bullet* I ....."?

"You bet your ass she is, now get in and tell me 'bout last night."

Kevin held on tight as he bounced around in the front seat, his mind racing along with the runabout as Clay roared down the big river. This wasn't a slow chug with the Waterboys in the *Lucky Lena*, this was the *Bullet*, with Clay at the wheel, and they were flying. The same *Bullet*, the same runabout he grew up with in Chip's boathouse, the one he helped drive back from those trips to the Old Club, and as it turns out, the one hanging in straps above him in Clay's boathouse as they loaded the *Lucky Lena*. He gripped the windshield frame with his right hand, like he did hundreds of times before. He ran his hands over the same cushioned seat he'd sat on during so many earlier adventures. It had the same feel, the same smell. And now he was racing again, down this river of vapors, in her once again.

"So, how'd you get her? Where'd you get the *Bullet*?" Kevin inquired.

"Bought her off the family of the old man."

"Leo's family?"

"Yeah, that's it. So what about last night?" Clay hollered above the roar of the wind and engine noise.

"What?"

"Last night, hell, what's with you man?" Clay yelled. "Tell me about picking that dude out of the drink."

"What about it, didn't you talk with Whitey?" Kevin responded, not happy about being hijacked once again, but hoping some conversation would help ground his reeling mind.

"Yeah, but only that you picked this dude up out of the water," Clay said, "and that we needed to hook up to try to help him. Not many details."

"I saw it. I'm the one who saw it."

"So you're the one who saved him?"

"Well, we all did," he reflected.

"But you saw him go over, right?"

"Yeah, I saw him go over," Kevin said half to himself as he began replaying the event. "I was riding on the bow of the *Lena*, heading up stream, coming back from the bar, where the band was."

187

"Brown's right?" Clay stated.

"Yes."

"Good band, eh?"

"Very good," Kevin said, then after a pause in which he recalled dancing with Renee to the throbbing beat and engulfing sound of the B-3, "very good."

"And?"

"What?" Kevin inquired as he hung tight as Clay approached a large cruiser running ahead, and without slowing turned to port and jumped the large wake, putting them airborne for a moment before slamming down and slicing through the first set of waves in an explosion of sparkling clear spray that engulfed the *Bullet*, and covered them in spray.

"Shit!" Kevin hollered.

"What?" Clay laughed.

"Your boat man, is that good for her?"

"Ha, she's fine, she's tough. I run these runabouts, I don't show 'em," Clay hollered as they blew past the cruiser and continued on down river.

The two hunched over seeking shelter from the windshield as they shouted back and forth.

"You were saying?"

"Well, we were headed back in the dark, and I remember thinking what a mysterious moment it was, the setting man, I was feeling it."

"Feeling what?"

"I don't know, the moment, I guess, the magic of it."

"Of the river, like when you were a kid? She can do that to you."

"Yes, I guess so, I mean it was night and everything was dark, the river, the sky, the shore line, with everything punctuated by lights, all reflected off the water. And we come up on this freighter, an old tub, like the one we saw the night before, pokin' along up stream. I remember thinking it all seemed like a dream, or like a scene from a movie, and recalled what The Waterman had said about Humphrey Bogart the night before."

"And Sidney Greenstreet?"

"Yeah, him too."

"Ha, he's always talking 'bout those two, eh?"

"Anyway, I'm watching this dream scene unfold before me and Whitey runs the *Lucky Lena* up the back of this tub, just off the stern, and I see this guy out on the deck, leaning on the railing, and I was about to wave, when he looks about, and waits a second or two and freakin' jumps over the side."

"Holy shit," Clay laughs.

"I couldn't believe it, still can't in a way." Kevin said.

"Did you freak?"

"I was surprised how calm I was, at first anyway. I didn't start freaking till I had a hard time snapping Whitey and Jeff out of their stupor and into believing what I was yelling at them."

"Then what?" Clay inquired.

"Well, then we couldn't find the dude, and I really started freaking because I began wondering if I really saw him jump or was hallucinating."

"Ha," Clay howled into the wind.

"Hey, it's not funny," Kevin protested.

"Sorry, but it is, a little funny," Clay said. "The Waterboys circling around in the river looking for a guy who might not be there, Ha. What was Red doing?"

"Hell, Red's the one who spotted 'em. Well we thought it was him until he turned out to be a seagull."

"What, he was a what, a seagull?" Now Clay was laughing in earnest.

"Well, we saw something in the water, shit man, it was dark, and the water was choppy with wakes, and reflections, and we come on this object we thought was the jumper, till it flew off."

"Shit man."

"And the longer it took, each time we circled, we knew it was taking too long, and if someone was in the water, we were probably going to find them dead," Kevin stated bluntly. "And I started imagining pulling a body aboard and then what the hell would we do?"

"Got pretty tense I bet," Clay shouted.

"Sure did," Kevin said. "It sucked."

"Yeah, but it was great eh?"

"What?"

"It was great, right?" Clay said looking at Kevin with that half-crazed glimmer in his eye that he and the Waterboys got at times. "I mean it was exciting, right?

"I suppose so." Kevin mumbled.

"Then what, how'd you find him?"

"Well, all of a sudden a pretty big tree branch appeared."

"A log-a-gator, of course," Clay confirmed.

"Yes, whatever you guys call 'em, anyway," Kevin carried on, "I wanted to make sure Whitey saw it, and as we approached, what we thought was a branch sticking up off this log started to move, it was an arm, and we all realized it was no log. It was a person.

"Holy crap," Clay shouted.

"Holy crap is right," Kevin said. "It was creepy, and scary, but we snapped into action, Jeff jumped in, and before we knew it had the dude aboard the *Lena.*"

"Wow," Clay said shaking his head back and forth, "that's a first for the Waterboys," then added with a smile, "Jeff will be spinning this yarn till the end of time."

"I suppose so."

"Then what?"

"That's it, really. We got him below and dried off, got him dry clothes. We learned real fast he was Asian and didn't speak English, that we better get off the big river in a hurry in case they started looking for him. He was carrying a few pictures, and a newspaper clipping that appeared to indicate he was trying to get into Canada, to Toronto and that's when Jeff and Whitey figured it was time to call you."

"Yep, we're going to just make another run, and instead of dropping off Glenlivet we'll be dropping off, say, what's this guy's name?"

"Hell, I don't even know," Kevin pondered.

The two rode in silence as the powerful machine roared down river blasting through wave tops built by the increasing wind. Scenes from the previous night's rescue flashed, out of sequence, across Kevin's mind, their reality difficult to grasp, yet one fact was beyond reproach,

"We saved him didn't we?" Kevin said, the idea sinking in deeply for the first time.

"You sure did, you saved the guy's life, and if we can get him across the river in a few hours and to Toronto, we will have saved his ass as well," Clay hollered into the wind.

Kevin turned his head to peer through the shinning spray and noticed the outline of Holy Cross on the shoreline as they flew by Marine City, "Hey, where are we going anyway?" he shouted at Clayton.

"What?"

"Where are we going?"

"Where are we going?" Clay repeated. "Hell, were going to deliver that shipwrecked sailor home to Toronto."

"Now?"

"Sure."

"What, I can't do that," Kevin protested.

"Why not?" Clay inquired.

"I have to get back, I have to finish at the show, I still have shit to do," Kevin responded with growing anxiety.

"Don't worry, you'll get back."

"When?"

"Eventually."

It's not that Kevin didn't give a damn anymore, he needed to finish the article and send it off, couldn't mess it up. He needed the money. It's just that his focus had shifted, his priorities altered, and his mind numbed by the combination of unexpected, outrageous adventures and lack of sleep. Or maybe it was the realization that he was ensnared in the Waterboys' web of intrigue and he was finally tired of fighting it, and accepted its inevitability, or some combination of both. Either way, he gradually sat back in the seat of the *Bullet*, sighed deeply, and became one with the roaring, racing runabout of his youth as it powered down river. Spectacular, shinning spray washed across, and over the windshield, dampening his face. The noise and power of the machine was all consuming, the vibration reverberated through his entire body. He turned to his right, where only a few feet away, water displaced by the speeding hull exploded ten feet in the air, sparkling water, accented with rainbow colors against a deep blue sky.

Clay pushed the *Bullet* hard, staying in the middle of the river. It was difficult for Kevin to locate where they were through the spray and constant bouncing of the rough ride, the shore a good distance away. At one point a freighter suddenly appeared off the starboard side, his side, the *Vandoc*. They went airborne, again, launching off the ship's bow wake, raced along her side hull where he caught a fleeting glimpse of the ships black stack with large white P emblazoned on it. They picked up even more speed when they cleared her stern and entered the smooth water just below her stern. Clay ran hard all the way to Algonac where he pulled back on the throttle at the head of Russell Island, where the river split and started its descent into the mystical world of the Flats. He followed the South Channel and tucked in close to Harsens Island, cruising slowly along the dock line, out of the increasing west wind, and in calmer water.

"Best burgers on the island," Clay announced as they slid past the Sans Souci Bar, with its red shingled, domed roof.

They motored on along the dock line till the river split again at the head of Bassett Island, the St. Clair Cut Off and the Bassett Channel opened off their port side as Clayton turned the *Bullet* to the west and rounded the southeast bend of Harsens Island. The turn removed them from the shelter of land and they found themselves heading into an increasing west wind and the choppy waters of the South Channel. They entered Kevin's favorite part of the island, the stretch of cabins, homes and hideaways tucked onto small plots of tree filled yards interspersed with small canals and channels running this way and that, a multitude of watercraft, all kinds, all sizes, all shapes floating at door steps, at small docks or immersed in the reeds and bushes. He remembered it from two days ago. He remembered it from 20 years ago, the same as it ever was.

Clayton pulled the runabout off the Channel into one of the small openings and pulled the engine into neutral. The *Bullet* drifted then slowed to a stop in front of the homes and cottages. Although the tree tops rustled and swayed in the wind, low on the water it was peaceful, and still.

"What's up?" Kevin inquired. "What's this, this a rendezvous spot?"

"No, this is the site of the hotel, Joe Bedore's Hotel."

"Yeah?"

"Yeah, thought you might want to know where she once stood. Red said he mentioned it to you."

"Yes, he sure did," Kevin stated as he remembered the conversation in the cabin of the *Lena*.

"Red sure likes to tell stories, loves to talk, eh?"

"Sure does."

"He's a beauty, eh? We all love Red."

"He also said you're related to this Joe Bedore fella, right?" Kevin inquired.

"So I was told. He was my great-uncle, or great-grand dad, something like that. But one of 'em was adopted I heard, or maybe, so I'm not actually sure of the details."

"Yeah?"

"Yeah and," Clay paused, "Well, I never looked into it much, doesn't mean that much to me, really kinda' confusing, all that ancestor, family tree stuff."

"Well," Kevin stated with a smile, "you got the name and it appears you're carrin' on in his style."

"You think?"

"Sure, you're connected somehow."

"That's what they say, and I heard it all when I was a kid. I heard all the stories growing up, about Joe and his hotel which was right here," Clay said pointing to a few homes on the canal. "It closed down around the time I was born and was torn down when I was around 18."

"Red said he was a legend."

"Who, Joe or himself?" Clay said with a laugh.

"Looks like both to me," Kevin smiled.

"No shit, man."

"What about Joe? What about his hotel?" Kevin inquired.

"Of course I never knew him, but I heard the stories, mostly from my grandfather and sometimes, when he told me tales he'd pump up his French Acadian, you know, Cajun accent to drive the stories home."

"Yeah?"

"Yeah, he'd say everyone talked about Joe's way of inviting folks to the Flats, I think someone even wrote it down once, made it a poem, a lady named Daland, or Holand, I think, I got a copy of it hangin in the boat house. I do remember her first name though, Hulda."

"What?"

"Hulda, what a name, eh?"

"Never heard that one."

"Well anyway, he'd belt it out."

194

"Yeah?"

"Sure," and with that Clay offered, "hello my friends, an' how you find yourself, all right? Dat's good. You ax what fetch me here? I come for feed. My place eez full o' folks, dem ceety folks, what feesh dis time o' year. Dey ketch much feesh? Don't ax me dat, my frind. Dat's not my beeziness to spile de fun. Come on de Flats and sateesfy yourself, I let you take my fishpole an' my gun."

Kevin smiled at Clay and stated, "Is there more?"

"I Garrruntee."

"Then carry on."

And Clay did, in perfect Cajun, "Well you say nothing, then I send my boy wid you, he take my scow an' punt you troo de marsh. He's good for dat. He ketch you lot o' feesh - nobody knows – jes give him leetle cash. Folks feesh dat way? Don't ax me dat, my friend. Come on de Flats an' stay all night wid me. You hear de bull frog croak, de mud hen sing. You bring home plenty feesh. Come up an' see."

"Wow man, that's great," Kevin laughed.

"Yeah? It's been a while since I pulled that one out."

"You say the place was right there?" Kevin inquired as he pointed towards the small piece of land.

"Yeah, that's the spot. Just about where those houses are now. It sat right out on the South Channel, a small peninsula surrounded by water and intersected by a canal. On one side was a landing for fishing boats and smaller craft and right out front, straight off the front door, ran a long dock where passenger boats from Detroit off loaded guests."

"Like the *Tashmoo?*" Kevin inquired. "Red said he rode up here on her with his father when he was a kid."

"Oh yeah, the *Tashmoo,* she'd be the first to arrive, she'd leave the foot of Woodward in the morning and head north, up river and across the lake, making stops along the way. Other ships as well."

"Yeah, that's what Red was talking about."

"Red would have been comin' after Joe had passed." Clay said.

"When was Joe runnin' it?" Kevin inquired.

"Well, turn of the century, around 1905 began the peak years. The place was legendary, a Mecca for sportsman." Clay said.

"It started out as Joe's house, and he expanded it with the labor of locals who he supplied with room and board, until it grew into the hotel, hunting and fishing resort. The place was built on these two small islands," he said with the wave of an arm. "One had a building that housed the dining room, kitchen, guest rooms, and bar. The ice house and boat house were also there, I think." He said removing his cap and scratching his head.

"And on the other island there was a wooden promenade and dance hall, and a picnic grove, and the bug-house."

"Bug-house, what was that?" Kevin inquired.

"A screened in place for the ladies."

"And an ice house, no 'fridges I'm guessing?"

"Nope, there was no electricity, no refrigeration and no electric lights, but I think there was Blau Gas at some point, not sure when," Clay added.

"What's that?"

"Kinda like today's propane."

"Cool."

"But it was all about Joe and his wife Marcella, they made the hotel the legend it was," Clay stated, "Nothin' special, not fancy or opulent, but a partyin' place, with his story telling and her cooking. It was their kingdom."

"It must have been great," Kevin said,

"Even after they passed, the place kept going," Clay said, "And during prohibition it was, as you can imagine, jumping."

Those times were gone, but for Clayton Bedore, he still lived a life connected to the Flats, entwined in everything the bayou embodied. He ran a fishing charter boat out of the Flats during the summer, and worked at a marina in Florida in the winter.

The two sat silently in the *Bullet*, just off the spot the hotel once stood, paying silent homage to a place that once permeated good times, good feelings, in natures basket, inspired by a couple of hard working immigrants who recognized their good fortune and relished in sharing it with all.   And if one tried hard enough, one could picture them sitting on the porch, oil lamps aglow, the aroma of fish, fowl and beer, highlighted with laughter, wonderful laughter as Joe told a tale below a low-lying moon, amongst the bull frogs croaking and ducks honking, somewhere across the distant Flats.

CHAPTER 12

Full Ahead

The smell of fresh varnish hung heavy in the warm humid air as Kevin Casey stood in the boat yard at the St. Clair Flats Marina, surrounded by wooden water craft; skiffs, runabouts, lap strake fishing boats and cruisers, sitting on cradles or trailers, all in various states of restoration. Some tore down to the ribbing, keel and chines, some with deck planks missing, others flipped over with bottoms being replaced, finished craft getting side hulls, decks and trim painted or varnished, all in preparation of soaking in slings to swell the wood. Off to the side, in a corner shaded by trees, lay a few carcasses, boats beyond salvaging, deteriorated beyond repair, picked clean of useful hardware, decaying dinosaurs, the grey boats, overgrown by weeds, relics of the past, their days of providing good times gone.

Clay had pulled the *Bullet* off the South Channel into a canal that lead to the marina, situated in a waterscape of small islands filled with cozy cottages, some rustic and ramshackle. And while Clay stepped into the small marina store and grocery, a converted two story frame home, Kevin wandered out back, drawn by the array of cradled boats. Warmed by the sun and entranced by the aroma of varnish and paint wafting on the breeze, he was suddenly at ease, happy he'd come, glad to find himself in this little corner of the boat life he'd not seen that provided new and interesting subject matter to shoot.

It was a constant process, a rite of spring, prepping the boats, some splashed early, on the front edge of the boat maintenance cycle, where little needed to be done, much of the process finished in previous seasons, or owners who had the work done by the marina, and showed up when she was already afloat in a slip, gassed up, and ready to go, a turn-key. On most craft there was more to be done, always more, and by owners themselves, limited to weekends and by bad weather, hoping to splash sometime that season, while others were clearly in over their heads and might sit on land for an entire season, or longer. But for the true waterman, even this was acceptable, for it was a way of life, this life in the boatyard, built on an understanding, and supported by strong camaraderie, that even if they were dry-docked, stuck on land, they were boating.

This day happened to be one of those weekend days, a sunny, Sunday, and a dozen or so folks were busy working away towards their eventual launch date. It didn't take long for them to greet Kevin, one smiling back through a hole in the side hull of an old cruiser.

Moments later a voice sounded from behind, "Good afternoon."

Kevin turned but saw no one.

"Up here," the voice repeated.

Kevin searched upward to find a jovial face peering down from the back deck of a cradled cruiser.

"She's heating up isn't it?" the man said as he looked skyward toward the sun.

"Yes it is," Kevin answered, noticing that standing between the boats, and out of the breeze, it was very hot.

"Want a cold one?"

"Well, sure, why not," Kevin answered after a dry, parched swallow, and climbed the step ladder leaning against the boat's swim platform. He found himself standing face to face with a bearded, rotund, middle aged fellow who handed him a cold bottle of beer, very cold. Kevin took a swig of the brew, relished in its refreshing chill, and thanked the man with feeling.

"No problem, it's better in a bottle, eh? Don't you think? Hell, I do, it's always better in a bottle, cold beer in a bottle, can't beat it, I never drink it from a can anymore, that ruins a beer, just not the same, tastes shitty, taste like tin, it sucks, don't you agree? Beer in a can sucks, especially on a hot day like this."

"Ah, I guess so," Kevin said, and adding, "This may be the best beer I've ever had," not lying, as the cold liquid soothed and cooled him.

"Well, I might as well join you," the man said as he turned to pull a bottle from an ice filled cooler, spun, and in one motion, dropped heavily into a folding lawn chair on the cruisers back deck, and without hesitation, twisted off the top, took a swallow, and added, "What brings you 'round here, picture taking? Looks like a fine camera there."

"Yea, it gets the job done," Kevin replied looking down at the Nikon hanging around his neck.

"What you shootin' the woodies?"

"Yes, those and the yard, mostly the yard, I..." Kevin began, but before he could continue the guy began a preamble that included, "Those old woody's are great all right, I used to have a couple, a small, fast one and then I moved up to an express cruiser, but they were too much work, so I got me one of these glass ones. It's still work, but a hell of a lot less," he said looking about at the snake pit of extension cords, lines, boxes of parts and tools that engulfed his chair.

"But ya know boatin' is boatin', whatever floats ya, whatever gets you on the water, right?" And before Kevin could answer he repeated, "It's whatever gets you on the water that counts, or near the water, for it's all about getting back to the water, eh, the water, the giver of life, the keeper of life, where it all began. It's in everyone, the pull of the water, some just don't know it, I do, and it appears you do. It's the life, on the water, and if not on it, as near as you can get to it. The life dock side, or in the marinas, or in a boat-yard like here," he said with a wave of his hand from his perch on the back deck. "It's the dock life, the slips, sitting in a boat's cabin, listening to the water lapping against the hull. You don't even have to shove off, just sitting aboard, or the boat yard life, hell, even if you don't launch, the connections there, the smells of varnish, cut

201

wood, engine oil, bilge water, hot, overheated electric tools, the marina shop, readying the boat, cleaning, sanding, scraping, scrubbing, commissioning the engine, painting, varnishing, the beer, the sun, the surprise bad weather, the stories, the reward of the launch, from the straps to the splash, the slide off the trailer, the soak, the float, spring in a boat yard, like baseball and spring training, the annual anticipation of the coming season, that first smell of water in the spring, back to the water, back to that feeling, THE feeling, back to the water, back to the spirit of the water, mother nature's pool."

Kevin just looked at the guy who was staring across the yard at the cottages, water and Flats in the distance, said nothing and took a drink of his beer.

"Hell, I might not splash her this year, I didn't last either." He suddenly said turning towards Kevin.

"No?"

"Nope, not only did I not hit the water, I stayed on her all winter, right here in the yard."

"Really?" Kevin stated skeptically.

"It was great, best winter of all, best off-season I should say, 'cause from late September, October on, it was gorgeous, and quiet, so silent at times, and," he added, "it was a good deal for me, I got to stay here for nothin', kept an eye on the place, and didn't have to pay for any storage in exchange."

"Nice," Kevin stated.

"You bet it was nice. It beat staying at my sister's place, indoors on the damn couch all winter long, the damn TV blarin' away night and day."

"So you lived here, slept right here, in the cabin." Kevin inquired starting to piece together what that must have been like as he scanned the back deck and peered into the open cabin door.

"Hell ya, that's what I'm saying and here's where I'm staying," he said as he took a quick look around. "I had a heater, a stove, key to the store for facilities, and most important, I had quiet."

Kevin never got another question, or word in, just a few head bobs in agreement as the guy continued on about the magic of the water and the boating life that he was immersed in. When Kevin turned his attention to the activity in the yard and fired off a series of photos the guy rambled on, stopping only for the occasional swig on his beer, or stare head down into his lap. It appeared everyone was getting work done but this ancient mariner, especially the busy family clamoring around a small glass cruiser on a trailer a few boats over. A young couple with two small children who were busy spraying each other with water instead of the boat's side hull, as dad lay on the ground, rolling paint on the bottom and mom unloaded supplies from the trunk of the car.

Kevin fired off a few more shots, lowered the camera and noticed Clay strolling through the yard, glancing upward before steadying his gaze on the western sky above the tree line.

"Looks like something's blowing up," Clay shouted as he headed towards the *Bullet*. "I'm going to put her inside."

Kevin finished his beer, thanked the boating Buddha, he never did get his name, climbed down the ladder and walked the short distance across the yard to a door at the back of the boat house. He stepped out of the bright sunlight into the darkness of the interior, feeling his way along a narrow dock, removing his sunglasses in time to keep from falling into the water. When he regained focus he found most of the doors on the waterside of the building open, providing the light that illuminated a row of eight-to-ten wood runabouts of various era's and styles, most hung in straps, a few floating in the water, all masterpieces, waiting silently to be started up, and run, again, across the blue water of the Flats. The rustling of trees and bushes on the increasing wind swirled about the building but it was eerily quiet inside the boathouse, like a museum, only the chirping of birds in the rafters and the occasional lapping of water broke the silence. A damp, musky air filled the old boat barn, a stew of smells, the grease of the hoists, the aged wood of the building, the now familiar aroma of antique machines, a combination of wood, caulk and oil, all stirred together with the scent of shallow water below. It was a peaceful moment, like in a gallery, alone, among works of art, knowing the intense, ancient skill and craft of creativity was all around. Or in an old church, in the afternoon, with no one else around, when the senses grow acute and the wonder of it all heightens.

The silence was broken when Clayton fired up the *Bullet* docked in the canal just outside the boathouse. Kevin could feel, as well as hear the roar of the engine, the sound echoing around the interior, louder as the runabout slid nearer. It startled him from his moment of serenity. It would be his last peaceful moment for some time.

Clayton swung the craft into an open well and tossed Kevin a line. As the boat slid forward Kevin carried it to the front of the slip and held off the bow with his foot. Clay shut off the *Bullet's* engine but the low rumble of an idling motor continued, and as Kevin looked up, saw the *Lucky Lena* slip into view. Clay moved to the stern of the *Bullet* to chat briefly with the Waterboys before the *Lena* backed down the canal to a spot along the wall.

"What's up?" Kevin inquired.

"Time to go," Clay replied as he stepped from the runabout and moved down the dock towards the boat house door.

"Yeah?" Kevin said as he turned and followed.

"You bet. The boys are here with your sailor and we gotta go now, it looks like the weather may get nasty."

"My sailor?" Kevin said.

"Well, you helped rescue him."

"Yes but."

"So, are you going with us, help get this guy to where he wants to go?"

"No, I mean I hadn't really planned on it, I got ...."

"I know," Clay interrupted, "You got work to do."

'Well, that's right, I do," Kevin protested as they walked out the door and through the yard towards the *Lena*. "I mean this worked out great, me coming along with you down here, stopping at the old hotel spot, learning about Joe, and this place is great, I got some great shots."

"Good," from Clay, "Glad to hear it."

"But I got to get back," Kevin said, before adding with stark realization. "How am I going to get back?"

"Don't know," Clayton stated as they arrived at the *Lena* idling along the breakwall. "You can wait here till we get back I guess."

Tom White appeared from under the canvas, "Hey man, what are you doing here?" the crew having not seen him in the shadows of the boathouse.

"Oh yeah, he rode down with me," Clay stated as an afterthought. "He was picture taking in the yard."

"Nice day for that," from Tom.

"Get some good ones?" Jeff asked as he stepped into the sun on the back deck.

Kevin replied in the affirmative as he mulled over how to avoid another adventure with this crew, another dreaded river run, another illegal mission into the Flats, no matter how admirable, still not legal, and how the hell he was going to get back to the boat harbor and finish his story. As he stood there working out his dwindling options his quandary deepened when Renee suddenly appeared from the cabin.

"Hey, Kevin, what are you doing here?" she inquired with that wonderful smile of hers.

"With Clay, I rode down with Clay," is all he could get out. Nothing about being shanghaied again, about at first not wanting to go with Clay, but stepping aboard anyway, only to experience the most enjoyable ride ever, an exciting race down river in the *Bullet*. The *Bullet*, the runabout of his youth, nothing about his thoughts of all things river and water, and life, all tied together by this old machine, connecting past and present, and evidently the future, and the reward of arriving at the picturesque boat yard and the shots he

205

fired off, or the boating monk. The only thing he got out was, "I came with Clay," followed by, "What are you doing here?"

"Oh, the boys picked me up at the harbor," she said. "Just like the other day. I was standing on the back deck, with my dad this time, and here comes the *Lena*, sliding into view, just like when you and I were there, remember? And Jeff asked if I wanted to go for a ride."

Of course Kevin remembered as he glared down at Jeff who was working with lines off the transom.

"So," she continued, "I said sure, and here I am," and after an extended pause where no one spoke but all were waiting, she laughed, and added, "Oh yeah, then I met this guy," she stated as she turned and pointed towards the cabin door.

Kevin glared down at Jeff, shocked and pissed that he would pick up Renee while the sailor was aboard the *Lena* without telling her, therefore including her in the Waterboys' harebrained scheme. When he looked at Whitey with an 'are you kidding me' stare Tom just shrugged his shoulders and said nothing. Then, as Kevin turned back toward a still smiling Renee, his angst subsided as he began to think things might not be so bad. Actually, things might work out just fine, thinking that he could wait at the marina with Renee while the boys sailed into oblivion, for surely she will not be going with this ship of fools on their misguided adventure. Even the Waterboys would not allow that. Visions of he and Renee filled his head, sitting together along the canal, shoes off, feet kicking the warm water, under the low hanging branches of a willow tree. Then running hard, hand in hand, to the shelter of the boat house as the oncoming storm cut loose, and falling together, into the back seat of a runabout, laughing and rolling on the leather cushions.

"So, you coming with us dude?" the Waterman asked.

Before Kevin could reply, Renee added, "Yeah, Kevin, are you coming along?"

"Are you going?" Kevin asked, shocked by the question.

"Sure, why not," she smiled.

How many times on this crazy weekend had he stood there perplexed, confused, needing to make a decision, in a hurry, every one waiting for him to decide, go or stay, go for it or not, wondering what to do, lost. This was another. As before, his initial reaction was to stay behind, not do anything extreme, out of the ordinary, against somebody else's rules, but on this wild weekend he had gone for it, each and every time, like it or not, voluntarily or not, and expanded his life experiences a hundred-fold in a few days.

"Well?" Captain Jeff said impatiently.

Kevin looked at Renee and her eyes pulled him aboard like a magnet. If she were going, how could he not, he needed to man up. He couldn't leave her alone with the Waterman, Jeff Waters the river pirate, where she may see him at his courageous best.

In moments Whitey was at the wheel, turning the *Lucky Lena* around in the narrow canal, and heading past the last small island of cottages for the South Channel. Jeff, in anticipation of high seas, went below to man the hatch cover and cabin windows. Kevin and Renee sat on the back-bench seat. The Sailor remained below, out of sight. Clayton suddenly shot past in a fishing boat, and with a wave, raced out of sight.

Most of the angst Kevin felt towards climbing aboard, for what he perceived to be a doomed voyage, was eased by the presence of Renee, but even that was blown away on the stiff breeze when Captain Jeff emerged from below and announced, "Hang on, it's going to get rough."

At that very instant the *Lena* pitched forward and rolled heavily to starboard as Whitey fought to right her. They were headed up stream and the growing waves rolling up the South Channel pushed on the boat's stern causing her to pitch and roll. The stern rose on each wave, just before it washed against the transom, then dropped as the wave rolled forward along the hull, causing the bow to rise and the *Lena* to slow, caught between swells, then suddenly race forward as the next roller pushed from behind, raising the stern again, to repeat, over and over. The rollers came at a slight angle so a side-to-side roll accompanied each up and down movement. It quickly became a rough ride. Whitey, feet spread-eagled at the steering station, fought the wheel to keep the *Lena* on course, turning to starboard as a wave lifted the stern slowing the cruiser, then spinning the wheel hard to port as she surfed down the front side, preventing them from getting caught sideways between waves.

Captain Jeff folded down the seat at the port side bulkhead and stood across from Whitey, turning on occasion to watch the following seas. Renee moved closer to Kevin on the bench seat. It was becoming an uncomfortable ride, very uncomfortable. Kevin just sat there, trying not to regret his decision and hoping he wouldn't get sea sick, and throw up. By the second rock and then roll Renee slid closer to Kevin and placed her hand on his knee.

"It's like a carnival ride isn't it?" she exclaimed, and before he could reply she added with glee, "Don't you love it?"

Kevin had regained his sea legs somewhat in the past few days, was doing alright adjusting to the rhythm of the current ride, but was a long way from loving it. Noting his trepidation Renee leaned closer and shouted above the wind, "You O.K.?"

"Sure," he answered, manning up for the second time in twenty minutes.

"I hear you were awesome," she said.

"What?"

"I hear you were awesome," she repeated louder.

"When?"

"Last night, when you pulled Minh from the water," she said pointing toward the cabin.

"Who?" Kevin inquired.

"Minh, the guy you rescued."

"That's his name?" Kevin replied. "How do you know that?"

Renee looked at him quizzically before answering, "Ah, he told me."

"Really," Kevin said as he tried piecing together a picture of that conversation.

"Anyway, like I said," Renee carried on, "I hear you were awesome last night."

"Who said that?"

"Jeff," Renee said.

"Yeah?"

"Yes," she said with a smile.

"Really?"

"Yes, and more than once."

"Yeah, what did he say?" Kevin said turning to look at her, trying to focus on, like she said, a carnival ride.

"He told me the whole story, about you manning the bow deck, you being the one who spotted Minh, being part of the crew, a true Waterboy."

"He said that?" Kevin said glancing toward Jeff.

"Yes, and on the ride down here he told me the whole story. He introduced me to the sailor, Minh. How exciting. So unbelievable, so far out, I wish I had been there."

"Introduced?"

"Well, you know," she laughed. "I went below to meet him after Jeff told me what had happened and we shook hands and smiled and nodded a few times, I said I was Renee, he said Minh a few times, till I figured it out, that's about it. Anyway, the rescue must have been great. I just wish I had been there."

"Really?" from Kevin.

"Oh yeah, I mean, how many times do you get to experience that, you're so lucky."

"Lucky?"

"Sure, real lucky"

"Well, it's not over yet," Kevin said looking into her eyes. "We'll see how lucky I am. We'll see how lucky we all are."

"I know," she said then added. "This is great! We'll be alright, remember this is the *Lucky Lena*."

Shortly after her pronouncement the waterscape darkened. The ill wind that had been building all day, bringing the morning humidity at the Willows, the rough waters on the *Bullet's* river run, and the menacing rollers to the South Channel, now delivered the front it preceded. With the eerie darkness came an even stiffer wind.

The flag flying from the *Lena's* transom stood straight out, snapping at Kevin and Renee. Noticing this Jeff stumbled aft on the pitching deck, catching himself on the transom, separating the occupants of the bench seat at the last second. The captain balanced with one hand and yanked the flag pole from its chrome base with the other and fell back to sit on the engine cover. He rolled the flag around the pole and stuck it in the side hull between two life jackets.

"We'll be out of this soon," the Captain yelled as he looked shoreward.

"What about Clayton?" Renee inquired. "Is he out here in that little boat?"

"He'll be fine, he'll run the dock line on this side and avoid these big ones," he said looking past Kevin and Renee at the swells. "Then he'll cross over at the head of Bassett Island, shoot for the Canada Club. That'll be a rough stretch but it's only a quarter mile or so, but he'll be fine. He knows what he's doing."

They beat hard up the South Channel, the distance made longer by the deteriorating conditions. The first sheets of wind driven rain hit them as they approached the tip of Bassett Island. Kevin and Renee scrambled for the cover of the cabin top squeezing between the Waterboys. The *Lena* got sideways between waves as Whitey tried to cut across the rollers and round the head of the island. The cruiser rolled violently and after bouncing and colliding with each other once too often, the Captain ordered Kevin and Renee below. This was fine with Kevin, at least till he flopped down at the cabin table, and remembered the worst place to be in high seas was below decks, with no view of a horizon to focus on in an attempt to help the brain adjust to a topsy-turvy world. It was claustrophobic. Now he felt worse. Renee fell into the seat opposite with a reassuring smile still displaying that excited 'this is great look.' Together they turned towards Minh sitting on the bench seat opposite the cabin table.

"Hey, how are you doing?" Renee asked her smile more than enough to make up for their inability to really talk.

"Yeah," he replied, with his own smile, reflecting an appearance of complete calm and relaxation, as if he hadn't a care in the world, as if he was about to say, like Captain Jeff, 'this is no big deal.'

"Yes," Renee repeated with an added nod in the affirmative, then turning to Kevin, "He's picking up a few words."

"Looks like it," Kevin said as he grabbed the edge of the table for support as the boat rolled. "Man, look how freakin' relaxed this guy is."

"Well, what did you expect?" Renee laughed. "This guy is a sailor, the real deal, a real sailor of seas. This is probably nothing for him."

Kevin suddenly felt the fool, again. Of course this little river run was nothing for him, of course he had way more to worry about then a rough ride in a small boat, he had the whole man overboard thing going down. He could claim he accidently fell over on that one, but the escaping, running, illegal entry problem were life changing events, even life threatening, and about to happen, and happen soon.

Kevin observed Renee, who was also handling everything with calmness and courage, and 'a go for it' confidence. Only he was stressed, and struggling, worried about everything, especially throwing up. His building anxiety grew until a burst of adrenalin, unrecognizable and source unknown, prompted a renewed effort to get it together before anymore doubt might engulf him.

"Yeah, Ohrono" the sailor repeated as he pulled a post card from his waist band and handed it to Renee.

"Oh yes," she smiled then repeated, "Yes, Tor-on-to."

"Oh-ron-o," he uttered slowly.

"Yes."

"Where did he get that?" Kevin inquired of Renee.

"Whitey gave it to him," she replied as she looked at the card, the Toronto skyline and CN Tower above a blue Lake Ontario. "He said he took it off the refrigerator door when he was home grabbing food."

"Yeah, Ohrono," the sailor said to Kevin, addressing him directly for the first time. Kevin was surprised how young the guy was. He appeared much younger than him, younger than any of them, too young to be in such a perilous position. Again, Kevin wondered what led to this situation, was it a twist of fate, a preordained path, a justified journey, and what would the outcome hold?

Suddenly, Kevin noticed the ride becoming smoother, the rolls less dramatic, the rocking much calmer. He felt relief as the *Lena* settled into a more comfortable rhythm on the water. Whitey had guided the cruiser around the top of the island and was running south down the Big Bassett. He had tucked the *Lena* in close to the east side of the island which absorbed much of the winds power providing the smoother water. The rain stopped. The sailor grabbed a map, also given to him at the Willows, where the Waterboys went over the plan, over and over and over, tracing the route on the Rand McNally, and handed it to Kevin. The sailor stood, moved next to Kevin, spun the map around on the table top and pointed, "Ohrono, me Ohrono."

He hit the target perfectly, his finger landing directly on downtown Toronto, and as Kevin turned towards him with a smile the young man flashed a hardy, thumbs up. Renee laughed at this and reached over to give him a pat on the back which turned into a short, affectionate rub.

Kevin scanned the map, from the metropolitan area to the far south west corner where he found the Flats, briefly tried to figure out where they were, and where he thought they were headed, traced an unknown route through the marshes, found Wallaceburg and the road to Toronto. He wondered if the guy would make it, and if he did, what was in store upon his arrival, and would any of them ever see him again.

Suddenly the cabin door flew open and Captain Jeff ordered, "Get up here. You have got to see this." The three occupants of the cabin exchanged glances as Renee leaned across the table to draw back a curtain. At that precise moment a golden ray of sunlight

212

burst through the cabin window to wash her face and a corner of the cabin in golden light.

"Wow," she exclaimed.

And wow Kevin thought, mesmerized by her beauty, abruptly bathed in outrageous gold. It was awesome, she was awesome, it was magic, she was magic, and yet again, he focused, and fired the perfect shot with the camera of his mind.

"Let's go," she said as she leaped up the cabin steps, and after a brief pause, followed by Kevin and the sailor.

The wet back deck of the *Lena* glistened in brilliant light and the entire Flats beyond were bathed in the brightest, heaviest, deepest golden color any of them had ever seen. They stood silently in wonderment, the moment extraordinary. None of them had noticed, what with the long river runs, time at the marina, the long channel crossing with darkening skies and accompanying rain that it had grown late, it was day's end, it was sunset time, and now, the sun slipped into a small hole in the parting storm clouds to illuminate their world for those few magic moments. And it was certainly magic, how else to describe that orb hitting such a small opening in the clouds perfectly, allowing for the pandemonium of colors, what a cosmic shot!

Kevin raced below, grabbed his camera, and was topside in an instant, firing off shots of the marsh, awash in tones of red and gold, and the sky, which exploded in colors without names that washed together, creating a Turner like firmament. He shot west across the tops of the reed beds, through the trees at the piercing sun, turned to shoot up and down the channel, colors dancing across the water with cloud bottoms illuminated by the suns spotlight, and to the east, the black wall of recent rain shimmering as it hung in the sky.

Then, in an instant it was over. The hole closed by the shifting clouds and like a thrown switch the light was gone, the colors gone, the moment gone, the incomparable wonder of it all, gone, and suddenly it became dark and ominous again, with the wind building, again.

"What is that?" Rene asked.

All aboard turned to see a white cloud wall appear on the western horizon where the sun had glowed only moments early.

"A fog bank, is it a wall of fog?" Kevin inquired.

"I doubt it," the Captain answered.

"It's blowin' too hard," Whitey said just as a blast of wind raced across the Flats striking the crew on the back deck with enough force to blow the caps of Jeff and Kevin. Jeff retrieved his from the deck as Kevin leaned over board in an attempt to fish his out of the channel.

"It's a squall, it's a fuckin' squall line," the Captain hollered.

"That's not good," Whitey shouted back.

"I've lost my freakin' hat," Kevin shouted as he returned his attention to the crew. "A squall?"

Just then Clay pulled alongside the slow-moving *Lena* and tossed the Waterman a line which he tied off the spring cleat.

"You see that?" the Captain yelled through the building wind.

"Of course," Clay barked. "Saw it building about twenty minutes ago. We've got to shit or get off the pot here, real quick."

Kevin watched as the Captain grabbed the brim of his cap and looked across the marsh at the building sky. To Kevin it was beginning to look more like a mountain side then a cloud bank.

Jeff turned back toward Clay "What do you think?"

"I think we gotta go for it."

"Yeah?" Jeff inquired, looking over his shoulder one more time. "You think?"

"Yes, and now," Clay shouted from his seat in the fishing boat, a bit surprised by the slight hesitation in the Captain's voice.

Jeff Waters knew Clayton was right. There was no turning back. They never turned back, no matter the cargo, no matter the circumstances. The plan had been set in motion, arrangements had been made, Gord and Billy were in place, others waiting, cars obtained. The coast was clear, he hoped.

"Should we tuck in here or cross now?" Whitey shouted from his place at the wheel.

Jeff turned to look at the foreboding sky one more time, then at his crew, all watching him closely awaiting an answer. He looked at Renee who stared at him with anticipation, hoping for the chance to jump into action, waiting for the Captain to give her an order, holding on for his command. He waited a moment more, smiled at her, turned towards Whitey and hollered, "Full ahead matey!"

With that they were off, the *Lucky Lena* roaring down the channel, the fishing boat tied alongside with Clay, head down against the wind, holding on tight. All on board took frequent glances to the west, off the starboard side, at the approaching cloud bank building on the dark horizon. They continued on till Clay, searching the east side of the channel raised his arm and hollered. Whitey pulled the cruiser back to an idle. The trailing wake rolled under the *Lena* as Jeff moved to the side rail to converse with Clay.

"Is this where we were the other night?" Kevin inquired of Whitey.

"Pretty close," Whitey answered. "It shifts around, the reed beds and openings move about, especially in these conditions."

The party idled on further, the Captain and Clayton scanning the marsh beds as the wind continued to build. At last, Clay pointed ashore and Whitey wheeled the *Lena* toward a spot that neither Kevin, Renee nor the sailor saw as any different then what they'd been endlessly running along.

The Captain checked one last time with Clay, turned toward the crew and barked, "O.K., let's go, you guys down below."

Simultaneously, as Whitey wheeled the *Lena* to port, crossed the narrow channel and entered a small opening in the reeds, a massive blast of wind, accompanied by a wall of horizontal rain, struck the cruiser from the stern. In moments they were soaked from a wind driven rain that pushed them against the cabin bulkhead. As they turned to squint through the deluge they saw the black cloud wall just before it hit them.

"Shit," Kevin yelled, "what should we do?"

"Clear the deck," the Captain hollered above the wind. "It's coming straight at us and there's nothing we can do."

215

Kevin, Renee, and the sailor went below, glad for temporary shelter from the storm.

"I'm worried for those guys," Renee said.

"I know, but hey, they're the Waterboys right, they know what they're doing," Kevin stated, hoping as he grabbed a ball cap from a hook on the bulkhead and tugged it on.

Suddenly, a large thud echoed around the cabin. It sounded as if the *Lena* had struck something. Bang, and bang again.

"What is that?" Renee hollered.

The sailor looked anxious for the first time.

Bang again, louder, this time with a shudder that raced down the cruisers keel.

"I bet its Clay's boat hitting the side," Kevin announced. "He's on that side."

Kevin drew back the curtain of the port side cabin window in an attempt to check but could see nothing in the tempest that boiled outside, his face sprayed with water penetrating around the cabin window frames.

It's strange what happens to time, one's perception of time in these moments, its importance nullified, as the *Lena* plowed forward through the churning uproar. At some point the Captain threw open the cabin door and hollered, "O.K., hold on tight," and the *Lena* suddenly accelerated.

"We're here," Kevin exclaimed. "This is what we did the other night."

"What?" Rene shouted.

"They're going to pick up speed so they can beach her so hold on, we'll hit pretty good."

Kevin was partially right, they beached the *Lucky Lena* as on Friday night, but without the heavy load of boxed contraband, this grounding was much softer, but still enough to toss the occupants forward in the cabin. They had stopped, the bow of the cruiser aground, as the storm raged on outside the cabin. Whitey kept the engine running, in gear, to keep the *Lena* beached. Thunder crackled all around. Clay beached the fishing boat and stood on shore.

Captain Jeff again stuck his head threw the door, this time to announce, "Let's go, matey, make it snappy."

The sailor looked up at the Captain, grabbed the small duffle Carol had given him and headed up the steps, stopping to smile, and nod at Renee and Kevin and was gone through the cabin door. Renee jumped from her seat and followed.

"Where are you going?" Kevin asked.

"To say good bye," She shouted back. "To say something, I mean this is it, we should at least say something."

Kevin followed and shortly after the crew huddled together under the canvas top in the elements as the storm raged around them. Captain Jeff Waters shook the sailors hand and wished him luck, Whitey took one hand off the ships wheel to pat him on the back, and Kevin also wished the sailor well with a handshake. The sailor looked at each, and with what appeared to be tears in his eyes, hugged each of the three with feeling.

Renee was last. She removed a leather necklace and placed it around Minh's neck, and hugged the heroic young man goodbye. Just as the two parted, the world detonated in a simultaneous explosion of light and sound that, in those few nanoseconds convinced each of them that they surely were about to die, if they weren't already dead, for they had been shot, or collectively, blown up. They were paralyzed, ears roared, internal organs swelled, hearts stopped. Their brains crackled and buzzed, then went numb. In a fleeting flash the Waterboys believed the *Lena's* engine had exploded. Kevin thought he'd been shot, the sailor thought they'd been taken out by a tank, or rocket, or torpedo. Only Renee got it right, for she was the only one facing in the right direction. She saw the lightning bolt explode out of the marsh, not 20 yards away, and climb into the sky at the same time as the explosion.

They stood there in the tempest, staring at each other, unable to speak, their mouths wouldn't work, their minds cooked. The water around them fizzed and bubbled.   They were anesthetized, temporarily paralyzed, till Minh looked through the driving rain, back at each crewman one more time, then climbed over the side, ran his hand affectionately along the hull of the *Lucky Lena*, and walked ashore towards Clayton, into Canada.

CHAPTER 13

The Wheelhouse

One thing Kevin Casey confirmed while spending the past few days immersed in the Waterboys' water world was that these guys knew what they were doing when it came to all things nautical. They knew everything about the waterways they lived on and the ways of those waters. They read the books and knew the charts, knew the depths, bars, shoals, and seaweed beds, where the deadheads were, the wrecks and hazards. They knew all about the weather and how it affected the waterways and how those waters affected that weather. They knew how to deal with the multitude of ever changing situations that arise cruising those waters, night and day, rain or shine, fog, high wind, choppy waters, currents, dangerous rollers and whirlpools. And they knew the boats they went to sea in. Every inch of them, how they were built and the engines that drove them. They diagnosed problems almost instantly and knew the quickest way to fix them. They were masters of the jerry-rig. They showed great respect for the water and rarely placed themselves in dangerous situations. They knew what they were doing.

They also knew that some who plied the same waters had no freaking idea what they were doing. Often venturing onto the water clueless, motoring about as if driving a car on shore, confusing traffic rules of the road with ways of the water, or not knowing the rules at all. That combined with a total lack of awareness of weather conditions and mother nature's tendencies put many boaters in dangerous situations, sometimes escaping without even knowing it, oblivious to the dangers surrounding them. And even though these fools often provided the Waterboys with entertaining moments; jumping off boats and missing the dock, splashing into the water; or docking as if in a car, way too fast, and crashing into a dock, sometimes launching crewmembers overboard, if lucky into the water, or if not, onto a splintered dock; motoring along a shoreline, too close, waving to folks ashore, as they clipped the lines of irate fisherman; running out of gas; racing along, oblivious to buoys and running aground; starting up an outboard motor, revving it, turning it hard, and watching it drop off the transom and spin, churning in the water till it disappeared on its way to the bottom; dragging anchor lines and entwining with others; approaching a beach too fast, running aground, then throwing the anchor overboard. More times than they wished to count, these events forced the Waterboys, out of compassion, to come to the rescue of wayward boaters.

However, there was no humor in the fact that these amateurs were not limited to weekenders and part-timers. At times designated officers of the law hit the waters with the same reckless cluelessness as the innocent travelers. Empowered by a uniform and badge, received after a boating class ashore, and God forbid, a gun, these 'save the world' warriors patrolled the waterways, usually on weekends imposing their newly gained power on any poor souls unlucky enough to drift across their path, often creating situations out of nothing with their unnecessary confrontations. Auxiliary sheriff or Coast Guard patrols, burning through government gas, powering up and down the waterways in their officially marked boats, breaking the same rules they were supposed to be enforcing. Even the official Coast Guard, with their crews of kids from Kansas, could occasionally annoy with over the top search and seizures. However, the Waterboys surely never confused the real guard with the rent-a-guards. They had a long standing, strong respect for the Guard, for they were the real deal, who had come to the aid of the *Lena* when needed, and countless others, and generally left the Waterboys alone, which was a good thing on rumrunning nights, but the part time patrollers were a pain in the ass, and that's exactly who the *Lucky Lena* encountered when they slipped from the marshes back into the Big Bassett.

"Holy Shit," Whitey exclaimed. "I don't believe this."

"What's up?" Jeff inquired from the back bench seat.

"We got company," Whitey barked as he pulled back on the throttle and leaned forward to peer through the windshield, "And I think it's those idiots we ran into before."

"Who?" Jeff asked as he jumped up to stand at the side rail.

"You know," Whitey hollered. "Those dicks in the $300 boat with the $3,000 radar."

"Are you shitting me?" Jeff hollered as he moved around the engine box to the starboard side rail. By the time he observed the cruiser through the fog and diminishing light Whitey had already spun the wheel hard to starboard. The cruiser, about the same size as the *Lena* but sporting a tower of electronic equipment and lights so large it gave the boat a comically top heavy look, was moving downstream and in seconds the two passed in the narrow channel.

The crew of the patrol boat, members of the Canadian Coast guard Auxiliary, may have been more startled then the Waterboys, as it took them a while to react, as it appeared all were tucked into the enclosed steering station or below in the cabin, sheltering from the recent storm.

"Maybe they didn't see us," Jeff stated.

"They had to, we passed within 15 yards of em," Whitey answered.

"Yeah, I know, but our lights are off, right?"

"Yes."

"Well, it's dark, their windows are probably fogged, and, you know...... they're idiots," from Jeff.

"Yeah, they're probably having a few beers," Whitey laughed.

"Ha, and rigging their gear gettin' ready to fish. Why else would they be way the hell down here?"

The moment the words escaped Jeff's mouth he and Whitey had the same, trembling thought, 'why are they way down here in the

Flats?' The last time they encountered these fools it was 30 miles upstream, much closer to their home base.

Whitey turned and looked directly at the Captain and with no command needed slammed the *Lena's* throttle forward, the engine roared to life, the stern dug deep into the calm water and in moments the *Lena* rose on plane, and raced up stream, lights out, into the dark, damp, descending night.

By the time Jeff turned to check, the patrol boat reacted, and though they may not have known it was the *Lena* and the Waterboys, they knew someone had passed them and was now fleeing, with lights out.

Instantly, they were back in the thick of it, snapped from the solitude of the past half-hour or so spent in quiet reflection, after the lightning explosion deadened their senses and the sad farewell of Minh's departure. They'd waited silently at the drop-off point, waiting as the storm dissipated, the rain gradually stopping, the heavy saturation transforming into a layer of fog building over the marsh, the only sound the *Lucky Lena's* idling engine tapping rhythmically along, the exhaust spitting in time. Clayton had emerged from the bushes ashore, pushed the *Lena* off the beach and hopped into his fishing boat, gave a wave and headed north, disappearing in the reeds. Whitey had turned the *Lena* about and headed west, retracing the route of their arrival. Each member of the crew rode silently with thoughts of what had transpired, each still partially traumatized by the electrical explosion from the heavens, till they reached the channel. The Waterboys usually headed south into Lake St. Clair when exiting the Flats, to avoid retracing their route when possible, but that all changed, with the appearance of the auxiliary cop boat and its self anointed, save the world posse.

Kevin and Renee, who had gone below to warm up and make a pot of fresh coffee, stumbled back on deck, struggling to maintain their balance.

"What's going on?" Kevin shouted.

"We've got company," Whitey replied with a nod of the head toward the pursuing craft.

Kevin looked over the stern of the flying *Lena* and couldn't make out much until they were hit by a burst of blinding, white light emanating from the chasing cruiser.

"Who the hell is that?" Kevin barked, shading his eyes from the spotlights with his forearm.

"It's the Auxiliary Coast Guard," Jeff stated.

"What?" Kevin shouted above the engine noise, "The Coast Guard?"

"The weekend boys, not the real Guard," Whitey said.

"Canadian's," Jeff added.

"What the hell, are they chasing us?" Kevin hollered, panic growing in his voice.

"It appears that way," Whitey calmly replied with a glance over his shoulder.

"What the hell for?" from Kevin.

"Not sure," Captain Jeff stated, "just on routine patrol, or fishing, or," he paused.

"Or what?"

"Or, there's maybe a slight chance they were down here looking for someone."

"What, looking for us?" Kevin exclaimed.

"Us, or someone, anyone."

"For Minh?"

"I don't know, Minh, fisherman without licenses, rumrunners, I don't know." Jeff answered.

"This is great," Kevin moaned. "This is just fucking great. Why did we split, take off? Couldn't we just talk to 'em? Minh is gone, there's nothing aboard is there? Booze, smokes, anything, is there?"

Jeff replied in the negative.

"Then why are we running?"

Jeff remained silent.

"I took off, it was my call," Whitey stated from his spot at the wheel. "We don't want to be hassled again by these ass holes, plus," with another look over his shoulder into the bright lights of their pursuers barked," they'll never catch us!"

"What do you mean again?" from Kevin.

The Captain interjected with a quick synopsis of the *Lena's* previous run in with the patrol boat, how on a sunny, weekend day, with the Waterboys anchored on the middle ground with a few friends, having a few beers, minding their own business, this boat charged down river, cut dangerously across the sand bar and pulled alongside, way too fast, almost cutting their anchor line, and causing enough wake to throw people on the *Lena* from deck chairs, spilling their beers. The crew of the gung-ho patrol boat, identified themselves, and stated they had gotten a report of an overcrowded boat, on or near the middle ground. The Waterboys informed them that they had seen such a craft, an 18' bow rider with about 18 people on board heading over the middle ground, down river, and that they even commented on their possible impending peril, but it certainly wasn't the *Lena* they were looking for. After a moment of discussion amongst themselves the posse announced they were coming aboard.

I said, "No way, buddy."

They replied that they were coming alongside.

I told them they couldn't, that they had no jurisdiction because they were in American waters.

"Ha, that's right, now tell 'em what you said next," Whitey laughed.

"Well," the Captain paused.

"Go on," Whitey shouted.

"Well, something like, hey Dudley Do-Right, keep that piece of shit away from us, I don't want you digging up my side hull, and with that we fired up the *Lucky Lena,* pulled anchor, and motored away, rising to serenade the warriors with a few verses of "Oh, Canada," and headed for the Pine River, a good day ruined."

"Is it the same guys?" Kevin inquired.

"Same boat, not sure about the crew, but we're not sticking around to find out," Whitey said.

"Those damn lights," Kevin wailed, squinting.

"Don't worry about those lights," Whitey shouted. "They're doing me a favor, showin' me the way."

"Can we out run them?" Renee coolly asked.

"We just need to get to U.S. waters, like I said, they have no jurisdiction there," Jeff stated.

"Can we?" Renee inquired.

"No problem," Whitey said reassuringly with a smile. "Like the Captain likes to say, this is no big deal."

While Kevin was unnerved by the reckless run up the channel in the fog shrouded darkness, Renee was excited, full of adrenalin, Jeff was used to it, and for Whitey at the wheel, it really was no big deal, how dangerous could it be, compared to other escapes through other deltas? This sudden escape through a marsh with night descending and lights out was similar to the many he made a decade or so earlier in the marshes of the Mekong Delta in Vietnam, while on patrol, carrying out missions that amounted to little more than trying to stay alive. All except for the being shot at part, at least so far. He was a gunner who became wheelsman when the trained one was killed. He often ran the marshes at night, at the wheel, racing gauntlets of lights bursting with gunfire and explosions, the pings of ricochets bouncing around the boat. His buddies loved Whitey being at the helm, for while all were engulfed by the adrenalin driven collective insanity of the firefights, he had the ability to punch that throttle forward, and roar headlong into the madness, into the darkness. He steered by feel, as they zigzagged through the insanity, always just missing the many objects of their demise. He had the proven ability to bring them back to the dock, time after time. No matter who the Captain ordered to the helm, the crew refused to depart unless Whitey was at the wheel. For Tom, this escape was a small taste of the once powerful rush he experienced in that previous life, a dangerous, reckless, run up the channel in the fog shrouded darkness, but it certainly was no big deal. Another certainty was whoever was at the wheel of the perusing patrol boat, they didn't have the skill, the wisdom, or the balls of Tom White.

225

"This is madness," Kevin hollered, squinting into the spotlight of the chasing boat.

"This is so cool," Renee stated calmly.

"No," Kevin protested, "this is fucking crazy, and may I add, totally unnecessary."

"What?" from Renee

The *Lena* rounded a bend in the channel leaving the pursuers behind, returning the wheelhouse to darkness.

"This chase wouldn't even be happening, we wouldn't even be here if we'd just left Minh back at the Willows, he'd be O.K. there," Kevin stated.

"But he wanted to go to Toronto," Renee replied.

"Well," Kevin stumbled for something to say, "At least he'd be in the States."

"But his people, his family, are in Toronto. He wanted to go there," Renee responded with annoyance.

The patrol boat rounded the bend and after a short scan of the marsh the spotlight found the *Lena* again, flooding the back deck and wheel house with white light.

"Shit," Kevin spit as he squinted into the light again.

"Would you relax," Captain Jeff barked at Kevin. "We are gaining separation. We are starting to pull away," then added, "What did you mean by at least he'd be in the States?"

"I don't know," from Kevin, "You know, he'd be in America, isn't that where everyone wants to be?"

"Ha, I don't know," Jeff laughed with a glance toward Whitey, "do they?"

Whitey recognized immediately where the Captain was headed with that question. It was time for the great American - Canadian debate, usually held with Gord and Billy aboard to represent the great white north, but in this case Jeff would play that role, which was fitting, as he was considered by many to be an American hoser.

"I guess so," Kevin stammered. "I think so. You're an American, right?"

226

"Sure," Jeff replied, "But that doesn't mean everyone else wants to be one," then glanced Whitey's way.

"They should," Whitey stated on cue, then followed with a, "USA, we're number one."

All on board looked at Whitey, Jeff thinking he may have overplayed his hand too quickly added, "Ha, number one? What, everything's reduced to a football game, or sporting event?"

"Well, all's I know is without the U.S. there'd be no Canada," Whitey bellowed, going straight for the long bomb.

"What?" Jeff barked. "There always was, and always will be a Canada, a great place."

"True, but it's no America." Whitey replied.

"What, home of the brave, land of the free?"

"Sure, that's it!"

"Ha, that's Canada too."

"Yes, but without America, who would protect you?"

"We watch out for ourselves, plus," Captain Jeff added, now flush with pride of a Canadian, "we don't need protection, people around the world love us. Nobody hates us."

"Yeah?" Whitey barked.

"Yeah, not like you guys, always bombing the shit out of someone, always on a crusade, telling folks who don't want to hear it, what they should believe in, how to live their lives. Always trying to run the world, always on a crusade, always marching to some war beat you created."

"Oh yeah," Whitey shouted, "The world needs a protector, and it's us, plus," he paused to check on the perusing patrol.

"Plus what?" the Captain inquired.

"Well, plus America created all the great stuff."

"What?" Jeff laughed, "like what?"

"You know, cars, movies, jazz, TV, freedom, Chris-Craft's."

"Yeah?"

"Yes, and important stuff, like Rock-and-roll."

227

"You bastards are crazy," Kevin interrupted with a glance over his shoulder. "What the hell are you talking about? What the hell are you doing? What are we doing?"

"Go on," Renee smiled, "I like this."

"Yeah," the Captain paused then shot back at Whitey, "Well Canada has better beer and invented hockey, what could top that?"

"Touché," Whitey yelled with a laugh.

"Good one," Renee' added with a smile.

Kevin wasn't amused as he turned again to search in the darkness for the perusing patrol boat before barking, "What are you talking about? This is bullshit."

"Ah man, relax, were just playin' with you," The Captain said. "It's all good, Canadian - American, it doesn't matter, because around these parts the common denominator is we're all Lakers, Great Lakers. You see a line running down the middle of the river, or across the lake? There are no borders, we're all Lakers first and foremost, who just happen to live on opposite shores."

"That's right," Whitey laughed, "kinda boaters without borders."

The Waterboys' little faux debate helped take Kevin and Renee's attention off the pursuers, at least Renee's, and lightened the tension of the chase through the final few bends of the channel. By the time the *Lucky Lena* emerged from the head of the Big Bassett channel they had left the patrol boat behind. They entered the St. Clair River, put on the running lights and turned to port, heading for the American side of the waterway. The fog that laid heavy in the marsh began to dissipate over the open water of the river, yet they continued to race through occasional patches, temporarily blinding the crew. The first fog bank they entered appeared from nowhere engulfing the *Lena*. Whitey never slowed even though visibility was near zero. Just as Kevin was about to holler an order to slow they emerged, as quickly as they had entered. Pin-pricks of light from a few boats appeared through the darkness, a burst of red light from a channel buoy flashed momentarily in the distance off the starboard bow, and a string of deck lights from an up bound freighter emerged off their port beam. Whitey turned the wheel slowly, starting a long arc to starboard, heading the *Lena* between the two without changing speed. Shortly after another grey wall atop the water appeared before them and suddenly they were engulfed by another bank of fog, this one larger and heavier, causing Whitey to pull back on the throttle, slowing the cruiser. Moments later they burst into the open expanse of the river again, the flashing buoy light now 90 degrees off their starboard side and the lights of the freighter left behind.

"We should be good," Whitey announced upon emergence from the second bank of fog, "we're back in U.S. waters now."

"Thank God," Kevin exhaled.

A quick survey by the crew found the *Lucky Lena* much closer to the Michigan side of the river with shore lights visible through breaks in the haze. Whitey pulled further back on the throttle beginning a steady, comfortable, run up river.

"Well Kev my friend, you can relax now, all is good," Jeff Waters announced.

Kevin turned to look at the Captain and inquired, "Yeah, you sure? I've heard that before."

"Yup," and with a slap on Kevin's shoulder smiled and added, "Not only that but we are taking you back to the Inn 'cause this adventure is over. As a matter of fact this crazy weekend is over, and besides, Whitey and I got to be to work sometime today, right Tom?"

"That's right," Whitey added, turning to face the two, one hand on the ships wheel. "And may I add it's been great having you aboard. It was like the old days, eh? I mean I know we busted your balls a little, but…"

"A little?" Kevin interrupted, at which the Waterboys laughed in unison.

"Well, maybe more than a little, but believe me, a lot of what happened was, you know, spur of the moment, shit just kept happening, and you, and Renee here, were just in the, you know, the middle of it all, right Jeff?"

"That's right."

"And, my man," The Captain said addressing Kevin, "like I said before, wasn't this more fun than covering that boat show, I mean those boats are great and all, but wasn't this more fun? And you got your pictures and all, got what you needed, right?"

"Yes, I did."

"And," Renee added with a smile, "Those shots back there, after the storm, down in the marsh, they have to be awesome."

"Yeah, I hope so."

"So there you are," the Captain added. "Not only your boat shots but your art shots, what could be better eh?"

"Well, I'm not done yet, I have to finish the article and get it in, and," he paused as the anxiety that accompanied him to some degree ever since he ran into the Waterboys on the dock of the restaurant bubbled up again.

"Don't sweat it man," Captain Jeff added, "we're headed back now. You'll finish it. You have it all done in your head, right? And in a few hours it will be finished."

"I guess so," from Kevin.

"That's right and it will be great," Renee added as she stepped toward Kevin and placed her arm around his waist.

"Yeah, and I want a copy of that magazine when it comes out," Whitey stated.

"Damn straight, and a free one," from Jeff bringing laughter from all.

"Say, Kev, here, why don't you take the wheel?" Whitey announced as he stepped back from the steering station.

"What?"

"Sure," Captain Jeff added, "That's a great idea. You've done well these past few days, very well I may add. You're boating skills sure came back to you in a hurry this weekend haven't they?"

"Yeah, I guess so."

"They sure as shit have," Whitey smiled, "and you've done everything but steer, so here, grab this wheel and bring us home."

"Oh, I don't know."

"Do it man," Captain Jeff ordered, "put your hands on the wheel, feel the *Lena* in your hands, her vibration, the way she moves, the way she handles, yes, feel the way she feels."

Kevin looked at Whitey who nodded, at a smiling Renee, and back at Jeff who barked, "Go on man, she's beginning to swing."

So Kevin stepped up and placed both hands on the ships wheel and quickly discovered the Captain was right. The vibration of the cruiser, from the pulsating engine, to the spinning shaft, to the quivering of the canvas top and the rattle of the cabin door could be felt through the wheel. Kevin tightened his grip and leaned forward to glare through the windshield. He knew they'd just passed the channel marker off the starboard side, so they were good on that side and the Michigan shore was off the port side, so he was on the lookout for other boat traffic. He felt the steering, reacted to the heavy cruisers drifts and shifts on the ever-changing waves and currents of the river, quickly learning, then remembering to compensate for the *Lena's* response time. He searched in all directions again, forward, aft, port and starboard, and then again.

"We're good man," Whitey said from his seat opposite the steering station, "Once a Waterboy always a Waterboy, right?"

"Yeah," Kevin replied with mounting enthusiasm as he grew more comfortable at the wheel. Memories of the days and evenings steering the boats of his youth returned, and the Waterboys were right, he had quickly remembered the ways of the water, of the boat, and had promptly become a competent helmsman again.

They rode in silence for some time up the river, in the darkness, headed for home, with Kevin at the wheel before he again surveyed the river in all directions. As he looked past the light on the stern flag pole for any boat coming up from behind his eyes lowered to find Captain Jeff and Renee seated together on the back-bench seat. Earlier, when caught up in the moment of piloting the *Lena*, he'd

231

thought nothing of it, but now the gained confidence in his performance gave his mind time to wander, and off it went. Straight to; no wonder he wanted me to steer, so he could be with her. Yes, he felt the vibration of the cruiser through the wheel, the way she handles, the way she moves, but he'd rather feel that of Renee, not *Lena*, as the Captain was, then Kevin turned again to see Jeff with his arm around her, both smiling, both laughing. He turned back to stare through the windshield, with less interest then before, wondering what they were laughing about, talking about.

What the two were talking about was the Captain involving her in the river run to the marsh, without mentioning the delivery of Minh part, and how pissed off Kevin had seemed about it. And in general, what a wild and wonderful, and crazy weekend it had been, with Renee expressing it was just what she'd needed, and not giving a shit what happened, and the Captain agreeing to all she said while trying to convince her into talking her father into keeping the *Captain Jack* in town, at least a few more days, knowing Kevin would probably be leaving that day. Kevin heard none of their conversation, until the lovely Renee burst forth with laughter......

"Oh, I don't mind, this is great. I was kinda hoping it wouldn't end."

Shortly after, she got her wish, it wasn't about to end, for out of nowhere a bright light exploded, destroying the darkness, then swept across the *Lena*. It was another spot light, from a boat behind them. The bright beam shot out across the river and swung back over the cruiser before settling on the back deck, engulfing the crew in white light.

CHAPTER 14

Navigating with Interest

"What the hell's that?" Kevin hollered.

"A spot light, a goddamn spot light. What does it look like?" Jeff responded, obviously annoyed.

"I mean, who the hell is it?" from Kevin.

"I don't know," Jeff said, an edge building in his voice.

"Out of the way Kev, let me in there," Whitey ordered as he stepped across the deck to take over at the steering station.

"Is that the same boat? Are those the same guys from earlier?" Renee inquired.

"I don't think so," Whitey replied. "But what I do know is I'm getting a damn stiff neck from looking over my shoulder all night."

"It shouldn't be those idiots," from the Captain now staring past the stern into the light. "We're obviously in U.S. waters."

"Maybe they radioed ahead," Whitey suggested.

"Probably," Jeff said.

"Well, let's get out of here," Whitey shouted as he jammed the throttle forward, the engine roaring to life, the crew shifting on deck to gain new balance as the cruiser dug deep into the water.

So once again the *Lucky Lena* and her crew were off, racing up the Big River, roaring into the dark yonder, pushing the unknown, pursued by some boat manned by an unknown crew bent on chasing them down, and that couldn't bode well. As on past river escapades over the weekend, Kevin, though growing accustomed to such insanity wasn't happy, "This is so fucked," he yelled into the eye of the search light. He knew when he first made plans to return home he'd eventually run into the old gang, was even going to try to hook up with them at some point, but had no idea what was in store. Ever since their chance meeting on the dock of the restaurant things had gotten crazier and more out of control as the weekend wore on, and now, it had all become too much, he was following these madmen over the edge, lunacy at a new level, beyond the pale, yet he found himself accepting this fate, resigned to the crazy ride, somehow unable to stop. He couldn't abandon ship, he'd been pulled in by the excitement, drawn to the adventure and engulfed by the aura of Renee and, because of her there would be no turning back.

As for Renee, she tilted her head back and yelled into the night sky, "This is great," for she was truly thrilled. Her dreams of some new adventures in her life were coming true. Since meeting the Waterboys, including Kevin and Minh, she'd exploded with life. She had become a commanding presence in their company, and long periods of drifting aimlessly, filled with anxiety and trepidation, had been released with the force of a freighter's great horn that burst forth across the water. Any tension with what was going down with her father, after their loss of the women who had been the anchoring force in their lives, had all turned for the better in the past few days. Her dad even seemed to like the Waterboys, like sons he'd never had, and enjoyed their company, and liked the way they loved the river, the lakes, the freighters and reveled in the world of old wooden boats. She wasn't sure, but she thought he may even have a sliver of admiration for their piracy, if he ever found out, maybe.

The Waterboys were now the anxious ones. Without saying much, they both knew they were most assuredly being chased by U.S. authorities, and that the Canadian patrol had called ahead, and it undoubtedly was about Minh, and now they were running till they came up with something better.

"What we need now is another fog bank," Renee shouted from her place along the side rail.

"No shit, that would be awesome," Whitey replied as he turned again to look at the search light. "We aren't gaining any separation yet."

"Whitey!" Jeff warned. That's all he got out as he stared through the windshield. By the time Whitey turned his head, a fishing boat flashed into view not more than 10 yards off their port side as they roared past, then was sent rocking by the *Lena's* wake. The lone fisherman, drifting in the darkness, startled by the near miss, raised an arm in defiance, then disappeared off the *Lena's* stern.

"Holy Crap," Renee hollered, "That was close."

"Too close." The Captain said.

"I never saw him," Whitey conceded.

"He had no light on, or it was so dim, shit, idiot," Jeff stammered, "We would have crushed him."

The crew squeezed behind the bulkhead staring into the darkness, searching the river, the beam of the trailing search light providing occasional assistance in finding their way as it scanned the water.

"Where are we?" Kevin inquired. "Are we anywhere near the boat house, Clay's boathouse, can we get there?"

The Waterboys turned and stared at Kevin before the Captain stated, "We're past there, and no, we can't go there. Why would we lead them there?"

"I don't know, I'm just wondering …."

"Well don't," Jeff barked his anxiety showing.

"Looks like they're closing the gap," Whitey stated after another look over his shoulder.

"There's another fishing boat, or two, maybe three," Renee shouted from her spot at the bulkhead.

"See 'em?" From the Captain.

"Yup, got 'em," Whitey replied as he began a course that swung the cruiser port, towards shore, to avoid a string of bobbing, white lights. He cut perilously close to the docks that extend from the shoreline, avoiding the group of fishing boats, never slowing.

"Ha, they must be bitin' here, look at all those lucky bastards," Whitey hollered, "They're catching all the goddamn fish."

He positioned the *Lucky Lena* between the line of docks and small fleet of drifting fishing boats, guided by the single white lights

235

of their stern poles. He never backed off on the throttle. All aboard knew the reckless danger they were putting themselves, and others in, but they had faith, blind faith, in the man at the wheel. Whitey's only concern was the shit he was dumping on his fellow fishing mates, throwing a serious wake at them as he ran through the fleet like a yahoo, the kind they always cursed. As they moved north, away from the fisherman it appeared they'd gained some distance from their pursuers but not enough, for after a short scan of the river, they were again hit by the spotlight.

The chase continued up river in silence, all scanning the water, the outcome still a mystery, until they rounded a bend just south of the rapids where Renee's continued cosmic, wishes come true, aura bending effect on the *Lucky Lena* and crew manifested again as another fog bank suddenly appeared.

"Wow, look at that," Kevin exclaimed.

Whitey and the Captain could only stare, Renee just smiled, and each thought about the luck of catching another break, but not for long, for things were happening way to fast. They collectively, silently, submitted to the good fortune of their fate, deciding to ride the magic to whatever lay ahead inside the fog bank.

Moments before entering the wall of fog they held their breath in anticipation, for surely hitting a wall of anything this large and ominous, at the speed they were traveling, would produce some kind of collision effect, a bounce, a split in the fog, a sound, something, but nothing happened, like the Waterboys knew, only the strangeness of the event.

Once inside the Captain gave the order to slow.

"You sure?" Whitey asked.

"Yeah, I'm sure. This is a pea-souper."

Whitey complied, pulled back on the throttle and in moments the roar and speed morphed into the subtle clicking of the *Lena's* idling engine as they slowed. Their ears hummed as they adjusted to the sudden stillness as they drifted to a crawl, carrying just enough speed to work upstream against the current, totally engulfed in fog.

"Visibility is only 20 feet," Captain Jeff stated.

"If that," Tom White replied.

They could hear the *Lena* slicing through the water. The air was heavy, saturated inside the cloud that sat atop the river.

"I can't see a thing," Kevin said as he turned in all directions.

"This is pretty creepy. Have you seen it like this before?" Renee inquired of the Wateboys.

"A few times," The Captain said. "But usually we try to avoid these."

"What now?" Kevin inquired.

"We wait," from Jeff.

"For what?"

"For this to clear and then we'll get out of here. But this is good," he paused as he scanned the river over the back deck, "Yes, this is real good. There's no way that patrol will find us now."

"How do we get out of this stuff?" Kevin inquired.

"We'll motor ahead slowly, keep our eyes and ears open, and wait it out, as long as we have to. We can't see shit so we have to listen our way through this, listen real hard," the Captain said.

"We'll need someone on the bow," Whitey added.

"Kevin."

"What?"

"On the bow," the Captain ordered.

"What?" Kevin repeated."

"Get out there on the bow and listen."

"For what?"

"For everything, boats moving through the water, waves, horns, motor noise, anything. You'll hear something before you see anything."

"Go ahead man," Whitey stated. "You were out there the other night, you found Minh."

"That's right," Jeff added. "This is nothing compared to that."

"Look, there's something, a light I think," Renee announced.

The crew looked over the stern to a large circle of distorted light moving through the haze. It reminded Kevin of the first night out with the Waterboys, shore lights in the fog, but this was moving all over the place, back and forth, up and down, disappearing, returning, brighter and dimmer.

"Think that's the patrol?" Whitey inquired.

"Probably," from the Captain, "Let's be goin'."

"Get up on the damn bow," Whitey announced.

"Let's go," Renee said to Kevin, "I'll go with you."

The two entered the cabin, climbed through the hatch and sat on the damp cabin top. Kevin was back on the bow of the *Lena*, at night, like the night they pulled Minh form the river, but this time immersed in a cloud, and engulfed in a bone chilling dampness. Kevin shook like a dog drying off. Noticing, Renee moved closer and placed her hand on his knee. When she leaned over and kissed him on the cheek the cold sogginess that consumed him disappeared.

"Hey, pay attention up there," the Captain barked. "Keep your ears open, you'll hear another boat before you see their lights."

Kevin and Renee turned to scan the river but with visibility limited to a few yards they turned their heads and tuned their ears to hear water slapping the bow and running down the hull, outboard motors in the distance, along with other indistinguishable sounds hidden in the deep, mysterious thickness.

"Hey," the Captain yelled again through the open windshield, "Move, we can't see through you. Kevin, you take the port side, Renee the other, and pay attention."

"O.K, you're the Captain," Renee replied, complying with Jeff's orders as they set up on opposite sides of the cabin top. Kevin wondered about the order. What could they be blocking? No one could see shit. He also wondered if Renee would do anything the Captain ordered her to do.

The crew fell into a time vacuum, not sure how long they scanned the waters, Captain Jeff off the stern, Kevin and Renee the bow, port and starboard sides respectively, and Whitey at the wheel. The distorted light of the pursuing patrol boat appeared with less regularity.

They listened and watched till their ears buzzed and heads ached. They heard a few boats in the far distance but nothing came close. They saw nothing in the fog cloud. So far so good, except for the spot light, that damn spotlight that kept appearing and suddenly seemed to be getting closer. Gradually the *Lucky Lena* began to rise and fall in the bow. Kevin and Renee seated on the cabin top noticed first. The cruiser began rolling side to side on ever increasing waves. Was it a wake Kevin wondered and if so where was the boat that made it? Again, the probing search light appeared off the stern, this time port side, and noticeably closer. As the two bow riders tracked the probing light the pursuing boat suddenly appeared out of nowhere. Instantly, the fog cleared and there it was, the patrol boat was right there, in the clear. Just as Renee shouted toward the wheel house Whitey hit the throttle and yelled, "Hold on."

The bow rose tossing Kevin and Renee back against the windshield where they grappled for hand holds on the cabin top rails and each other. The patrol boat search light nailed the *Lena* with a direct hit of blinding light and turned to starboard to close the distance.

"Shit," Kevin barked, "This is it."

Suddenly the light moved away to train its beam ahead, across the water, into the distance. Kevin and Rene followed the path of the light and turned forward just as the *Lena* planed off, and as the bow lowered saw what the patrol boat had, another hill of fog. The patrol boat veered sharply to port disappearing in the bank. Moments later the *Lena* followed, slowing as the cloud thickened. Rollers on the bow continued to increase.

"Where are these waves comin' from?" Kevin yelled.

"Not sure," Renee replied.

"Got to be from a boat."

"Yes."

The two bow riders didn't have to wait for an answer as they emerged from the fog again to see the stern of a ship looming ahead. A very large ship, a freighter, and the *Lena* began rocking and rolling on her wake. A stream of steam appeared from near the top of her huge stack and moments later a blast of sound filled the river.

"Shit," Kevin shouted.

"Wow," from Renee.

Whitey wheeled the *Lena* further to starboard and increased her speed. The cruiser rose and dove on the ships wake. Kevin and Renee held tight as they bounced around the cabin top. As they gained on the ship, approaching her starboard side they noticed she was a salty, like Minh's. Another fog bank appeared. The ships horn blasted again. The bow riders felt the vibration run through the cabin top. They wanted off the deck, bad, but could only cling tight to the hand rails. The fog thickened and suddenly the ship disappeared from sight. They knew she was there, not 50 yards away, but saw nothing. The great horn blasted again.

"Shit," Kevin hollered again.

"Wow," Renee repeated.

The rolling slowed as they moved ahead, out of the stern wake, but waves from the bow were soon to follow. Bursts of clearness appeared as the ship moved in and out of the fog and the *Lena* rose and dove as she drove through its bow wake. Kevin took a quick glance at the freighter. She appeared to be a tanker. As they emerged from the cloud they found themselves just ahead of the freighter and clear of her bow wake. Kevin tried to make out the name on the freighters bow but his attention was grabbed by the sight of the patrol boat emerging from the other side of the ship, also racing up the river at top speed. Five short blasts from the freighter, the signal for danger, roared across the water. Whitey spun the wheel and pulled back on the throttle to tuck in behind the patrol boat as it raced across the path of the ship. The move left the *Lena* perilously close to the approaching ship, the ten-foot-high wall of water, pushed by the bow, roared at them, a collision eminent. Just past the last moment, Whitey slammed the throttle forward and the *Lucky Lena* dug deep with all she had. She didn't fail them. A good thing, for even one plug misfire, one cough from the suddenly flooded carburetor would have caused a hesitation, dooming the cruiser and her crew. As it was, they only cleared the danger with the help of surfing down the wall of water created by the ships massive bow. All aboard turned to look up, almost straight up, as the wall of black steel slid past off their stern. All stunned, all breathless.

"Wow," Whitey yelled, "How about that?"

The wheelsman's move had worked, to the point of buying some time as the Patrol boat didn't catch it at first, and by the time they reacted, another wall of fog filled the river. Five loud blasts from the ships horn erupted again, and again, till it sounded like ten in a row, and again till it was one continuous series of warning salutes echoing across the water.

Kevin and Renee looked at each other then made their move for the hatch cover, inching along the wet cabin top. They managed to get the cover open and Renee swung her legs around, and into the opening, sitting for a second on the edge, catching her balance as the *Lena* rolled, then dropped through, her feet resting on the bunks below, her head and arms top side. She held the hatch cover as Kevin made his move. Just as he leaned to swing his legs around the *Lena* rolled violently, Renee turned her head to see the cause, the patrol boat emerging from the fog dead ahead. When she looked back Kevin was gone, only his hand grasping the edge of the open hatch. She grabbed hold as he dangled over the side, feet dragging in the water. Renee struggled to keep hold, fought with all she had. They locked hold to each other's wrists. Kevin's weight pulled her half way out of the hatch, to the point they could see each other over the edge, eye to eye. Heavy fog again engulfed all and Whitey suddenly swung to starboard, accelerating, the move breaking their grip, and Kevin was overboard, all the way, in the drink. The last thing he saw was her hand reaching, fingers spread, straining.

Going down reminded him of jumping off docks as a youth, into the same river, how the underwater world always sounded so different, so mysterious, and how strange boats and their engines sounded, like the *Lena's* prop as it passed close by in the darkness, very close. He kept his eyes closed. He didn't know why, he always had. Habit, or the fear of not wanting to see what was going to hit him, or the ancient, large fish that was about to brush by. As he sunk deeper a low, guttural, moaning permeated the density of the river, followed by a deeper, throbbing sound. He remembered the freighter as he felt the displacement of water. At the bottom of his drop, for a moment, he accepted a fate that included returning to the river of his youth, passing through it to the next life, and thinking there were certainly worse ways to go, and that the Captain would surely get that. He also remembered going down deep into the river, like when jumping off tall pilings, the water getting colder the deeper he sunk and that being the time for the big leg kick that would start one's journey to the surface. That's what he did, with everything he had. Why? Instinct, or the vision of Renee's face, but he kicked a second time as well and reached his arms upward. There was always that other big unknown, how far was the surface and when will he reach it. In the daytime he could see the light, but even then judging the distance was difficult, at night, impossible. He hoped it would be soon, he kicked again, please hurry he thought. Another kick and his hand broke the surface but his head stopped just short. He panicked, kicked again and pulled with both arms, his head breaking the surface. He gulped air. The underwater silence was gone as sound exploded into a chaos of noise, splashing water and the continuous blast of the ships horn.

The bedlam around him came into focus as water ran from his face and he wiped his eyes, surprised his glasses had remained in place. To his left, upstream, he saw the freighter; he was adrift in its smooth after wake. He turned down stream to see a boat approaching, small cruiser, white hull, could that be the *Lena*, he hoped, prayed, and it was.

"Yes," Kevin yelled into the night as the *Lena* approached. He couldn't believe he surfaced right in front of her. His mind raced calculating the odds. He couldn't fathom his good fortune. He gulped more air and treaded water. Members of the *Lena's* crew couldn't believe it either.

"Holy shit man," Whitey barked over the side hull as the cruiser slid alongside. "Good timing buddy, you lucked out," he shouted as he leaned over with an outstretched hand.

"I can't believe it," Renee cried out as she appeared alongside Whitey then flung a ladder overboard almost striking Kevin. "Are you all right," she cried out.

"I can't believe it. I can't believe you went over, and here you are!"

Kevin saw their mouths moving but couldn't make out much of what they yelled for his ears were filled with water. What he started to make out was the ships horn still blasting across the water.

Renee hooked the ladder on the port side rail as Whitey leaned down, grabbed Kevin's wrist, and in one motion hauled him up. His feet scrambled to find the ladder steps and in the next motion landed on the *Lena's* back deck, spun and flopped onto the back bench.

"Oh Kev," Renee said as she sat and gave him a hug, "Are you O.K?"

Kevin didn't reply, or couldn't, or wasn't sure yet, if he was actually, O.K. What he did know was this wasn't the first-time Tom White had saved him.

The first was in junior high school, when Whitey stepped in to rescue him from a group of tough, high schoolers who threatened to kick Kevin's ass on a daily basis just because he accidently hit one in the head with a snowball. It had happened months earlier, in a mass snowball battle involving dozens, but somehow Kevin had been singled out, and he would pay. The day of reckoning didn't arrive till summer, on a warm, sticky night at the basketball courts outside the city pool, where the gang of toughs approached, picked Kevin out of a crowd, and announced it was time.

Kevin knew Tom White as a classmate, a star athlete popular with the girls, but not a close friend. Not close enough to call him Whitey. But there he was, emerging from the growing crowd of bystanders to intervene on Kevin's behalf. The challenges were tossed down, a time and place set, and all scattered peacefully into the night. Kevin's pals laughed, slapped him on the back, he had been saved.

Later that night while cruising the back roads of town with a friend's older brother, they found themselves on a stretch of dirt road brightened by a wide swath of light. They slowed, but there was no room to turn around. They cautiously approached to find 20 or more cars circled, headlights illuminating the center of the road, silhouettes of people moving in and out of the light, and in the middle two guys duking it out. As they slowly passed the combatants, never stopping, Kevin, wide eyed, peered out the back-seat window and saw Tom White land a right hook in his defense as they rolled by. Later, it became known Tom White had his own agenda with the guy, but for Kevin it forever was Tom saving him, and from that point on he was a good friend whom he called Whitey.

The second was the summer after high school, before he and his peers dispersed into the unknown; to school, or into the service, with a good chance of going to war, or getting a real job, or getting married, or both, or into the float zone, waiting for a path to appear. A diverse group of friends planned a road trip that took them to as far away as they could imagine, north, to the U.P., Michigan's Upper Peninsula. They spent one afternoon jumping off the cliffs of Presque Isle Park in Marquette, into the frigid summer waters of Lake Superior. At one point late in a day of partying, they explored the rugged shoreline, climbing the rock cliffs. A group that included Kevin found themselves on a rock outcrop a good fifty feet or more above the jagged, shore line, waves busting ashore. The only way across to reach a wider, safer path was a climb up, and over a promenade, a short distance of free climbing on the face of the rock. Others made it with relative ease. Kevin went last and the wait had given him time to think about the maneuver which caused his hesitation, at the wrong point, which led to his feet slipping off the rock, his weight pulling him from his hand hold. For a second he dropped, feet kicking, till a hand grabbed his arm. He looked up at a smiling Whitey.

The third was upon Whitey's return from the Vietnam War. He came back alive, while others from their small High School hadn't, but changed. He appeared gaunt and more reserved and had a faraway look in his eyes. However, he adjusted quickly, reverting to the Whitey his friends had remembered. He never talked about Nam and Kevin and the others never asked. Until one time, while sitting around a camp fire on an island in the middle of the river, after a long day and night of partying, out of nowhere, he just started talking and got it all off his chest. He described the horror of it all, in enough detail to make them frightened and ill to their stomachs, talked of the senselessness and meaninglessness of the missions he was sent on. Then he ordered those present, especially those about to be drafted due to low draft lottery numbers, which included Kevin and several others, not to go, no matter what. Do whatever necessary. Don't go. Go to Canada, its right there he pointed across the water. You'll be fighting for no cause. Only after you get there, when it's too late, will you realize you're only fighting for each other but that's all. Don't go. This from the toughest guy they knew.

And now, yanked from the river.

"Kevin, are you all right, can you hear me?" Renee inquired again with a worried voice. "I can't believe we found you. I thought that ship had run you over."

"Hell yes, he's O.K," Captain Jeff barked from his position at the wheel. "He's out of the drink, sitting there, he's just freaked out."

"Kevin?" Renee repeated.

"Yes, I'm O.K.," he said after a pause, then looked around at the crew and added, "Thanks to you guys, and especially you man," he said addressing Tom White, "Once again, you have saved my ass."

Renee responded with a hug for the shivering, soaking survivor.

"Hey, we're pretty good at pulling people from the river, eh?" Whitey stated, "Good thing we found you before that patrol boat."

"How did you know," Kevin mumbled. "How did you know where to be?"

"Oh, just lucky I guess," Whitey smiled. "Like everything else on this trip."

"It's 'cause they're the Waterboys," Renee stated emphatically, followed by a laugh.

"Well, we don't have time for this sentimental shit," the Captain shouted from the steering station. "We gotta get out of here, plus," he added stopping to peer through the wind shield as more fog filled the river.

"Plus what?" Whitey asked.

"These goddamn freighter horns are everywhere now, in freakin' stereo.

"Yeah," Whitey stated, turning.

"Yeah."

"Think there's another freighter?" Whitey inquired.

"Might be."

CHAPTER 15

Back of the Front

Red saw what the Waterboys couldn't, a second ship moving down river through breaks in the fog. He stood at a window in the back room of his great home overlooking the river. The room he loved. The place he and Whitey spent many hours.

It had been a long, rough night for Red. When Whitey dropped him off after a stellar but strenuous afternoon and evening of river runs culminating with the bender at Browns in the Flats, he'd made it as far as the couch, where he passed out. He never heard the scolding Rose covered him with, along with an afghan, yet he dreamt of her. Poor Rose, poor sweet Rose, always telling him to take it easy, take your medicine and stay away from those Waterboys, all that drinking and swearing, didn't he know he was too old, way too old to be behaving as he did when around them. The drinking, didn't he remember what his doctor said about the drinking, too much drinking, and swearing and drinking. She didn't understand him Red thought, and what the Waterboys were to him, that they lived the way he wished he'd done more of, that they cherished the river like him, that the retirement thing was boring, all's it gave him was empty time, time to think of what he'd missed. Time to think how it was going to end, the fear of being in a home, he couldn't imagine the Waterboys ending in a home. It was messed up, for he knew Rose was the greatest thing that ever happened to him, but he couldn't listen to her now, not now. His new job, his purpose in what was left of his life, was to stand sentry over the river, for he'd watched his beloved waterway change over the decades, for the worse, and how it was continuing, faster and faster, and he wasn't going to go down quietly. Someone needed to speak for the river, the way it was and the way it needed to be, or the entire, glorious system would be altered till it was unrecognizable, unusable and uninhabitable. He wasn't a crazy old man, he wasn't, and the Waterboys knew that. They understood what he said, and more importantly, they wanted to hear what he had to say.

Red was awakened by the continuous blasts of ship signals that rose up the hill on the warm, humid, post storm air and through the open windows. He was soaking wet with sweat, his heart pounded, and he gasped for breath. He gargled a call out for Rose as he pulled himself to a sitting position. He listened to the continuous blasts of the ships horns. What the hell he thought?

"Rose," he blurted again, but wasn't sure at what volume, "come down here."

He dragged himself to one of the large open windows and steadied himself with one arm placed head high on the frame. His squinting eyes adjusted and he caught his breath just as the down bound freighter came into view through a break in the fog. His mind cleared, the freighter blasts sounded, in stereo, from port and starboard, and he quickly realized exactly what was up; two ships were headed straight for each other, one up bound, and another coming down bound. It was just a matter of avoiding each other, would they? Ships passed each other in this stretch of the river, but rarely at night and never in these conditions. Maybe there was a mechanical error, loss of steering, loss of an engine, or an incompetent pilot or helmsman, but he doubted that.

"Rose, we could have a collision here," he shouted again, and as he focused on the down bound freighter added, "Well, I'll be, it's the *Grand Venture*, it's the goddamn *Grand Venture*, the Dukes water ship."

"Rose," he thought he yelled, he felt light headed, "It's the goddamn *Grand Venture*, that son-of-a-bitch has done it, he's loaded her up with fresh water from up north, sucked it out of the lake and now he's headin' for some goddamn desert. He's done it, that bastard is taking the water."

The cacophony of blasts coming from the two ships merged in Red's head, five at a time, continuously, 5-10-15-20, like some countdown to a game of hide-and-seek. He felt dizzy, his arm hurt.

Red saw Dukes freighter sliding slowly past his window through breaks in the fog, heard the blasts from its horn signaling eminent danger mixing with the warning salutes of the north bound tanker, and heard the agonizing grind of steel upon steel as the two collided. The low crushing sound ground on for what seemed an eternity in the dark, fog shrouded valley of the river, just south of Red's. When it finally ended, the ships horns, which had stopped during impact began anew, but with less distress, as if the crews knew it was too late. Eventually, Red observed the aft end of Duke's water ship swing out of a fog hill stopping just short of the dock line extending from shore. It was the last thing Red Holtz ever saw.

The last thing he ever heard was his own voice howling with laughter, at least he felt like he was laughing, as he lay upon the floor of his beloved back room. This was it, he thought, I'm done, but he was O.K with it, he was really all right with it. He was. He thought of Rose, where was she? Again, he was O.K. with it, with leaving her behind, alone, for he knew time would heal his passing, and with him gone she wouldn't have to deal with his stress inducing shenanigans any longer. It was all good. He went down on his beloved porch, on his beloved river, with his last visual a freighter, and it was the water robber's ship, and it would sink, ruining his crazed plan to siphon off water from the precious Great Lakes, the leakage of oil minimal, but enough to scare river lovers into action, and the final howls of laughter that filled his mind was knowing he was right.

The crew of the *Lucky Lena*, like most along the river, had heard, and felt the collision. Many residents a good distance from the river spoke of being awakened by the crash. After rescuing Kevin the *Lena* moved east, toward the safety of the middle ground, clear of the ship channel, and despite being on scene, the crew never witnessed it due to the fog. Like many, they'd been overwhelmed by the ships ceaseless warning blasts filling the night, followed by the frightening sound of grinding heavy metal. It was a sickening sound, so excruciating in length, the low decibel grind. A noise none of them had heard before and hopefully would never hear again.

They rode in silence, Whitey at the wheel, Captain Jeff at the port side rail, Kevin and Renee on the back bench. They were exhausted, drained, sucked dry of energy and emotion. The Captain kept glancing back in the direction of the wreck, as if repeated looks would somehow correct the distorted visual in the pre-dawn haze. Right after the collision, just after the horrific sound abated, he'd extolled the good fortune the crew of the *Lucky Lena* had been gifted, by the bad luck of the freighter crews, for in an instant, the patrol boat, and all other craft soon to arrive no longer would be looking for the them, and he was right.

Whitey, also aware of their luck, had time to run a wide arc around the scene, north, then down the shore line, squeezing by the dock line and the wreck. When they turned south, Red's boathouse appeared out of the fog, a solitary structure atop the water, its long dock connected to shore hidden in mist. As they drifted bye Whitey turned back, and as the boathouse disappeared again in the fog, wondered how Red was doing, then moments later, read the ships name while passing under the freighters grounded stern.

"Say," he wondered aloud, "Isn't that Dukes ship, the freakin' water boat?"

"Shit," I think your right," Jeff said staring up at the rounded hull.

After a short pause Whitey added, "That's kinda funny, don't you think?"

"Well actually," Jeff answered, "That's great. That guy was a dick. And this," he added looking back at the ship, "this is fuckin' great."

"Ha," Whitey laughed, "I'm sure Red will get a kick out of this. Yep, I can't wait to talk to Red, he'll be thrilled."

Dawn brightened the eastern horizon lighting up the back of the front as it moved away south and west. The rising sun began burning off fog from atop the river. The *Lucky Lena* continued downstream past the Inn, just south of the hulking wreck of the two freighters. The Dukes water ship sitting sideways, blocking the river, her nose pointing toward the middle ground and Canada, her stern aground along the Michigan dock line, a huge whole torn in her side. The tanker sat close to where the collision occurred, anchor dropped, nose blunted. A crowd of hotel guests, some in pajamas and bathrobes had gathered, gawking at the unfamiliar setting. Kevin, wrapped in a blanket, soaked and cold, sat staring straight ahead. He knew it was finally over, this floating folly, and they were headed in. Renee couldn't wait to tell her dad about it, at least most of it. Along the boardwalk, just past the Inn, town folks started to gather in the park, waiting for the fog to dissipate, to get a view of the ships lying still in the river.

"This is good here," the Captain suddenly barked, "bring her in here."

"Here?" Whitey inquired.

"Yeah, put her along the wall," from the Captain who turned to Kevin and asked, "This O.K. with you man?"

"Sure," Kevin replied, surprised that the time had actually arrived to go ashore for good and suddenly overwhelmed with emotions. He thought he had more time, thought they were headed for the Willows, he thought he had more time to collect his thoughts, what he'd do next, sort out his assignment, and Renee, what about Renee, was he saying goodbye, would he see her again he wondered? He mechanically rose from the damp seat, as if he had no control, dropped the blanket and stepped to the side rail as Whitey spun the wheel to starboard and brought the *Lena* alongside the boardwalk.

"Here you go man," Jeff announced as he held the cruiser off the wall.

Renee followed Kevin to the rail and as he stepped up and off the boat she turned him by the shoulder and gave him a quick kiss. "I'll talk to you soon, right?" she asked.

"Sure," he answered.

"You have my number, right?"

"Sure do," from Kevin.

"Don't forget to call," Renee smiled.

"I won't," Kevin replied.

"Take it easy man," Whitey shouted above the engine noise, "Let's do it again, it was real."

"Well, maybe," Kevin said, managing a smile.

"Come on man, what a trip, eh? At least now you have something to tell your landlubber pals when they ask you what you did over the weekend," he laughed from his place at the wheel.

"Ha, that's right Kev my boy," Captain Jeff smiled as the crew shared one last laugh.

Whitey was right, Kevin thought as he stepped up on the side hull and then off the *Lucky Lena*, it had been the wildest, craziest weekend he'd experienced since, well, since the last time he ran with these Waterboys years ago, and now he wondered if he really wanted it to end.

"Keep in touch" the Captain shouted then turned to Whitey and barked, "let's get out of here."

"Wait," Renee hollered, just as Whitey spun the wheel and started to slip the engine into gear.

"What?" from the Captain, "Wait, wait for what?"

"I want off too," Renee replied.

"What?" Captain Jeff repeated?

"I'm going with Kevin."

"What for, where?" Jeff inquired.

"I don't know," she answered looking at Kevin standing on the boardwalk. "But I'm going with him." Then she broke the uncomfortable pause that followed, turned to the Captain and added, "Because I want to move on and I know at this moment, Kevin is, and you're not, and probably won't, 'cause you'll never leave this river, your river, ever, she is your lady."

Before the Captain could say anything Renee turned and kissed him with a kiss he would never forget and climbed out of the boat. From the boardwalk Renee saluted as Whitey put the *Lena* in gear, turned from the break wall, and motored away, downstream. Whitey looked back, stepped from under the canvas and returned the salute, the Captain didn't.

Kevin and Renee walked the boardwalk in silence, the only ones not focusing on, or talking about the wreck. They strolled into the riverside entrance of the Inn as curious guests and onlookers pushed out. No one seemed to notice the wet, miserable looking guy, plodding through the lobby. They both had much to say but were too exhausted to get anything out. They were comfortably content in each other's silence.

Kevin bumbled around the hotel, literally; trying to get his land legs to work, realizing he'd spent little of the past three days ashore, as well as figuratively; struggling to organize his thoughts with a burnt out, frazzled mind. Renee, not as spaced out, walked him through the morning which passed in a curious day-dreamy kind of way. It was a resplendent, summer day when they headed for the marina; the previous night's post storm heat and saturation cleared away on the breath of dry, cool breezes out of the northwest, the result of the ever-changing weather patterns of the lakes. By the time they reached the harbor it was empty, the boat show over, and most town folk headed in their craft for the scene of the wreck. Renee's father was not on board the *Captain Jack*.

"What now?" Kevin wondered aloud.

"I'm not sure," Renee answered, looking about the empty docks. "But let's get out of here."

"What?" from Kevin.

"Let's go somewhere. Let's get out of here," she said. "I don't want to be 'round here anymore, not now. Let's split."

"Split, where to?"

"I don't know."

The two stood silently on the empty dock alongside the big Chris-Craft cruiser, heat building with the climbing, morning sun, sea gulls and their ever-present calls filling the skies.

"I know," Rene exclaimed, "Let's go to my Aunts."

"What? Where?" from Kevin.

"My aunt's, in Muskegon," Renee replied. "She has a little place there, in the dunes. My dad and I were headed there anyway. I'll just go a little early."

"In the boat?" Kevin wondered.

"No, no silly," Renee laughed. "We'll drive. We'll take your car."

Kevin just stared.

After a short pause, Renee went on. "Well, what do you think?"

"What about your dad?"

"I'll leave him a note, give him a call and hook up with him again later."

"Now?" Kevin replied, "Right now?"

"Sure, why not?"

Kevin started thinking of reasons not to go, they'd dropped his film in a mailbox on way to the harbor, but he still had to finish and send the article. Take his car she said, his car wasn't running that well and he had little money left, but one look in Renee's sparkling face, her magic eyes, and he replied the only way he could, and quickly, "Sure, why not."

They hit the road still rockin-n-rollin from the long days and endless nights afloat. He had a tough time driving, the tightness of the car's wheel compared to the sloppy play of the *Lucky Lena*. He missed the freedom of roaring up the river, all the wide-open expanse. After a few heart pounding near misses they exited the freeway, opting for the slower but calmer two-laners. He had a glove box full of maps they didn't use. They just followed the sun west. Much of the time they rode in silence, headed west but looking back east, from where they came, and all that had happened and wondering if it had all been real.

They stopped at a crossroads gas station somewhere in the middle of Michigan, a two pump, one repair bay, groceries, beer, and lotto tickets for sale place with a restaurant add on around the side. They went into the eatery to find the restrooms and realizing they were starved, stayed to eat. They were the only non-locals among the half-filled tables, and felt like a couple in the setting, ate too much, which took the edge off, and departed needing naps.

They rolled along till they hit water again, this time, big water. They didn't shut the car off till they were parked at Pere Marquette Beach in Muskegon, overlooking majestic Lake Michigan across a desert of white sand. The blazing, descending sun, changing towards red, turned cloud banks on the horizon into seascapes of unimaginable colors.

The Waterboys motored into the Pine River and docked at the Rocky Dock after dropping off Kevin and Renee. The restaurant was closed, chairs still on table tops, but the boys knew the manager, who cooked up some bacon and eggs for his frazzled friends. Jeff washed his down with a beer. Whitey talked with their friend about the wreck, while the Captain ate in silence, until the first whop, whop, whop, of helicopters sounded in the distance. Jeff looked up from his plate, then at Whitey, before turning towards the open windows overlooking the river.

"The press, it's the goddamn press," the Captain shouted as he jumped off the bar stool. "I can't believe I didn't think of that. Shit man, let's go."

Whitey thanked the barman then followed Jeff, who had instantly been snapped from his funk, and was already untying the bow line. For Whitey, once again choppers, three of them, were flying in, low, up a river, out of a morning mist, the noise overwhelming. These set down in a parking lot at the mouth of the Pine River, in view of the wreck.

Soon after the *Lucky Lena* entered the big river, jammed with reporters, cameramen and equipment, all bouncing and staggering around the back deck. All were anxious to get to the scene, a few looking squeamish on the suddenly rolling cruiser, all having paid the crew a pretty penny to get on board.

Halfway to the wreck, with Whitey at the helm, Captain Jeff turned to shout across the back deck, "You see, the great thing about this river is it presents us with endless possibilities. It's a waterway to adventure. It's a waterway out of here. It's the water of life."

D. Chase Edmonson was raised on the St. Clair River in Michigan and has traveled extensively throughout the Great Lakes. After college, he explored Europe and lived in London, England. Upon returning to Michigan he opened Chapter One Bookshop in St. Clair before moving to San Francisco. He moved back to Michigan to live and work in Ann Arbor and St. Clair. He currently lives in Pittsburgh where he has worked in Sports and Entertainment for over 30 years. He is drawn back to the Great Lakes each summer to boat on the St. Clair River, the Flats, and Lakes St. Clair, Erie, Huron, Michigan and Ontario.